# PRAISE FOR L. J. SHEN

"A great debut read by L. J. Shen. I instantly liked Blaire, especially her inner monologue that had me chuckling quite a few times at her silly banter. I also really liked Ty, like a lot. He was super hawt and had a good amount of alpha to him."
—Meli Mel's Book Reviews, Goodreads

"I was captivated and devoured this book in no time from the moment I picked it up. Ty was easy to hate in the beginning but shit… I fell for him hard when I learned more about him and his outer shell he showed to those not close to him. Boy oh boy… I want a man like him!"
—Star Angel's blog

"Un-freaking-believable that an author right out of the gate gets something so right."
—Carolyn, Goodreads

"I would recommend this book if NA is your thing, you love sexy, confident MMA fighters and you're looking for a good romance with a little angst, some laughs and sweet times. This was an enjoyable debut novel and I look forward to what else Ms. Shen has in store."
—Suzanne, Goodreads

"*Tyed* was a beautifully written first book! Lots of sexy & funny & suspensy & frustrating & adorable moments! GO AND BUY THE BOOK!!!! You don't want to miss Tyler!"
—BJ's book blog

"Well done. Tortured/redeemable hero and adorable doesn't-know-how-hot-she-is heroine. Believable HEA in spite of hero's major errors in judgment. I liked it a lot."
—Smexy book blog

"My lovely L. J. Shen, you've got yourself a fan for sure!! Can't wait for your next book!"
—Lin Tahel, Goodreads

# TYED

**L. J. SHEN**

# ACKNOWLEDGMENTS

To my amazing husband, who has been nothing but supportive throughout this journey and convinced me that I'm not crazy for pursuing this dream (Granted, I'm crazy for other reasons, but *not* because I decided to self-publish a book).

To my close group of friends and beta readers for tolerating me through all this—Eliya Orman, Lin Tahel Cohen, Lilian Nahum, Ilanit Adani and Linda Mizrahi. You rock. I don't think you even realize how much I love you.

To my editor, Karen Dale Harris, for turning this from an okay book to something I'm actually proud of.

To my mom and dad, for telling me I should write a book. I'm pretty sure you had something entirely different in mind when you suggested it, but here we are.

To my readers and reviewers for encouraging me to continue writing. You have no idea how important you are. I feel so incredibly lucky to have you guys in my life. Thank you for your feedback, for your support... and yeah, thanks for the snarky comments, too. You sure know how to keep me on my toes.

Shane and Izzy have been nagging me for months, and I finally started writing their heart-wrenching story. Hopefully you'll join their journey, too, because these two are even crazier than Ty and Blaire. (Luckily, Ty and Blaire are going to make a very cute cameo in book #2).

If you made it to this list, I want you to know that I love you. I really do.

L. J. Shen

# DEDICATION

For those who told me I could
And for those who told me I couldn't
Here's to chasing my dream, one word at a time.

# CHAPTER 1

I hate going to college.

Not that my parents give a damn what courses I take. They only care that I get my communications degree.

Especially after I failed at my first year of college,

So they are paying fuck-knows how much money (they could tell me the exact tuition amount, I'm sure) for me to sleep through Journalistic Reporting class, studying a profession I never. Want. To. Work. In.

Fuck my life, right?

I make the commute from my Walnut Creek apartment to Diablo Hill School of Art almost every day. The university is located between San Francisco, Oakland and my internal wish to kill myself. I'm putting in my time and counting the weeks, days, hours and nanoseconds until graduation.

I have two months and twelve days left until I'm free. Two months and twelve days until I have to face the harsh, unforgiving reality: I have no idea what I want to do with my life. At the moment, my biggest plan for the future consists of a take-out pizza and re-watching the first six seasons of *Sons of Anarchy*. I'm nurturing a monogamous, not-at-all disturbing relationship with Charlie Hunnam's work right now.

(Don't judge.)

Today is a Tuesday, so I'm taking a hard-earned nap after

1

Creative Writing and Ethics classes. I always doze off in Journalistic Reporting. This shit would make a hyperactive kid snore his way through Halloween. Charlie and I are just about to re-create the part where he impregnates Tara Knowles (though I should note our on-screen chemistry is much steamier) when I feel a sharp elbow jabbing into my ribs.

Okay, this nudge is definitely not Charlie's. Ouch.

"Wake up, dopey."

I raise my head slowly, wiping the drool off my chin as I struggle to unglue my eyelids. "What's up?" I ask the owner of the elbow

"Final assignment." My best friend, Shane Kinney, jerks his chin toward the whiteboard at the front of the room. His messy blond hair swishes like he's in a goddamned Head and Shoulders commercial.

I blink at the board. "I'm too sleepy to decipher all the letters and words."

"It's called a sentence. Jesus, Blaire. You have to start taking fewer night shifts at Ned's. "

"I need the money. Groceries are expensive." I pull my hoodie down to cover my face. Thankfully, class is over and everyone is stuffing laptops into their backpacks. Shane stretches, curling his fists as he yawns. Hypocrite. He's bored too. His bellybutton makes a cheeky appearance from underneath his shirt, and I poke my pointer finger into it, making a funny sound.

"You could move back in with your parents," he suggests when I shove to my feet. "It would save you some money."

"Dumpster diving will save me money too, but I'm not desperate enough to do that either."

"Are you saying you'd rather be homeless than live with your folks?"

"I am saying we could be having this conversation while drinking a double shot of espresso outside."

"I don't know, B. You look like you need more than coffee to pull through the day." He winks at me and grins, picking up both of our bags.

I smack his shoulder with the back of my hand. "Seriously, pot at school?"

"Beam me up, Scotty!" His smile widens as we pour into the flood of students streaming down the hallway.

Once we grab our coffees and take a seat on our usual, secluded red bench in a corner of the main quad, Shane produces a cigarette pack he keeps especially for his rolled ones. He lights up and passes a blunt to me. I take a long drag, closing my eyes and savoring the sunshine.

"So what's our assignment?" I finally ask.

Shane gives me the brief. Apparently, while I was busy reliving steamy scenes with CH, Professor Penniman, who is crazy anal about her reporting assignments, gave us our biggest challenge yet: a two thousand word, in-depth piece on a topic that is totally foreign to us.

Shane explains, "She's randomly assigning each of us a subject, but she wants to switch up gender roles. She basically said that the guys could expect to write about crap like romance novels and postpartum depression and the girls are going to dig deep into stuff like muscle cars and first-person shooter games. We'll get our individual topics via e-mail tonight by 10 p.m. And, oh yeah, switching isn't allowed."

"Great. I already hate journalism, and now I have to write about a subject I most likely want nothing to do with."

"Yeah, but you hate everything. Maybe it's time to branch out a little." Shane knocks his Levi-clad thigh against mine. Shane's a journalism major. He's been smooth-sailing the whole university experience. In fact, he was the one who suggested I take this class so he could help me out with this course.

He's wearing his usual uniform of jeans, Timberland boots and a tee shirt with something funny written on it. Today, his shirt says "Step Away, Coffee. This Is A Job For Alcohol." He always smells of cinnamon, Abercrombie cologne and opportunity. Always.

Shane is crazy cute, but he's just not for me. He's like the brother I never had, and I'd like to keep things that way.

"What are you up to this weekend?" He glances sideways at me with his teal eyes.

I shrug. "I'm working Friday night. I'll probably sleep all day Saturday, then roll up a blunt and catch up on *The Walking Dead* or something."

"Care for some company?"

"Can the company bring avocado egg salad sandwiches

and sweet potato chips from Pinder's?"

"Can Floyd Mayweather dodge a punch?" Shane opens his arms wide with a grin.

"I have no freaking clue who that is, but I'm taking a wild chance here and guessing the answer is yes."

"You're killing me, B." He laughs, hooking his arm around my shoulder and pulling me into a friendly hug, messing my hair with his free hand. "Now what am I going to do with you?"

"Dirty, naughty things that will make my twin sister blush?" I arch an eyebrow and feign a devilish laugh.

Shane jumps off the red bench like he's been slapped. Jaw clenched, he strides to a concrete trash can, discarding the evidence of our blunt. "I've got to go," he tells me.

I cough, wondering why my little banter pissed him off. It's like I pushed the very-wrong button.

ও৵

It isn't until almost midnight that I remember about our Journalistic Reporting assignment. Between shopping at Target, visiting my parents and an early shift at Ned's, I managed to forget all about the promised e-mail.

I fire up my five-year-old Dell, and it occurs to me that I'm probably the only person under thirty in the Bay Area who doesn't have a MacBook. Izzy, my twin, says that a twenty-three-year-old working on anything else is the uncoolest thing she's ever seen. But I secretly believe I'm way cooler than everybody else for giving zero fucks about what anyone else thinks.

My e-mail screen finally graces me with its presence and notifies me of two unread messages. One from Professor Penniman and the other from Shane. Apparently he's over whatever upset him earlier today.

I open Professor Penniman's e-mail first:

Ms. Stern:

As per my instructions in class, I would like a 2000-word article, no less, excluding the headline, on the subject below. Your whole grade depends on this assignment, so please take it as seriously as I do. I want you to interview people who work in the industry. Follow them around to understand the ins and outs of their line of work. Your article is due the first day of exam week, June 1. This should give you plenty of time to complete the assignment.

Please DO NOT e-mail me back, call or otherwise approach me about changing your subject. You may ask for further guidelines or clarification about the assignment itself, but the subject is mandatory.

Subject: MMA

I wrinkle my nose. And just what exactly is MMA? The initials sound vaguely familiar. A government agency maybe?

I jot down the three letters so I won't forget to Google them, and then I double- click on Shane's e-mail. He wants to know what subject I got and why I'm not answering my texts. Oops, I put my cell phone on silent when I was having dinner with my parents. House rules.

I turn on my phone now and see a text from Shane asking the same question.

I type: **MMA. Wtf?**

Shane replies almost immediately: **Mixed Martial Arts. Lucky you. My roommate Josh works out in an XWL gym in Concord.**

I text back: **XWL? More initials?**

Shane translates: **Xtreme Warrior League. Josh says you're better off trying to find another gym because this one is full of jerks. Anyway, I logged into their website. Talk to the general manager/coach, Dawson.**

He includes a phone number for the gym.

Then he texts: **Don't forget our TWD binge Saturday night. TTYL.**

I realize he's signed off before he even told me his topic. Maybe he was so busy helping me he forgot. The thought makes me smile. Where would I be without Shane?

We've been friends forever. He grew up down the street and has been my closest friend for as long as I can remember. When Shane traveled the world for a while after high school, I felt like I was missing a limb. I'm not exactly a social butterfly and Shane has always stuck by me. Even when we were kids and Aiden, the lazy-eyed kid down our road built a tree fort and invited everyone (Shane and Izzy included) except me to come and play, Shane preferred to stick around with Boring Blaire. We caught fireflies with jars and, because my mother was concerned and guilty about my lack of social life, she pretty much let us raid the kitchen and gorge on sweets.

I know Shane dates a lot of girls. Sometimes he has less time to hang out, or he receives a sassy text or steamy call when I'm around, but he's a great friend.

Me? I'm saving myself for a fair-haired Englishman who is oblivious to my existence.

I enter Dawson's number into my phone, walk to my bathroom and start filling up a bath. I dust the coffee table while the water's running. My twin Izzy's the one footing the bill for the rent and pretty much everything else. I'm the one who does all the cleaning. It sucks, but so does everything else about being Boring Blaire in comparison to Sizzling Izzy.

I run the magic swipe along a picture of my sister and me. I'm petite, slim with curvy hips. Lily-white skin, full lips and dark, wavy hair with blue tips. I have freckles sprinkled on my nose and high on my cheeks. I guess I'm like, air-hostess hot. Meaning I look better than the average girl but nowhere near as perfect as those girls in the magazines.

But Isabelle? *Pffft*. She *is* that girl from the magazine cover. Taller, slimmer and prettier by a mile. Higher cheekbones, deeper shade of blue eyes and the aura of a goddess. Izzy basically makes me look like a beta version of her. So at eighteen, instead of debating what to do with her life (like me), she decided to become a model and make tons of money off her beauty.

Currently, Isabelle Stern is traveling the world as a lingerie-wearing Elizabeth's Passion Fairy, visiting everywhere and living the life, while I'm attending a shitty university and serving lukewarm beer in a neighborhood bar to make ends meet.

Even so, when I'm not working night shifts at Ned's and she's not rolling around on an exotic beach in her underwear, Izzy and I have a routine.

I hear my phone ringing, walk back to the bathroom, turn off the faucet and slide a finger into the water to check the temperature.

"Izzy," I answer and instinctively distance the phone from my ear.

"Sissy!" my sister squeals back. She may be gorgeous, but her high-pitched voice could crack double-glazed windows.

"Where's your skinny ass today?" I sit on the edge of the bathtub, circling my finger in the water.

"I'm in Singapore. You'd love it! It is so different and awesome and full of skyscrapers. Had an awkward incident when I landed here, though. Apparently it's illegal to chew gum here, especially in botanic gardens. I almost got arrested!"

We laugh as I slide my body into the water, letting out a sigh.

"You in the bath now?" she asks.

"Yeah. You?"

"Yup. It's giant, twice as big as the one in the apartment, and it has jets. Hey, you think we're freaks for liking to do this every day? Like it's a kinky twin-womb thing?"

"What, have baths while on the phone?" I chew my lower lip. "It's not exactly Dr. Phil material. I'd ask my therapist if I could afford one."

"You need money? You know I can always help you out."

"No." I clear my throat and quickly change the subject. "Anyway, what time is it there? I'm just about to head to bed."

"Like, 1 p.m."

"Taking a bath at lunchtime? You are a bit of a freak."

"Mmm, okay, Blaire. At least I'm not boring."

Izzy does have a point.

I chatter about my MMA assignment and about Shane acting weird. Izzy didn't even realize we were taking a class together. I must have forgotten to mention it. She doesn't seem very interested though and cuts our usual thirty-minute phone call short.

After she hangs up, I flop onto my bed with my laptop and decide to type *MMA* into YouTube. Might as well see what I'm dealing with here. The first video that pops up has a guy being knocked out so brutally the referee has to jump between him and the other fighter to stop the match. One fighter is unconscious, the mat beneath him as bloody as a

*CSI* crime scene, while the fighter on top is still trying to pummel his opponent into submission. The crowd is eating this up, encouraging more with claps and excited screams of "Choke him out!" and "Arm bar! Arm bar!"

I'm not into being mainstream or judgmental—some will even consider my profanity, ripped jeans and nose piercing uncivilized (join the petition led by my folks)—but even *I* recognize how sick this is. I'm not sure where the *Arts* part fits in Mixed Martial Arts. It's definitely not in the ring, where I just witnessed a guy being choked until he turned blue.

Further research into the subject reveals that there's a heated debate about whether or not MMA should even be legal. The defenders of the sport say it's consensual. But hey, crime can be consensual too.

This is pretty vile, I think as I slap the laptop shut and squeeze my thumbs into my eyelids.

I'm so going to fail this course. *Again.*

# CHAPTER 2

The good thing about getting MMA as my assignment topic is that the sport seems eager for any kind of attention it can get. I don't have to go through any snotty secretaries, PR agents or legal obstacles to score an interview at The Grind, a gym in Concord. All I have to do is ask. In fact, the only problem with Mixed Martial Arts is that it's Mixed Martial Arts.

I figured the violence in the first video I watched was a fluke. I thought that MMA must be like WWF wrestling, with a lot of flamboyant role-playing cowboys and heavy-metal knights. You know, when men in customs jump on each other after a theatrical twenty-minute speech.

But I was wrong. During my in-depth research (yeah, fine, I Googled it), I discovered the men of MMA literally beat each other up to oblivion. There is blood. Everywhere. There are black eyes, torn ligaments, broken bones and enough medical staff to open up a field hospital at every match. It is all real and painfully brutal.

My initial conclusion is that any guy who would want to be an MMA fighter must be brain damaged. When I hit Dawson Alba with this psychological assessment this morning on the phone, the trainer serenely confirmed, "Yeah, the guys all get hit pretty seriously in the head."

Fun times ahead, right?

As I pull into the parking lot of The Grind on Saturday, I'm shivering not because it's a chilly afternoon, but because the thought of researching this bloody sport is grossing me out to the max. I stare at the huge, two-story hangar on the outskirts of town. The XWL logo is proudly painted in red, white and black on the front and sides, the stylized symbol seemingly visible from every freeway in the Bay Area.

I park my pink Mini Cooper among the black Ram trucks and Jeeps. I inherited the Mini from Izzy for free so I shouldn't complain, but it's so devastatingly pink, it stands out among the other testosterone-fueled vehicles like a juicy pimple on a prom queen. A half-dozen guys stroll by and peer through the window, staring at me like I got lost on my way to the nearest mall.

A tall guy shakes his head in amusement as I release the custom-installed, pink-patterned Hello Kitty seat belt. Damn you, Izzy. I want to yell that a supermodel chose the car, not me, but keeping a low profile seems to be a higher priority right now.

I stumble my way out and light up a blunt, frowning at the guy through my Wayfarer sunglasses (another discard from Izzy) as I attempt to calm my nerves. I'm not going to smoke the whole thing. Just a few drags to take the edge off won't do any harm, right?

Say what you will about my pink car, there's no mistaking me for Izzy and her designer clothes once I step out in my Subhumans black tee and Boyfriend ripped jeans, my messy bun tied carelessly at the nape of my neck. We're a different species, she and I. I take another deep drag, frowning.

*That's it. Breathe in, breathe out.*

I'm getting kind of good at it.

"Yo. You're not allowed to smoke here." It's the tall guy again. He's wearing a black-skull bandana mask covering the lower part of his face, presumably because he thinks it makes him look badass. (It kinda does.)

"I'll put it out in a second." I grunt my irritation and puff a cloud of smoke skywards.

"Oh, man, you're smoking pot?" He jerks out his SkullCandy earbuds, puffing his cheeks. He is athletic and muscular, his chest and thick arms bulging through his black XWL tee. I scan his gray sweatpants and flip-flops and catch a glimpse of the huge snake tattoo crawling up from his back onto his neck.

Crap. I need to say something. "We're outside. How the hell is it your business if I smoke here." I puff my blunt coolly, but inside, my pulse is racing. "Keep walkin', cowboy."

*No, not that, you idiot.* I want to shut up. Correction, I need to shut up. He is three times my size, pure muscle and male arrogance, and he has this dusky stare that makes my skin tingle.

But I can't seem to stop myself, and to my horror, my mouth continues firing more stupidity. "If you care so much about your health, second hand smoke should be the least of your worries. You realize getting punched on a regular basis damages your brain. It affects memory and all kinds of other stuff."

*Fantastic, Blaire. You basically just called the guy brain dead.* My chances of leaving here in an ambulance have just dramatically increased.

He closes the space between us and plucks the blunt from my lips, flicking it to the other side of the parking lot with his thumb and forefinger. My mouth is still agape when he pulls his bandana down to his neck, exposing his whole face.

"That's a very bad idea," he warns in a low, husky voice. His breath smells of mint gum and mouthwash, and he is standing so close I can feel the heat pulsing from his body despite the fact it's ludicrously hot today as it is.

"You mean smoking or running my mouth at you?" My voice cracks. I'm tongue-tied. It feels like my mouth is full of cotton wool.

"Both," he says, removing a lock of hair from my forehead.

Wow. I mean, wow. Hot Parking-Lot Dude is so sizzling, calling him beautiful would be the insult of the century. He's lucky his nose is slightly crooked, like it's been hit one too many times, because otherwise, he'd be sickeningly pretty. What the hell is he, anyway? Latino? Asian? Mixed Caucasian? He looks like he's been Photoshopped by a bunch of horny teenagers. He has pouty, perfectly shaped lips, slanted Asian eyes and the chiseled, Brad Pitt-like bone structure girls shit themselves over.

Quick reminder:

I'm a girl.

I'm standing in hazardous vicinity to him.

And I'm clearly, unbelievably fucked.

"That's some car you drive." His bedroom eyes narrow to a spot behind me.

"Problem?" I bat my eyes slowly, trying to look bored.

"Na, figures." He's so pretty I can't concentrate on what he's saying. Or what I'm saying, for that matter. Then he pivots in the other direction, and before I realize what's happening, Poof, he's gone.

It takes me a minute or ten to regroup.

I lean back against my hood, practicing deep breaths and trying to calm down. Everything is under control. I just had a brief encounter with a personal-space invading maniac. Who happens to be unfairly gorgeous. But the gym is huge and my chances of running into him again are slim.

Besides, Dawson is waiting and I can't afford to be late. I need to focus on this assignment in order to graduate. Mom and Dad will kill me if I fail again. No, I will kill myself if I fail again.

I enter the gym, and I'm greeted at the counter by a ginger-bearded dude with a man-bun and a black XWL tee just like the one Hot Parking-Lot Dude wore.

"Hi, I have a meeting with Dawson Alba. My name is Blaire Stern." I offer a polite smile and try not to look like the place is freaking me out. Which is difficult, especially since the gym is painted in floor-to-ceiling black.

I adjust the messenger bag hooked over my shoulder and try not to feel conspicuous in my ripped jeans and black chucks. The scent of aftershave, sweat and testosterone assaults my nostrils. I see tons of Iron-Man-sized dudes punching stuff and rolling around on the floor, and even spot a few women lifting super heavy barbells. These women mean business and are nothing like the soccer moms at my mom's gym, the kind on the treadmills with their makeup still on, walking at the pace of a dying turtle.

"Okay..." Ginger-Bearded Guy looks distracted. "Sorry, can't leave this place unattended." He shifts his weight from one foot to the other. "The boss's office is on the other side of the gym. Let me get someone to show you the way, cool?"

I nod. So they are not all bossy jerks. Ginger-Bearded Guy is nice and helpful. He motions someone over to the desk while I drink in the place with my eyes.

"Here we are! This is Ty. He'll take you up to Dawson's office," GBG announces behind me.

I turn around to greet the Good Samaritan who's come to my rescue, and my jaw drops to the floor. Hot Parking-Lot Dude is standing in front of me, sexy galore. "You!" I squint accusingly, for a reason beyond my grasp. Other than putting out my blunt, he hasn't done anything wrong. Then again, I guess it was a no smoking area. And, well, pot is still illegal, and stuff.

Hot Parking-Lot Dude, now officially identified as Ty, fights the slow smile that's spreading on his lips. Is he laughing at me or with me? My cheeks flush and I look away immediately.

GBG's eyes shift between us. "You two know each other?"

"No," we both answer in unison. I think Ty is still looking me. I wish he'd stop. Why am I embarrassed? It's very unlike me.

"Right. Then Ty, could you show Blaine where Dawson sits?"

"It's Blaire." I grit my teeth.

"Right." GBG waves my correction away dismissively.

I follow Ty's broad, triangle-shaped back as he separates the ocean of gym rats like Moses parting the Red Sea. His dark hair is buzzed extremely short, and I study the tattoo of a giant snake winding up his neck. The snake's face is a zombie skull that looks like it's about to sink its teeth into one of his ears. His ears look deformed and lumpy, so I try to focus on them and his tattoo, soothing my out of control hormones.

Final verdict? Ugliest tattoo to ever be inked on human flesh, but Ty somehow pulls it off without looking like a serial killer. The guy has such an attraction to death that I'm surprised he is still alive. Skull bandana, skull headphones, skull tattoos.

Other than my pounding heartbeat, we walk in silence. Ty takes a set of metal stairs, bypassing an elevator, probably hoping to avoid the awkward elevator conversation. Can't blame him. I don't know what to say, feeling embarrassed about our earlier encounter, and also because it's becoming evident that Hormones are taking over Brain.

He's not my type, mind you.

I always go for the preppy hipsters, guys like Shane, who are into deep stuff like indie music, beat-generation books and... Lord help me, his butt is just so firm and round when he climbs up the stairs, how is this even anatomically possible?

I don't trust myself around this guy. My body can get rebellious sometimes. Charlie Hunnam can testify.

Upstairs, Ty leads me down a catwalk, then stops and tilts his head at a closed black door. "That's your guy."

"Thanks." I send him a tight-lipped smile.

He nods grimly.

"Sorry about earlier," I say. "I rarely smoke pot. I may have relapsed the last couple of weeks, but it's not a recurring thing." Oh my God. I'm babbling like an idiot and I bet he doesn't give a damn. *Get to the point, Blaire.* "I'm just so out of my element here...." I circle the floor with the toe of my chucks, arms behind my back. "I guess what I'm saying is I needed to... I had to... well, never-mind. Thank you."

It's amazing that I'm studying communications, considering my lack of ability to articulate a full sentence.

Ty nods again.

"Jeez, are you a chatterbox, or what?" I say. "Shut up for a sec!"

He ducks his head to hide a slight smirk, and that's when I see it. His unbelievably boyish smile, with dimples and all. No wonder he's trying to fight it. He looks like such a sweet, innocent guy wearing this smile, even with the tattoos and buzzed hair. Before I realize, I'm smiling too.

We're beaming like two idiots, for a bit longer than socially acceptable. I look down and he fiddles with the black rubber bands on his wrist.

Ty is the first to wipe the grin from his face. "Take care of yourself, huh?" He takes a step back, momentarily allowing me to pick up the pieces of my heart without having my butt metaphorically kicked. "And stop smoking pot."

"Yeah, whatever. Ciao."

I knock on Dawson's door and watch Ty already heading back the way we came. I can't help but feel a pang with his departure. He must be a mind reader, because just when I'm about to let out a gloomy moan, he turns back in my direction.

"I know you'll do the right thing, Blake." He's walking backwards as he speaks.

"It's Blaire!"

I see those dimples again. Is it wrong to be bummed about the fact he doesn't seem to want to remember my name?

Then Dawson Alba is opening the door and I remember why I'm here.

Alba wears his forty-something age well, and looks military sharp, with a natural tan and broad shoulders. He sits with his feet propped on his desk and talks to me enthusiastically about the XWL and what they do. Even though he knows my article will never see the light of day, he is eager to help.

"Way this thing works, every MMA gym has a group of elite XWL fighters who participate in professional matches. I've got a few, including two stars that are actually top fighters in their leagues. They travel all over the world, meet international opponents and fight them to the Xtreme Warrior title in their unique weight division. They make a living out of this thing and have dedicated fans all over the world. But clearly, they also have to make a living. You can't rely on the few bouts you take every year and the occasional endorsement. So they also work here and teach people what they know about the art."

"I admit, up until now I thought MMA was all about illegal cage fighting and broken teenage boys looking for redemption." I bite back an uneasy giggle, thinking about Ty. The posters behind Dawson's head, of upcoming events, make my skin crawl, and so does the crazy twinkle in his eyes when he talks about violence.

"But that's exactly what my guys are." His mouth curves into a smile. "What they were, at least. Now? Now they're a sliver of the American dream. Power, money, brutality. Can't get more primal than that."

I thank Dawson and arrange to visit his gym at least four

days a week while I'm working on my assignment, but he isn't satisfied with my huge commitment. Nope. Dawson insists I should participate in one of the gym's classes, see what all the fuss is about. I explain I'm grateful for the opportunity, but that I would probably kill myself by accident if I ever tried MMA.

After a long exchange of "no's" and "yes's", we settle for me participating in a class of my choice sometime next week. Yay, right?

Wrong.

I'm so out of my depth here. The sport, the blood, the men... the Ty.

I'm not even sure how he drilled himself into my head, but I'll probably outgrow our encounter within the next couple of days. It looks like Brain and Hormones are in for a fight. Just as long as Heart stays out of the ring.

৯৵

The next day I sleep until noon. Shane bailed on hanging out last night. Still, I'm exhausted from the thoughts swirling in my head in a jumbled whirlwind. The XWL gym is like a dancing flame. I'm intrigued, but I don't want to get burned.

I wish I could get Professor Penniman to let me change topics. I'm not looking forward to visiting the XWL gym again today. Dawson called after our meeting and he's arranged for me to meet with his two stars this afternoon. No classes, he promised. Just the interviews I asked to conduct with his two elite fighters. Well, at least I won't have to sweat.

I collapse on the couch and consider asking Izzy for advice. She's sent a bunch of pictures of Japan to my phone. She's moved on from Singapore to Tokyo.

The doorbell interrupts just as I'm about to call her. The chime shoots me out of my seat.

I'm not expecting anyone.

I gaze through the peephole and see Shane staring right back at me, pretending to hump my door theatrically. Laughing, I open the door, watching him troop into my luxury apartment— nine foot ceiling, designer finishes and all that jazz—holding a box from the bakery near my complex,

The Sweetest Affair. His favorite. My favorite.

"Such a pleasant surprise." I offer a devious grin.

"Don't make a guy blush."

"I'm talking to whatever's inside that box."

"Cupcakes. You know how much I love pleasing you, B." His words seem to hang in the air as he swings my fridge open.

He pours himself some coffee with milk, while I demolish half the box in one go, then let out a delicate burp.

"Always a lady," he teases, though I know Shane well enough to recognize that he does consider me too much of a tomboy.

He's always been drawn to the girlie type. Izzy is the one exception. She's about as girlie as they come, but he seems to almost hate her. I never understood why they don't get along. Neither of them explained why they stopped talking altogether shortly after he traveled abroad, and while I tried to milk some info about their beef, I didn't push the subject with either of them since I couldn't afford losing Shane as a friend or Izzy as a roommate.

"Well, this lady has to go to the XWL gym in Concord to work on that article Professor Penniman assigned. What's your topic anyway? You never said."

He rubs the back of his neck, squeezing his eyes shut. "Elizabeth's Passion."

The slow grin spreading across my face says it all. Hello, Shane, meet Fate.

"You mean you'll actually have to talk to Izzy and..." I fake a gasp. "Ask for her help?"

"I'm trying to find a way around it. Maybe my good friend here can help me out."

This explains the cupcakes. What it doesn't explain is why Shane is doing everything he can to avoid my twin. They used to be cool with each other growing up.

"You don't want me anywhere near your assignment. I'm college poison, remember?"

He grimaces, knowing how right I am.

"Whatever issues you have with Izzy, get over 'em. I'm sure she's way past the subject. I talk about you all the time and she's never said a word about you. She probably doesn't even remember who you are."

By the flare of his nostrils, I realize I just said something incredibly stupid.

I quickly backpedal. "Don't worry. Just talk to her. Anyway, wanna come with me?" I slap his thigh.

I could use his support. The Grind makes me feel uncomfortable, and the possibility of running into Ty makes me feel even more self-conscious, so I'd really appreciate it if my best friend would tag along.

"I came this morning in the shower, but I would love to come again." The next thing he does happens very quickly. I feel his hand gripping my thigh. And not just for a moment, but he actually takes the time to squeeze. It takes me a few seconds to register what's happening. So sudden, so unexpected, so... *crazy*. My gape travels from my assaulted thigh to his teal eyes as I sit on the barstool.

Don't panic. Don't scream. Do. Not. Pull. An. Izzy.

I bolt from of my seat, rushing toward my bedroom. "Need to get dressed, be out in a sec," I choke, disappearing into my room.

I rummage through my closet to make some noise. Maybe the clicking of the hangers will quiet the thoughts swirling in my head like a tornado, ripping every single house, tree and car in its way. My best friend made a pass at me out of the freaking blue. Brain. Does. Not. Compute.

I watch his frame in the reflection from my bedroom mirror as he runs his hand through his hair, probably thinking the exact same thing. This is bad. A calamity. A deal-breaker.

"I'll wait." His eyes lock on mine in the mirror. And I know exactly what he means...

৩৵৩

Driving to Concord, Shane and I try to regain our tension-free banter. We have this thing where he makes up stories to keep me entertained. They are always the stupidest stories ever, but he tells them with such conviction you can't help but laugh your ass off. This time he amuses me with a story about a baby anteater that went to boarding school with—you guessed it— ants. All the baby ants resent him and bully him for who he is, and he is lonely, sad and isolated, until he forms a punk band with a beaver and a frog and they become a national sensation in the Portuguese forest where they are all living.

No, we are definitely not smoking anything in the car.

Yes, I'm aware this sounds mega-stupid.

But it's working. By the time we arrive at the gym, my stomach hurts from the cupcakes, laughing and anticipation.

We jump out of Shane's Mustang and enter the gym, and I actually feel a tad proud when I lead our way toward the rings where the MMA fighters train. I first noticed the enclosed platforms when I climbed the stairs with Ty yesterday. I made a mental note to check them out next time I was here.

"Ich Will" by Rammstein is blasting through the speakers. The beat drops and bodies crush into one another violently, twisting and wrestling on the mats, mosh-pit style. That one's called sparring.

"This place is crazy, B. You'll develop testicles just by breathing the air here." Shane is puffing out his cheeks.

We stride toward Dawson, who is teaching a class. He is roaring at his students while they brawl. Shane's right. The levels of testosterone in this place are intoxicating and the music blasting through the speakers is threatening to burst my eardrums. In fact, my BFF and I are the only people who aren't soaked in our own bodily fluids head to toe.

"I don't know about testicles, but I may sport a mustache by the end of this assignment." I lean on a red and white sign asking the gym goers to Please Clean up Your Blood after Practice and Keep Our Gym Clean.

Shane rests his leg on a nearby wall, arms folded on his chest.

"Marco, you dropped to the ground!" Dawson thunders. "That's no good, man. The ground is your worst enemy!" He is pacing back and forth and looks like he's about to explode.

"Marco zero. Gravity one. Poor guy didn't stand a chance." I nudge Shane and we share a laugh.

But the truth is, I'm impressed. These men are doing their own thing, inching closer to their dream one punch at the time. What am I doing with my life? They have determination—

purpose. I want to feel as passionate about something as they do, sans the cracked limbs and mangled ears. I want to feel fulfilled and alive like them.

"Didn't you say your roommate is training here?" I ask Shane.

The dude has a gazillion roommates, each weirder than the other. I try to keep my communication with them to a minimum. This is a philosophy I apply to most of the human race.

"Yeah, Josh. Stopped coming here a while ago, though. Someone broke his nose."

"Damn," I say. Not that this comes as a surprise after the videos I watched. "No wonder he said the place is full of jerks."

"Yeah. The asshole really screwed up his face. Good thing I prefer to express my masculinity by watching NFL and running every once in a while."

After a few minutes of us silently looking at the guys dancing in semi-gay thigh grips and grunting like Anna Kournikova in a white skirt, Dawson approaches us.

"Yo," he says, shaking both our hands. "You can talk to these guys if you want or wait for my two stars to arrive. Remember I told you about the two pros that are ranked super-high in the XWL? Jesse and Ty. They'll be happy to talk to you when they finish practice in ten minutes."

Shit. I didn't know Ty was one of the guys I was going to interview. I'm not sure he's going to be all that happy to talk to me, but my heart skips a beat the minute I hear his name. It's pounding all over the place. One second it beats fast enough to jump out of my ribcage, and the next, it's slow and I almost feel faint.

*Get a grip, Blaire.* He's just a guy, and not a very nice one either.

"You okay?" Shane rubs my arm, his eyebrows pinched together.

I ease my arm away, still anxious about that earlier thigh grip. "Yeah. Cupcake overdose is all." If this is my reaction to hearing Ty's name, I'm dreading the thought of what's going to happen when I actually see him in the flesh.

"There they are, the men of the hour." Dawson raises his

hands to greet his approaching stars.

Ty strides toward us, accompanied by a taller, even more muscular, black guy—Jesse, I guess. Between them, they have enough tattoos to cover the whole of NorCal. They swagger toward us like B-movie gangsters. There's something incredibly cocky about the way they carry themselves. Everything, from their posture to their clothes to the way they chew their gum and the smug glint in their eyes. I'm guessing that Dawson referring to them as his "stars" doesn't help with piercing their inflated egos.

"This is the definition of douchebag-ism," Shane complains in my ear.

Figures. Sucks to be him, or anyone else with a dick in this room, for that matter. Talk about alpha-male dominance.

Ty's sleeveless shirt is soaked with sweat, and he is pulling its hem up so he can wipe off his forehead, revealing perfect abs. Not a four pack with a pouch, but a solid, I-can't-believe-it's-not-Photoshopped six pack. I don't find his sweat disgusting. At all. In fact, I wouldn't have minded snuggling into this shirt tonight. Or snuggling into him…

*Sheesh*! I need to get over this thing, whatever it is, fast. Hormones are bullying Brain again, even though Brain knows better than to like Ty. He was straight up rude the first time we met, when he plucked the blunt out of my lips. He is cocky. He is trouble. And most of all—he is a distraction. I need to get this assignment over with. I need to graduate. No, I *must* graduate. Hormones can keep on dreaming.

The next thing I notice is a huge welt on Ty's ribcage. I have an unexpected urge to stroke his skin, to soothe away the pain. Why does he make me want to touch him? I don't normally fall in lust with men I don't know.

"Meet Ty and Jesse," Dawson proclaims proudly. "This is the reporter I was telling you about—"

"Blake," Ty cuts through Dawson's introduction and winks at me.

"Blaire," I correct. I take a deep breath and try to look indifferent about his mistake. I'm not a girl who's into *Cosmo* and *Glamour* and stuff, but even I know that if a guy doesn't remember your name, you shouldn't expect a call from him anytime soon.

It's weird shaking hands with him now. Yesterday, his lips were inches from mine in the parking lot when he snatched that roll up out of my mouth, and he didn't seem too eager to talk when he showed me to Dawson's office. I'm expecting him to crush my clammy palm, but he treats me like a fragile doll. Before he lets go of my hand, he circles my knuckle with his thumb. A small gesture, but it makes the rest of my body tingle with pleasure.

Shane, however, is not awarded with the same treatment. Ty almost rips off his arm when he shakes it. Shane's limb practically raves in the air like a dancing balloon man. Shane jerks his hand free, massaging his wrist.

"Why don't you look around for awhile? I need to ask these guys some questions," I quickly explain. It was my idea to bring Shane with me, but I'm beginning to regret it. I need to focus on my task, to get this assignment over with and to get the hell out of here. What I don't need is more complications.

"Ask away." Shane hooks an arm over my shoulder and thrust out his jaw. It's an I'm-pissing-on-my-territory face. There's no other way to describe the look of challenge he shoots at Ty.

Ty's nostrils flare as he stares Shane down. If looks could kill, forensics would be all over these two. Everyone falls awkwardly silent.

"Fuck this shit. I'm out, coach." Ty grabs a towel from a nearby bench and drapes it over his close-cropped head. He walks away, not even bothering to grab his duffel bag.

What the hell is his problem?

I eye Jesse, who offers me a half-apologetic smile. "Ty's ego is bigger than his head. He'll come around. Let's do this interview, kid."

ৡৣৢ

We sit on blue plastic bleachers in front of a cage. I spend thirty minutes with Jesse Clement. He is witty and amusing and gives good quotes. In fact, he is journalistic gold. He speaks frankly about taboos like steroids and performance-enhancing drugs, about the reaction of people who hear he beats the shit out of guys for a living, and how sometimes the same guys beat the shit out of him. Every warrior in the XWL loses a battle every once in a while, even the champs.

"Why MMA, though? That's what I don't get. You look like you could have been an athlete in any sport. Why pick something so...?" Barbaric, dangerous, controversial... I could go on forever, but I leave it hanging in the air.

I take a quick glance at his tattoos. Jesse is inked head to toe, fingertips included. I wonder if he realizes he'll have to walk around with these when he's old and saggy when it looks about as cool as my dad's stamp collection.

"I didn't choose MMA. It chose me." Jesse cuts off my line of thought. "Cliché as it sounds, you gotta play the hand you've been dealt in life. Growing up in the projects, I had to fight to live. There were thugs everywhere, and they always wanted something. My money, my food, my new shoes. And sometimes they just wanted cheap entertainment. I survived with my fists, medicated on street fights. Then, at some point, I don't remember when exactly, fighting became a therapy and no longer a necessity. A way to take out my anger on this world."

I stare down. It hasn't crossed my mind that Jesse wasn't in another sport because he didn't have the cushy upbringing I've had.

"It's all good, though. I make good money doing what I do, and I love it. I get to travel the world, meet new people and stay in great shape all year round. Personally, I have a steady girlfriend that I adore, but if I hadn't met her, it's always a plus when chicks dig your job."

"What, MMA?" I raise an eyebrow.

"That's right." He grins.

"Somehow I find that hard to believe." My experience with competitive fighting might consist only of playing Tekken once or twice in my life, but even I can see it's thuggish and about as appealing as bathing in your own vomit.

Jesse lets out a loud laugh, like I just told him the earth is flat and populated by glittery unicorns. He's on the verge of tears, holding his stomach when he finally says, "Ask Tyler. He'll tell you all about the fangirls."

"Tyler?"

"Yeah, that's Ty's name. Tyler Wilder."

Tyler Wilder. Lookie here. Looks like I have a name to Google.

"Before you make any assumptions, I suggest you hit one of our classes and see what the fuss is all about. If you're going to write about it, you need to try it, no?"

I drop my head back and sigh, knowing he's right. I know Dawson wants me to try it out, and a happy Dawson means a happy interviewee.

"Okay," I say, feeling pushed to the corner.

Jesse gets up from his seat and chuckles to himself. "Besides, you kinda look like a tomboy. I think you'll have fun."

When Jesse and I climb down from the bleachers, Ty is waiting for us, leaning against a doorframe, ankles crossed, eyebrows raised and arms folded. He grits his teeth when I pass him, a devilish look in his eyes. I flip him the bird as I stroll over to join Shane, trying to look like I'm bored with his antics.

Jesse nudges Ty's ribs. "What's good, bro?"

Ty is jerking his chin at me when he returns gruffly, "Nothing's good. And there goes the neighborhood."

# CHAPTER 3

I fill up a bath and wait for Izzy's scheduled call.

Sliding into the water, I dunk my head, still fuming about Ty Wilder. How dare he bail on the interview I need! And why was he so bitchy after Jesse and I came back?

And did I mention he is not my type? Because he isn't.

The phone rings.

"Izzy."

"Babe!" she yells. My arm is already stretched to avoid the unfortunate scenario where her voice will make my head explode.

"Where's your skinny ass today?" I ask.

"Australia. Sydney is amazing. You should see the harbor. Everything here is so expensive but they have the best burgers and cutest accent. And the men! Blaire, the men are just to die for! This is almost my last stop. Only eight or so more weeks before I'm coming home."

I'm happy for her. 'Course I am.

I tell her everything about Ty and Shane. Izzy's take is that Ty likes me and he went all cold on me because he thought Shane was my boyfriend.

"I don't know much about this world, but I can smell flirting from a mile with earplugs and a trash bag over my head. This Ty guy, he was definitely flirting. Now Google his ass before I do. I will steal him. You bet I will, soul sista'."

I finish my bath in a hurry, make myself a giant cup of coffee and mentally prepare myself for some earnest, unforgiving journalistic investigating. That's right, I'm Googling Tyler Wilder.

The first thing I discover is that Ty has his own Wikipedia page. It doesn't give much detail about him, but it exists. He also has a Facebook fan page with over two-hundred thousand likes, but doesn't have a private Facebook page I can connect to.

I map out my plan for research. I'll start with Ty so I can come up with good questions for when I interview him. Then I'll move on and see what I can find out about Jesse and Dawson.

I establish some basic info first: Wilder is twenty-six years old. He was born in Martinez and has lived in northern California his whole life. He currently resides in Concord and is an avid Harley-Davidson fan. His favorite color is black (shocking, I know) and his culinary weakness is Mexican food.

There are some crazy hot pictures of him on Google Images, including a few where he's in a tux at an MMA charity ball two years ago. I also find lots of YouTube videos of him thrashing his opponents to knockouts and submissions. He is the darling of winning by decision too. Ty's ring nickname is "The Zombie." It suits him perfectly, with that ugly, snake-skull tattoo. To add a personal touch, he always breezes out of the tunnel and enters the ring to "Zombie" by the Cranberries, an angry grunge tune I overplayed as a teenager.

It sends a chill down my spine every time I watch him walk out of those tunnels in one of the videos, beer dripping on his head as the crowd erupts with screams, people clutching their beer cups, roaring and chanting. His lower face is always covered with the skull bandana, and he's looking at his opponents like he's going to butcher them alive. Every time the cage door shuts and I hear the secure click, the audience leaps to its feet in anticipation.

Not everybody is rooting for Ty, but everyone respects him.

He frequently wins by decision, which is prestigious, I guess. His wrestling and Muay Thai background makes him lethal in the cage, and his left hook is the best in the XWL, if the rumors online are true.

One of the commenters in a video where Ty sends a dude straight to the ER with a broken nose and blood streaming from his forehead points out: *Man, Wilder is ruthless. He shattered the dude to pieces like taco shells!*

Another commenter adds: *I love the intensity in his eyes. Truly, the gladiator of our time. He is an animal, and tall for the welterweight division. Most strikers don't stand a chance getting inside his reach.*

I read comment after comment. People praise him, curse him, love him and hate him, fear him and respect him. I seem to share those mixed feelings. He attracts me and repulses me at the same time. Like a car crash. Only I worry I'll be one of the casualties involved.

I quickly realize why Jesse was oh-so-amused with me thinking women don't find this sport attractive. Desperate, female fans are found in toxic quantities with every video I watch. Nearly every match online of him knocking out an opponent bears endless comments from adoring women, like: *I watched this video three times. Once with the door locked ;-)* And the less understated: *I want to sit on his gorgeous face!!! CALL ME TY.*

Cue to pass the puke bucket, please.

Evidently, I was wrong. Women like men who play hockey, football, basketball and golf (okay, scratch golf). Women love men who know how to fight.

Ty's ranking in the welterweight division is impressive, with experts predicting that he or Irish Eoghan Doherty could take the title from Brazilian Jesus Vasquez this year.

I spend the night gorging on info about Ty Wilder, creating a self-feeding monster. The more I find out about him, the more I crave. It's 3 a.m. when I finally slam the laptop screen with a bang, exhaling sharply.

Yes, I will research Jesse and Dawson. But I'll do it tomorrow. Tonight, I've seen enough.

On Wednesday, I decide to bite the bullet and take a class at the gym. The workout is both research and minor damage control, seeing as Shane is coming over tonight for our delayed *Walking Dead* marathon and he's bringing enough junk food to clog every artery in my body. Yeah, I guess Sunday is forgiven, despite the thigh-gripping incident.

Plus, I'm pretty sure taking a class will get Dawson and Jesse off my case, and I want to play nice with them. They've already helped me a lot, even when I e-mailed them each three times on Sunday.

I park my pink Mini in an exceptionally busy XWL parking lot, but this time there's no sign of Ty. Not that I'm looking for him.

Ginger-Bearded Guy welcomes me at the desk with a big smile, and even calls me "Blaire" a few times just to prove that he remembers my name. He also introduces himself as Scott, which, I admit, is far catchier than Ginger-Bearded Guy.

"So what class should I take?" I study the schedule on the board behind the desk. Every single class sounds foreign and intimidating. Muay Thai. Brazilian Jiu Jitsu. Tae Kwon Do. I run my hand over my hair with frustration. Guess there's no point asking when the next yoga class is.

"There's either kickboxing with Jesse or jiu jitsu with Tyler. Both start at six o'clock."

I think I'll get a better grip of how things work if I take kickboxing. Plus, Jesse is a cool dude, so that's a no brainer.

"Kickboxing, please."

"Cool. Go all the way straight, and it's the first door on the right. Ask Jesse for the gear. Break a leg, babe."

"Trust me, Scott. With my luck, I just might."

I stroll into class, and even though I'm ten minutes early, there are already fifteen people inside, chatting to each other and swapping class-related advice while guarding their favorite spots.

They obviously know one another and are comfortable as a group, and they all have boxing gloves, mouth guards and kickboxing gear. Being the newbie, I keep to myself. Which is easy, since no one talks to me. A pang of excitement pierces through me. I've always been the sporty one, Izzy being the delicate, girly twin. Me? I climbed trees, rolled around the mud and even played soccer. This could actually be fun, I try telling myself.

Five minutes later, the door swings open and Jesse walks in, hands on his waist. I sheepishly wave to him, grateful for his welcoming smile. He looks surprised to see me. I'd be surprised to see me too. But the truth is, Dawson pushed me to participate in a class, and I definitely don't want to piss him off. I need to nail this baby down if I'm ever going to get my degree.

Jesse hands me an old pair of boxing gloves. They match my lazy attire of black yoga pants and pink, loose crop top I borrowed from Izzy's closet. I listen patiently when he explains what we're going to work on today, and nod along with everyone else, even though he might as well be speaking in tongues.

He is using kickboxing lingo, and I pretty much understand only every fourth word. My mind drifts and I'm zoning out.

*I want an ice cream sandwich.*

*I should probably stop eating so much sugar.*

*Is the new Arctic Monkeys album out? I need to buy it.*

*Hey, whatever happened to that kid from* The Shining*?*

My grave contemplations are interrupted when the door flings wide again. Ty swings it with force, testosterone pouring from every cell in his body. Behind him is a large group of students wearing head and knee guards.

My mouth turns dry just from seeing him. He's wearing a wifebeater, black fight shorts and a baseball cap. The chatter stops, and all the women stare at him like he's a red velvet brownie.

His hawk eyes are scanning the faces, searching, until they land on little ol' me.

His gaze narrows and he shoots me a hard-edged smile.

He found what he was looking for.

"A word, bro?" he asks Jesse in an even voice, but his dark eyes are still trained on me.

They huddle in the corner for less than a minute, bobbing their heads in agreement before Jesse claps his hands and announces, "Okay, class. Change of plans. Today we'll have a special class. We'll mash and mix up the techniques and do both traditional kickboxing and jiu jitsu. You will be paired with the other class, and you'll work together. Both Tyler and I will be instructing this class, so this should be pretty damn good."

Yup, that's definitely it for me.

Trying kickboxing with Jesse might have been okay, but there's no way I'm chancing public humiliation under Ty's watchful eye. Every time I'm around him I feel like my limbs don't belong to me. I can't use them when he's watching my every move. I'm leaving.

I casually start for the door, resisting the urge to tiptoe, and I'm about to reach for the knob when a big warm hand snakes around me and grasps my wrist.

Goddammit.

"And where do you think you're going?" It's Ty, his voice filled with amusement. The asshat.

"Me? Oh, I think I'm going to pass today. I'm not really into... jiu jitsu." I try to sound cool.

"You don't know what it is," he says matter-of-factly.

"Hence I'm not into it," I deadpan. He shakes his head no and moves closer to me. I notice he does it a lot, invading people's personal space. I guess it comes with the territory of the occupation. You know, like thigh-hugging a guy's head in your crotch to cut off his blood supply until he passes out. That kind of thing.

"You're staying."

"Thanks for the offer, but no."

"Was there a question mark in my voice? It wasn't an offer."

Douchebag much?

"I'm sorry, okay, but I really don't want to do this now. I thought we'd be punching bags or something. I don't think I fit in here at all. I hate violence. Please get out of my way." My eyes are furious, and I hope they are shooting lava darts at his silky black pupils.

"Bullshit." He smirks, his dimples deepening. "You love violence. Every woman does."

"Excuse me?" I huff.

He circles closer, like a predator zeroing in on its prey.

The air freezes. Everyone around us seems to disappear. I have his undivided attention, and I have no clue what to do with it.

"Are you calling me a liar?" I try to keep my voice steady. He's pissing me off. I have a feeling he is assuming that I see whatever other girls find alluring in him. Watch him through the same veil of lusty desire. Well, he's wrong.

"I'm calling you a liar *and* a bullshitter. All girls like violence. Every woman wants to mate with the victorious warrior. It's okay, Blaire. It's in your DNA. Don't feel bad about it." His mouth curves into a devastating smile as he brushes his thumb down my spine.

What!

Brain finally kicks Hormones in the butt, grabs the gun at its temple and throws the weapon to the far corner of the room.

I ball up my fist and wave it at him. "I'm warning you," I hiss, "if you don't take three steps back from me this instant, you'll regret it."

I'd never hurt a fly. But he doesn't need to know that right now.

"Let me get this straight, you're threatening an XWL fighter with a punch?" He laughs, but his nostrils flare. I'm pissing him off. And I realize I like it. There's a lot of commotion in the room, people stretching and shouting, but we're both so oblivious to our surroundings, an alien spaceship could land right between us and we wouldn't even notice.

"Yes. We both know you won't hit back."

"Why?"

"Because I'm a girl," I say with conviction, eyes rolling. His face is so close to mine, I'm almost able to touch his lips. Hormones want to wrestle him to the mat-covered floor, and not in a professional, jiu-jitsu way, but Brain still has the upper hand.

Ty's warm breath caresses my skin, giving me goose bumps. I'm convinced my heart is thudding loud enough that not just everyone in the room can hear it, but everyone in the county. The air sizzles between us.

Jesse finally notices us and yells from across the room,

"Tyler! Get your ass over here, bro. We're about to start."

Ty doesn't break his intense stare and holds my gaze for a few more seconds.

"You wanna hit me? I'm game. Let's see if you're as good as your words after class. But you're staying." He thumbs my ribcage, and even though I want to run away, I stay put. Not because he tells me to, but because I sure as hell don't want him to think I'm afraid of him.

We start off with dynamic stretching and move to cardio, with lots of jump squats and walking lunges. It's intense, but I try to keep up. I don't smoke much weed, I really don't, but I'm beginning to reassess whether to ditch my new hobby altogether. I don't remember feeling so out of breath when working out, and I used to be a sporty kid up until my senior year in high school. Practically the best runner out of all the girls in my class. I feel dizzy and exhausted as hell, but my pride won't let me stop. I wish I had the same approach to college. It might have saved me time and my parents a whole lotta money and pep talks.

"Doing a great job there, kid." Jesse gives me the thumbs up as I complete another round of sprinting and crawling. At this point, nausea takes over my entire body, but I'm not giving up.

Tyler ignores my existence, but I somehow figured that he would.

After warm-up, we get down to business, and this is much harder for me to keep up with. I don't have the technique or the knowledge to compete with the person I'm paired with. As it happens, I'm teamed with a veteran kickboxer named Josie. Josie is a real ballbuster. She's well into her forties but could probably skin me alive and use my body as a living room rug if she wanted. I'm no challenge for her, and she's obviously growing frustrated with my inability to fight back. We take turns holding the pad for each other while the other person throws punches. Neither of us actually gets hit, but I get tired whenever it's my turn to spar and exhausted from holding the pad whenever she throws punches. I know I'm slowing her down, and she is losing patience.

"Put the pad higher toward your face. I don't want to break your pretty little nose," she warns for the fourth time as we're circling, shadow-boxing each other. "And trust me, Barbie, I can."

Whoa! Barbie?

"I've seen your pink Mini, hon. It's real cute, just like your glittery top, but I need you to focus, I don't get many chances to work out during the week," she explains.

"I'm trying, Jackie Chan Junior. Cut me some slack, this is my first time." I'm panting and constantly swiping sweat off my forehead with the back of my forearm. Maybe I shouldn't have gone all G.I. Jane and wasted all my energy in the first fifteen minutes.

"You wanna learn or you wanna whine, Barbie? Hold the pad higher!"

"I'm not a Barbie," I grunt, which clearly contradicts my point. Jesse and Tyler are moving among the sparring pairs, offering tips and instructions. The last thing I need right now is Ty butting into this thing. So, unsurprisingly, fate leads him straight to our corner.

Seriously? There are like forty people in this room.

"What's up, Josie?" Ty asks. He brought his irresistible mouthwash and Hot-Dude smell with him. Why'd he have to do that?

"She's getting it." Josie wheezes, tossing another blow. "But she hates it when I call her Barbie."

Ty's eyes light up like a Christmas tree when he hears my new, humiliating nickname.

"Suits her. Have you seen her car? Perfect name." He winks at me and then glues his mouth to my ear. "Stop firing aimless shots when you spar. Plan ahead, and don't hold the pad so tight. You're wasting your energy," he says and walks off.

"Oh, boy, you're in trouble now, Barbie." Josie laughs and throws another punch at me. This time she doesn't hold back on her strength.

My body bounces backwards from the blow, but the pad absorbs the hit. This time I don't wince. Josie whistles her approval, circling me with an interested expression.

"How do you mean?" I ask. I'm pretty sure it's her turn to hold the pad, but I'm not in a hurry to send more useless punches.

"I know Ty and I know how he is around girls. He likes you. But watch out. This one will eat you alive."

Are these people for real? Who talks like that?

I blush, biting my inner cheek.

"I think it's my turn now, Josie." I hand her the pad.

Josie looks disappointed, but she knows she milked the situation long enough. We change positions and I study her for a few seconds, debating how to go around it. I can throw aimless punches, or I can try and mimic the guy to my right. I've been watching him throughout class and he seems to know what he's doing.

I choose the second option and send a roundhouse kick and then a jab, trying to aim straight to the middle of the pad.

"Whoa, Barbie!" Josie's eyes widen, almost in slow mo, as she tumbles backwards slightly.

According to Josie, I just threw a combination.

Ty is looking at me, arms folded over his chiseled chest. The whole class stops to see how the newbie kicked ass against all odds. Confidence washes through me.

"Good?" I pant. I will never be able to do this again. Ever.

"Great!" Josie smirks.

"So can you stop calling me Barbie?" I ask.

"Sure thing." She wiggles her eyebrows and cocks her head in Ty's direction. "But he won't."

# CHAPTER 4

Jesse unwraps my hands from the tight boxing gloves while I'm babbling about my so-called combination. An uninformed person would suspect I had just taken down Arnold Schwarzenegger and Muhammad Ali together. I wince when I realize my knuckles are bright red and keep fidgeting with my fingers to help the blood circulation flow.

"You did good, Blaire," Jesse compliments. "You should hit class more often."

I smile and squeeze his hand. Jesse is nice, but I think I'll stick to running and hitting yoga classes every once in a while. I'm still freaked out by MMA, and it'll never be my scene. Plus, I'm pretty sure I was running on zero oxygen throughout the majority of class. Now I'm not a doctor, but this can't be good, right?

The room is beginning to empty out, but people are still milling around Ty, asking him questions. Especially girls. My hair is plastered on my sticky temples and my cheeks are flushed.

My tight yoga pants and pink top are soaked, but I feel absurdly invincible.

Finally, Tyler walks back to us, taking a sip of his protein shake. There are still a few people scattered around the room, talking about head kicks and whatnot. Tyler stares at me, his eyes unwavering.

"Everybody out," he orders, raising his voice. "Barbie stays."

The chatter stops and everybody's curious eyes are fixed on me. I fold my arms, trying to look indifferent, but my blush betrays me.

Jesse shakes his head, laughing to himself, and stands up from the stools we sit on. "Watch yourself, Blaire. This one takes no prisoners." He walks away, slapping backs and herding people out of the room.

Everyone seems to accept Ty's order and dashes off with no argument. He wears authority incredibly well. Another thing to add to the list of things I find irritating about him.

I watch the door closing behind the last person to walk out and close my eyes, inhaling all the oxygen I can get into my lungs. I can handle him. I can handle Ty Wilder.

Of course I can handle Ty Wilder.

I'm a (kind of) strong, (semi) independent woman, and I can. Handle. Ty. Wilder.

Jesus Christ. I so can't handle him.

He paces around me like a tiger, checking me out head to toe, and doesn't even attempt to hide it.

His eyes are scanning me like he's trying to decide whether he likes what he sees. I'm acutely aware of my body, and I instinctively suck in my stomach and straighten my posture. When I realize what I've done, I'm horrified. Every feminist bone in my body instructs me to get the hell out of here, but Brain is momentarily kidnapped by Hormones and has duct tape plastered to its mouth. I'm melting like candle wax from the intentness of his gaze. I'm freakin' mute. Just as well, since I doubt I'd make much sense when he is so incredibly close.

"Punch me, Barbie," he murmurs, his hooded gaze boring into my clothes, making me feel oh-so-very naked.

"Stop calling me that." I wet my lips, my mouth dry. He keeps circling me, his wifebeater tight against his muscular body.

"Punch. Me. Now," he barks into my face. "What the hell are you waiting for? Come on now. Give it all you got."

I lift my arm and send a weak punch into his bicep, barely

making contact. He throws his beautiful head back and laughs, showing off a string of pearly whites. His smile dies quickly.

"Harder, Barbie."

Thump.

"HARDER!"

Thump.

"H-A-R-D-E-R!"

I stop and stare at him. He moves closer. I know he expects it to throw me off balance, and I play along. I take a step back, so he takes two steps forward. He is now predictable to me, and I have every intention of taking advantage of it. Plan ahead, he said, right? We continue this stupid tango until I have him at an angle that allows me to throw a good punch.

"You get off on bullying me, don't you?" I build momentum and throw the hardest blow I can produce. My knuckles throb as my fist collides with his taut stomach muscles. Even though I'm the one hitting him, I'm also the one yelping like a little girl who just got wedgied. The impact is so hard, my shoulder almost dislocates. I'd like to think I managed to hurt him, but judging by the lazy smirk plastered on his face, I doubt he felt it.

"Seriously?" I shriek. He didn't even flinch.

He taps his lower lip looking upwards, pretending to think about something. "You do realize I'm a professional fighter, right?"

"Nah, I thought you were an astrophysicist." I bite my inner cheek and fold my arms.

His smirk breaks into a grin, and he pins me against the wall and boxes me between his massive arms. I gasp my surprise and feel the heat humming between us like electricity. There's crazy laughter in his eyes and I can feel his ribs and abs crushing against my chest. His forefinger presses on my lips as his weight shifts onto my much smaller body with force.

"Do. Not. Yell," he whispers.

Every hair on my body stands at attention. I battle for air, my gaze shifting from his eyes to his lips. I'm under a deep spell, and I'm beginning to forget the reason I don't want him in the first place. He is so sinfully sexy that it actually makes me angry. Angry at him, angry at myself, and especially angry at his mother, who raised a son who is so freaking sure he can have every girl he's ever laid eyes on.

Ty is staring down at me, calculating his next move under those thick, dark eyelashes. His jaw is clenched, and he looks like million things are running through his head at the same time.

"Tyler…" I clear my throat. My voice sounds foreign to me. "Don't kiss me."

I don't want to get hurt. And kissing him is hurling me in the fast lane toward a collision with this walking calamity. Cocky, over-confident, explosive.

And I have absolutely no control over my feelings around him.

"You're scared," he states evenly, his gaze steady on mine.

I nod, closing my eyes before I'm the one who kisses him.

"Good. You should be." He untangles me from his grasp and takes a step back. Air leaves my lungs once I'm no longer clasped between his arms, leaving me deflated and cold. He starts walking toward the door as I hold one arm against the wall, regaining my balance.

"That was a good punch," he mutters almost to himself, but the next thing he says is loud and clear and definitely meant for me to hear. "And you're right, to be scared. I would never hit you, Barbie, but I'll hurt you, alright."

He shuts the door behind him with a thud, leaving me to stand alone in the big, empty room.

I slide down the wall to the floor and clasp my head, shaking it as I try to figure out what just happened.

I'm in trouble. Deep, deep trouble.

৯৯

"I'm not sure eating an egg salad sandwich before watching *The Walking Dead* is a good combo." I moan, my head resting beside Shane's shoulder. We're both fighting our gag reflex, our eyes glued to the TV as a zombie's head explodes.

"I'm not sure eating and watching *The Walking Dead* is a

good combo, period," he says.

On the TV screen, Rick is doing some father-son bonding with Carl as they both kill a bunch of zombies. I sigh and burrow into Shane's "I Like Kids, They're Delicious With Ketchup" tee.

"How was the practice today, dopey?" He runs his fingers through my hair, and I let him. So what if he squeezed my leg the other day? He's also a close friend, and I'm sure he got the hint.

"Ten shades of super-weird. I did well during cardio and managed one good kick, but got really weird vibes from Ty."

Shane rolls his eyes. "That asshole almost crushed my hand. Don't let him hold any babies."

I giggle uncomfortably, wondering if I should tell him how Ty kicked everyone else out of the room so I could punch his arm for five minutes. Probably not. After Shane's recent I-Want-To-Get-In-Your-Pants vibes, I'm not sure spiking this disastrous recipe with Ty's action is the right thing to do.

"How's the Elizabeth Passion research going? Spoke to Izzy yet?" I ask.

"I'm sure Professor Penniman isn't expecting me to talk to someone who actually models for them. I got an interview lined up with one of their PR people next week. I got shit handled."

"You're kidding me, right?" I sit up straight, searching his face. "You grew up with one of their biggest models, and you refuse to get her help. What happened between you two when you traveled to France and met her there?"

Am I nuts for thinking these two did something behind my back that made them hate each other's guts? Last night when I tried to talk to Izzy about Shane she switched the subject to the weather. The weather!

"Nothing. Nothing happened. No drama. Don't act like we ever got along."

"You never avoided each other either. Well, up until recently."

"We move in different circles." He shrugs, his jaw tensing.

I sigh and shake my head. "Talk to her. Even if she acts

like she doesn't give a damn, I know Izzy. She hates it when people are mad at her."

As if on cue, my BFF presses the pause button and grasps my shoulders firmly. I immediately know we are going to have The Talk. You know, the one when you smash your friendship into a million pieces because one of you decides they want to know how it feels to take a roll between the sheets. I need to put the brakes on this thing, fast. We cannot have The Talk. I'm not ready for The Talk. Talking is overrated. Why can't we all just watch zombies being killed? (Sorry Ty, didn't mean you.)

"Listen, Blaire, we gotta talk."

Crap.

"What's up?" I cock my head with a casual smile, but my discomfort is evident. I wish I were the zombie Rick has just smashed a rock into and not my human, flustered self. I can't lose Shane, but I can't date him either.

He is perfect, just not for me. In fact, if anything, he is way out of my league. I see how girls look at him, laugh at his jokes, whisper when his Mustang drives by. He is friendly, outgoing, funny and most girls would find him drool-worthy. Just... not me.

I never really got how best friends can turn into lovers. I know too much about him. Hell, he knows too much about me. There is nothing mildly mysterious or sexy about our dynamics, and that's why all of this seems so crazy.

Guilt washes over me as Shane grabs his beer, tips his head back and drains it in one swig, slamming the empty bottle down on my table.

"Here goes... Blaire, you're one hell of a girl, but I suspect you already know what I think about you. You're the girl who can make a guy laugh, but also make him think. You can be one of the guys, but somehow remain so freakin' hot at the same time..." Shane looks down toward his feet.

Maybe I should fake a faint. Or pretend to throw up. Scratch that. I can totally throw up for real right now. It's just sad that all this delicious food will go to waste...

"And you," he continues with a humorless laugh, "you have no idea how beautiful you are, which kind of makes you even hotter."

Oh no, he's still talking. *So what's it going to be, Blaire? Faint or puke?*

I don't want to hurt him. He is awesome, and deserves someone far better than me. I'm broken, I'm raw, I'm in trouble.

"...and it occurred to me that seeing as we're both blindingly intelligent, passionately intellectual, sexy beasts, we could..."

I want to yell at him to stop. He's driving in the Friend Zone. He cannot switch lanes to Boyfriend. That's an illegal turn. Two double yellow lines.

"We could..."

Buzzzz. My doorbell rings.

*Phew.*

Talk about timing. I play exasperated, when in reality, Darth Vader could be standing on the other side of the door and I'd be completely okay with it. But... I'm not expecting anyone.

I dart toward the door like my ass is on fire and glance through the peephole. For some stupid, inexplicable reason, I hope to see Ty on the other side, despite the fact he doesn't have my address and I basically rejected him earlier today by asking him not to kiss me.

It's my mother.

"Mom?" I open the door. She rushes in, her hands full of paper bags.

"Hello little peanut!" she chirps, dumping the bags on my kitchen island. I stand in the middle of my apartment, shifting my eyes from a startled Shane to a cheerful Mom. Awkward doesn't even begin to describe this mess. My mom never shows up unannounced. She must come bearing a pretty insane piece of gossip. Shit, I hope Izzy isn't pregnant.

"Oh, Shane, honey, I didn't know you'd be here. I was just in the neighborhood and thought I'd drop by and bring Blaire some... some—"

Some more reason to let Shane know this conversation is over?

"—snacks. I didn't mean to interrupt your fun." She waves the air frantically, like she is putting out an imaginary fire.

"Don't be silly, Mom." I start helping her unpack the groceries. I don't rule out holding her hostage if it means I can avoid a confrontation with Shane. Seeing as this is my mom we are talking about, that says it all.

Shane stands up and puts his shoes on, hopping from one corner of the room to the other in an attempt to lace up his boots. He seems as comfortable as a cat trying to avoid the rain. "It's cool, I was just heading out, anyway," he assures. "How are you, Mrs. Stern?"

"Great. Thank you, Shane. And you? How is college life treating you?"

"Can't complain. Doing my best." He flashes his confident smile, regaining his composure. He's a slacker, just like me. Only Shane is too smart to fail at anything, anywhere.

They share an awkward hug, my mother's grin hinting she's intrigued at finding our ex-neighbor here.

"I'm so happy you two are still close." She scans the room, hoping to find what exactly? Evidence of a hookup?

"Yeah, well, I've always been a big fan of your daughter." Shane quickly adds, "The less famous one."

After a few more pleasantries, Shane leaves and my mom and I chat about work, Izzy (not pregnant) and everything in between. When she coos about how handsome Shane is, I refuse to cooperate. She then suggests I borrow one of Izzy's cute, designer outfits next time I meet him.

"So he can see just how pretty you can be," she suggests.

Gee, thanks, Mom.

Jane Stern would love for me to have a boyfriend. I wonder what she'd think if I introduced her to Tyler. Actually, I know exactly what she'd think. Hair buzzed close to the scalp? Cauliflower fighter's ears? An 80/20 ratio of ink to skin?

Nope, she would not be weeping with joy.

But she would be weeping, alright.

When she brings up the subject of school, I inwardly cringe. I don't have helicopter parents per se. They let Izzy get away with whatever she wants to do. Then again, she's financially independent. I, on the other hand, have always been the quieter, less confident one. For that reason alone, I was expected to shine academically, but instead, my grades were so bad that the only degree I'm qualified for is in communications, and up until this year, it didn't look like I'd manage even that.

"How's school, darling?"

"It's good." I shove something in my mouth. Donut holes? Sponge cake? I'm not even hungry, just stalling to be honest. Mom's powerful glare is burning holes in my face.

"If you're struggling again and need any help..."

"I'm not struggling." I cut her off sharply, hating myself for being so harsh but knowing my mother will never back down. "I'm doing fine. I'm doing great, in fact. Acing my courses and everything."

"I'm just worried about you."

"No..." I start clearing the living room table of the plates Shane and I left. "You're worried about the tuition bill you paid."

"Blaire!" My mother springs from her seat, but quickly goes back to her normal, unruffled self. "Don't say such things. I'm just doing everything I can to make sure you succeed."

Yes, including threatening to revoke financial support if I don't graduate this year. But I'm not in the mood for another argument.

"Mom, I promise, school is good."

After about an hour, our spontaneous get-together nears an end. Mom gathers her belongings and heads for the door. As I take a sip of my Diet Coke, she drops the mother of all atom bombs.

"Oh, by the way, your grandmother is getting married."

I choke, spraying my Coke all over my coffee table and carpeted floor. There's not a single hole in my face that isn't shooting soda right now.

"Nana Marty?" I ask in astonishment. The name clarification is totally unnecessary, though, because my other grandma, Sally, has been six feet under for a decade now and is probably not planning a wedding in the immediate future. "To who?"

"A man she met at the retirement complex. His name is Simon."

"Simon?"

"He's seventy-four."

"Seventy-four?"

"They're moving in together."

"Moving in together?" I choke again. My grandmother's love life is more eventful than mine, and she's like eighty-three. Doesn't that make her a cradle snatcher? Or a wheelchair snatcher? *Shit*. Nana Marty's getting married!

Mom delivers the wedding details through tight lips, meaning she is not happy about it. Well, is she ever happy, really?

"Right now she's leaning toward a vineyard in Sausalito. Beautiful resort. Marvelous. The place has Victorian-era gingerbread architecture."

"Sounds fancy. How many guests?"

"Not many. Most of Nana's friends are... well—dead."

"When?"

"The middle of June," she says cautiously, cocking one eyebrow to watch my reaction.

My mouth falls open. "I'm graduating the middle of June."

"Well..." Mom clears her throat and plucks at her pastel Ralph Lauren cardigan, removing an invisible lint ball. "There's still time and we'll see how and when and if..."

And *if*? My family doesn't believe I'll graduate? What the hell? I feel a knot forming in my stomach, but I know debating the point is a waste of breath. My parents made it clear that I entered their shit list the minute I failed a year of college. So I swallow the insult, as bad as it tastes.

"Thanks for stopping by," I say flatly, staring past her and motioning at the door. I can't make eye contact with her right now without exploding into pieces of insecurity.

My mother sighs in exasperation. "Little peanut," she mutters almost silently, before I hear the door shut.

# CHAPTER 5

"Two margaritas and four cosmos coming right up," I yell from behind the bar to Bree, the waitress on the other side. I'm shaking my ass to a heavy metal version of "Tainted Love."

Yeah, Ned's is that kind of neighborhood joint. Lots of 80s and classic-rock music, a little metal and punk, and zero pop and country crap. No jukebox, thank God. I get to pick the music on my shifts, as long as I don't go too loud or too indie, which is a serious plus when you're a music buff like me.

All the waitresses and bartenders are in their mid-thirties at least. Well, other than me. There's something very family-orientated about this place. Ned's belongs to a Texas-transplant named Mikey, who is loud and funny and probably the most good-natured guy you'll ever come across. Mikey surrounds himself with good people, affordable alcohol and great food, which makes Ned's a perfect combination and one of the best places to visit in Walnut Creek.

"Hurry up, I need to pee." Bree knits her legs together, dancing in place like a drunken marionette. She's mid-thirties, African American and a real, classic beauty.

I work fast to prepare the drinks, but I know it's going to take some time, because the table all went for girlie cocktails with a five-page ingredient list. People rarely order fancy cocktails here—Ned's is a beer and shots kind of place—so it's not like I'm used to doing this.

"Go ahead to the bathroom." I quickly line up tall glasses and take out tequila, lemon and cranberry juice, my hands loaded. "I'll deliver the drinks once I'm done mixing them. What table?"

"Nine. Thanks, Blaire. You can't miss them. Six loud, blonde girls with air balloons for boobs."

I nod, blending another cosmo, still singing horribly out of tune. Bree contemplates this for a second before I smack her on the ass with my dishtowel. "Go!"

She hops toward the bathroom, shooting me a relieved smile.

Bree is right. Spotting the blonde girls is not a difficult task. They all have this daddy-didn't-love-me pout, with extra short skirts, bleached hair and... are those fake eyelashes? Interesting...

When I serve them their drinks, they ignore me and keep talking.

"...so I texted him and said listen, I don't care who you are, I'm not waiting around here for two hours until you're done messing around with these three sluts. And he was, like, well, Nicole, no one handcuffed you to my bed—even though he totally did that at one point, if you remember the time we bumped into each other in Tahoe—and I was like, are you serious! Are we actually having this conversation over text? It's bad enough he's sleeping around with every single girl I work with! So I called him twice and he didn't pick up..."

Nicole's story piques my interest and hurts my feminist self at the same time. I decide to stick around and listen to the rest of it. I don't usually bump into juicy relationship stories. All my friends are dudes, and none of them are the type that pull this kind of crap. It's like flipping through the channels and stumbling across an old *Ricki Lake* rerun. You don't want to be caught looking, but damn if it's not super-fascinating on some screwed-up level.

"So I told him I was done with him. Went to his gym and told him it's over. Get this—the douchebag didn't care! I was so, so upset, you guys. I was literally crying, and he just kept training. I actually had my dad pick me up because I couldn't drive. Fast forward two days later, and the bastard calls me up."

Nicole's eyes briefly browse over me with a flicker of curiosity. I no longer have a valid reason to stand around like a bump on a log, eavesdropping on her heartbreaking monologue, so I pretend to dust the fireplace behind her table like a complete idiot.

Needless to say it's way out of my job description, right?

Mikey, who sits at the bar with Jaime, our manager, sends me a WTF look, and Bree, who's returned from her toilet break, looks puzzled too, wondering how come I haven't hurried back to my place behind the bar. I pretend not to notice their dumbfounded stares and keep listening to Nicole as the bar gets more and more crowded with people wondering why the hell the bartender is dusting the fireplace instead of pouring drinks.

"Na-ah, the assclown," one of Nicole's clones gasps dramatically.

"What a dog," agrees another blondie. Nicole is now approaching her grand-finale, and I pray to God it'll arrive before I get my ass fired.

"So he calls me up on Tuesday, right? And get this—he's talking as if nothing's happened! He's all 'Hey babe, what's up? Wanna come over to my place,' and I'm like 'What?' and he's like 'Is that a yes or a no?'"

Is Nicole going to get to the bottom line sometime in this decade? Because I'm running out of spots to dust and the bar is getting backed up with unattended drink orders. Luckily, after a few more seconds and complete violation of the use of the word "like," Nicole finally gets to the point.

"Long story short? I went over to his place. At the end of the day, he's the hottest piece of ass in this county, and I'm enjoying the mind-blowing sex. Guess Ty Wilder is my steady dip for now."

Wait... what?

I drag my feet back to the bar, stunned. He's had sex with her. And possibly with three other girls. I'm not sure why I'm surprised. This is exactly why I didn't want anything to do with him in the first place. All this Casanova behavior from an ultra-pumped MMA fighter is such a cliché. He slept with Nicole on Tuesday, the night before he almost kissed me.

Not that I should be mad. He's a free agent. He can do whatever (and whoever) the hell he wants.

But crap, this pisses me off too.

I trip my way behind the counter and grip it firmly. Judging by the worried looks plastered on Bree's and Mikey's faces, I'm guessing they think I'm in the middle of some kind of a seizure.

I can already see the humiliating headline: Bartender, 23, dies of heart attack caused by boy she doesn't know.

My hands move fast as I try to catch up with the number of orders that piled up while I was gone. I make horrendous mistakes. I pour the beer awfully and whenever someone orders a cocktail (which is rarely) I find a way to ruin it somehow. People are finally getting the drinks they ordered ten minutes ago, and all of them probably taste like whale sperm.

Bree plucks the cranberry juice from my hand before I pour it into someone's piña colada. "Sweetheart, are you okay?"

Maybe it's because I'm pale as a ghost and just about as jolly. Or maybe I'm lucky and she might just be referring to my cleaning the fireplace out of the blue.

"I just noticed all the... dust," I blurt.

Bree arches one brow as she scans me up and down. "And I'm just noticing all the bullshit you're feeding me. Start talking, girl."

Well, I have a long shift to burn and Bree has ears, so it makes sense to let her in on my latest adventures at the XWL gym. I have plenty of chances to share my love-life woes with her, because she has to keep returning the drinks I've prepared, people complaining they don't taste right. I remake all the orders, this time pulling myself together.

"So, you have a crush on a bad boy, huh?" Bree slides beers on a tray.

No. No. No.

Maybe.

"But you don't want to date him because you're afraid

he'll break your heart?" Bree—mother to fourteen- and twelve-year-old daughters—has adopted a don't-bullshit-me tone. It seems to be working just fine on twenty-three–year-old me.

I hitch a shoulder up and fish for a piece of gum. I need to chew my nerves away.

But Bree isn't done. "Well, let me make it easy for you. Bad boys? They're bad. Taming the bad boy? That's a good idea for a chick flick. Doesn't usually happen in real life, though. Sweetheart, you're far too smart to be another notch on his belt."

She's right. I don't want to become a statistic.

"Don't date the guy unless he makes it a point to show you you're different. Because you are." She cups my cheeks with her hands and smiles at me. "And I don't just mean your weird musical taste and the plaid boyfriend shirts no one actually wears but you."

"I'll bring them back into fashion," I say, pouting.

Bree throws her head back and laughs. "Of course you will, honey. Don't settle, d'ya hear me?"

"Yes, ma'am."

I spend the rest of my shift ogling Nicole and her look-alike friends, and thinking about Bree's advice. Nicole is hot in a busty sorority-girl way, but she has fake hair extensions, fake boobs and her clothes suggest she is an exotic dancer (or the least appropriately dressed teacher or business person in the world.)

But maybe I'm just being jealous.

Oh crap, I'm jealous.

I'm jealous of women who sleep with Ty.

I haven't thought about Charlie Hunnam once this week.

What is up with that? That's it, I'm locking Ty Wilder out of my mind and throwing the key.

*Just get this school assignment over with, Blaire.* And get the hell out of The Grind.

# CHAPTER 6

Two weeks after I receive Penniman's assignment, I begin to outline the first draft for my MMA article. I'm nowhere near ready, but for some reason, I'm excited about this task.

I have hard facts and statistics, and I'm going for the gold and have already contacted the chairman of the XWL, Ian Phillips, and his peers.

I've visited The Grind half a dozen times, making good on my promise to Dawson. I still need to ask him a few more things now that I'm more MMA savvy, and I still need to interview Ty because, unbearable or not, he could be the next XWL Welterweight titleholder, and I'd hate to pass on an opportunity like that.

Besides, my intuition cautiously tells me that, for once in a very long time, I'm doing a good job.

But the minute I set foot inside the journalism building, I start worrying about the last time I hung out with Shane. We haven't really spoken since *that* talk. We've both been busy with school and work. Now he is here, earbuds tucked in his ears, bobbing his head slightly as he makes his way down the hall toward the same lecture hall I'm about to enter. He is wearing an "I'm With Stupid" tee with a finger pointing to his crotch. A herd of cute girls hello him shyly, and he stops briefly for a chat, then notices me and plucks out his earbuds.

"How's it going?" He plants a casual kiss on the top of my head.

"Hey, good. What're you listening to?" I chirp awkwardly. I'm not even sure why since he seems cool and pleased to see me.

"Blonde Redhead. Listen, my roomie Josh may be able to hook me up with two tickets to I Prevail this weekend. You game?"

Jesus, of course I'm game. Or at least, I would have been a week ago. Now? I'm afraid it might turn into a date. I bite my lower lip, trying to calculate my next move.

"It's not a date," he says dryly, putting me out of my misery.

"Obviously, I knew that. Sure, I'm in. So how's your research going?" I tilt my chin toward class and we make our way, climbing up the stairs to our usual spots. He runs his hand through his messy blond hair and puffs out his cheeks.

"I called Izzy, but she didn't pick up."

"She's in Asia. You probably called her in the middle of the night. She'll get back to you." But somehow, I'm almost sure she won't.

"You?" he asks.

I blow a lock of hair out of my eyes. "I need to ask Dawson a few more questions and I still haven't interviewed Ty."

"Get it over with, B. Getting all the info and interviews is not even the hard part. Putting it together is the real bitch."

I chew on my lower lip. He's right. I need to get it done if I want to graduate. And I do want to graduate, even if none of my family members actually believe that I will. I make a mental note to pay a visit to The Grind and to yell at Izzy for not getting back to Shane.

Damn, since when did being a responsible grown-up suck so bad?

৵৵

On Thursday, I arrive at The Grind straight from school. Scott greets me at the reception desk with a smile and a fist kiss.

"Stern, Stern, Stern." He strokes his beard and scans me

51

over like I'm dinner. I guess I attract guys like Scott, with my casual wardrobe and low-maintenance vibe.

"You gonna work out today or are you here for more interviews? Gonna try to force everyone into verbal diarrhea mode again?" He cups his chin with his thumb and index finger, wiggling his eyebrows playfully.

"Interviews," I answer shortly. I'm not in the mood for chitchat, just wanting to get out of here.

"Too bad. There's a circuit training class at four, and it's the hottest class around nowadays." Scott tears open a cardboard box and stocks the shelves behind him with XWL baseball caps.

My convo with Bree still echoes in my mind, and the thought of Ty refusing to give me the interview makes me anxious that Mom's assumption that I won't graduate will actually end up being true.

"Where's Dawson?" I ask, scanning the venue.

"Upstairs in his office." He reads my mind, adding, "Ty said you kicked ass in class last week. You should really try circuit training."

"Interviews," I repeat. Why the hell was Ty talking about me, anyway? He's avoided me every time I've spotted him at the gym. *Remember, Blaire, you don't care.*

Scott boomerangs one of the hats in my direction. He grins at me when I catch it mid-air.

"Good instincts," he says. "By the way, the guy you're really looking for isn't here. He's filming a promotional video in San Francisco for the Eoghan Doherty fight."

I shrug off his remark and pretend to check my phone. My cheeks are so hot, I feel like I just got caught masturbating in a church.

"I have no idea what you mean."

"He'll be here in a couple of hours. I'll tell him you're looking for him." Scott shakes his head and resumes stocking the baseball caps.

"Whatever, I'm going to see Dawson." I wave my hand at him impatiently and leave.

Dawson makes time for me, even though I dropped by unannounced. I guess that's what you do when you're passionate about your job.

"You got pretty cool stuff for your article by now, don't you, Blaire?" He jerks his chin toward my laptop as I type away at some notes in his office.

I nod eagerly, still looking at my screen. "Yeah, actually, the only person I've yet to interview here is Ty."

"You gotta speak to him. He'll be fighting Doherty on June 13th in Vegas. It's a huge deal. If he wins, he might get a shot at the championship belt."

I stop typing and my head shoots up. "He's not very cooperative."

"He's got his issues." Dawson doesn't sound the least apologetic about Ty's behavior. "His life's a bit of a mess. He'll talk to you eventually."

"He's having a hard time dealing with something?" I ask, trying to dig for some info about Ty's life.

Dawson smirks at me and tosses the weekly class schedule into my lap to let me know this discussion is over. "Ty rolls with the punches."

I'm ready to shut down my computer and head back home, but I decide the schedule is a sign. I could use to let off some steam.

Circuit training is the perfect outlet. The class is taught by a guy named Angel. It's intense but has nothing to do with MMA, just a hell lot of aerobic exercises, and I end up dog-tired. After I sweat my own body weight, I opt for a quick shower before heading back home. I crawl into the girls' locker room and peel off my damp clothes. There's an LED TV mounted on the wall in front of the mirrors, and it's showing an old bout Ty participated in with a guy named Jason Monrose that I've already watched. (Ty won by submission.)

I step into the shower and turn the faucet on all the way, making sure the water is steaming hot. I stand beneath the stream, dropping my head backwards and enjoying the water against my bruised skin. It's easy to get lost in thought when you're in a hot shower.

The water is comforting against my skin, and my mind drifts to my favorite guy in the whole world: Charlie Hunnam. I wish Jax Teller were here to sponge my back. I allow myself to get lost in this fantasy momentarily when

Ty's stupid face floats into my thoughts. Sneaky bastard.

Get. Out. Of. Here.

My body is my temple and my temple only accepts blond British dudes who ride Harleys.

But I still can't believe he's banged someone else the day before he almost kissed me...

Right, I promised myself I'm not going there. *Shush, Blaire. Change the subject.*

I resort to singing in an attempt to drown my thoughts. I start humming "Blank Space" (the *I Prevail* version, of course), murdering the song cold-heartedly, missing every single note possible, as loud as I possibly can for distraction. Every windshield in the gym parking lot is about to explode into a million pieces. Wolves are howling their agony at the sound. And I continue, undeterred.

I roar the lyrics, shutting off the water and enveloping myself in one of the complimentary towels. I wipe the water drops from my face and peek around the plastic curtain separating the shower stall from the locker room.

*Bang!* My jaw drops to the damp concrete floor.

Beyond the mist awaits Ty, and he is leaning against the wall, between me and the locker where my clothes reside. His arms folded on his chest, a huge grin on his face.

I let out a hysterical shriek and pedal back into the stall, shivering.

"Really, Barbie? I'm the one who should be scared after this. Silence really is fucking golden."

I tug the towel tighter over my breasts, pulling at its hem to make sure my lady parts are concealed. This is so crazy I don't have the time to dwell on the fact he deeply insulted my singing. I can still hear the TV in the background. The host is talking about the guy standing in front of me.

*Since these two warriors first met, it seems like they've gotten under each other's skin. It's been escalating for a long time...*

"What are you doing in the girls' locker room?" I shriek again.

"Don't worry. I won't bite." His eyes scan me head to toe. He shakes his head, eying my hand clutching the towel. "Unless you want me to."

He is wearing a black suit, tailored perfectly to his wide

shoulders and a crisp white shirt open at his throat, revealing a tiny sliver of tattoo.

"Why are you here?" I repeat, squeezing myself past his lethal body to my locker.

"Pussy patrol." He doesn't butt out of the way, even when he sees me squirming in an attempt to escape the unavoidable brush of our skin. Then he must notice my face paling, because he finally awards me with a serious answer. "Scott said you were looking for me."

*Let's just hope both of them will fight clean,* the commentator says from the screen.

I tug my underwear and jeans up my thighs under the towel, extra cautious not to show any skin.

As usual, Ty is staring. And as usual, he isn't trying to hide it in any way.

"And did it not occur to you that it's the girls' locker room and that I might—shock, horror—be taking a shower?"

"It did. That's why I came in." He flashes me one of his signature, dimpled smiles.

*Whoa, good shot by Wilder.*

The more articles of clothing I put on, the more confident I feel. I get straight to the point before he bombards me with more reason to stutter. "I was looking for you because I want to interview you. Can you spare me ten minutes?"

"Nope." He swivels to the door and starts marching.

"Wait!" I cry. My head drops when I realize how desperate I sound.

I hate him. I hate him, I hate him, I hate him!

"It's vital for my assignment," I say quietly.

He comes to a halt, his body still angled toward the door. "I don't do interviews, and even if I did, it's not like the article will ever get published. It's just a stupid school thing. Don't have the time to waste on this shit. What's in it for me?" He suddenly sounds half-interested.

*Monrose is putting up a fight against Wilder, but Wilder is too loose and confident to make a mistake…*

"Don't be an ass," I tell him.

This makes him turn around.

"I see feisty Barbie is back." He takes a few steps closer, the right corner of his lips pulling into a crescent.

"Give me ten minutes with you." I swallow. I watch the TV from behind him, and see how he throws a head kick, his opponent dropping to the floor. Ty wastes no time leaning down and squeezing his opponent's head like a vicious snake, until the referee steps between them. Monrose taps the floor multiple times with his right hand, signaling his submission.

Ty takes a few long steps and stops when he is mere inches away from me. Face to face. Nose to nose. My pulse rate edges up three notches.

*Thump. Thump. Thump-thump. Thumpthumpthump.*

"Ask me," he purrs, sending tremors down my spine. I swear those dark, demanding eyes are drinking my soul, emptying out every coherent thought I possess, burning my skin, his pupils feeding the flames.

I stare at the vee of his shirt and wonder how the tattoo on his chest looks like up close. Jesus Christ.

*Stop being curious, Blaire. Focus.*

"Ty, can you please do a ten minute interview for my journalism project?" I roll my eyes.

He puts his hands on my waist and yanks me closer. I'm melting into him, beyond excited, and judging by the huge bulge on my thigh, so is he.

"Only if you'll go on a date with me," he says into my forehead, his breath tickling my hairline.

Another shiver travels down my spine, and this time it's bringing all of its friends.

His thumb is lifting the hem of my shirt and rubbing my waist in leisurely circles. It makes me giddy, and Hormones are clunking their champagne glasses as Brain, handcuffed in the far corner of the room, sarcastically exclaims, *She still hasn't answered him, ya' know.*

"No," I hear myself saying.

"No?" His brow furrows.

"I'm sorry. I don't think it's a good idea."

"And why's that?" Amusement laces his voice.

Because I built up walls, high and strong, and I don't let anyone through them. Ty wants in. But why should I open up to him? Because he's hot? Because he's used to getting his way? No, he needs to scale those long-ass walls, just like everyone else.

"I'm pretty busy this week." God, how lame do I sound? Super-lame, that's how much.

"Yeah? Well, so am I." He turns around and starts walking.

*Think about your assignment, Blaire. Think about shoving your degree in Mom's and Dad's faces. Think eyes on the prize.*

"Wait! Do you have a girlfriend?" I hear myself asking. I don't know what his current status is, but I'm not going to date someone who's taken. No matter the reward.

"No."

"So who's Nicole?"

If Ty is surprised, his face doesn't betray him. He is as relaxed and self-assured as ever. He doesn't even ask how I know about her. I bet he's searching his brain to remember which one of them is the long-legged blonde.

"I don't have a girlfriend."

"I'm not going to be another notch on your train-long belt," I warn. When I started high school, I made a rule never to chase after hard-to-get guys. Then again, judging by the last two years, apparently I also made a rule never to date any guys. Period.

Ty pauses the thumb action. He hovers close, gluing his luscious lips to my earlobe. Behind him, the crowd on the TV is cheering and chanting *USA! USA!* as his bloodied figure shakes hands with the opponent he just nearly killed.

"Trust me, Barbie, you'll be begging to get some of this long before I touch you."

"You're touching me now." I want to pull away, but instead I shift closer, craving his touch. *Damn you, Hormones.*

A young woman enters the locker room and squeals in shock when she sees Ty standing here. I know how bad it must look. He is leaning against me, fondling my midriff, his lips to my ear.

He turns around and commands, "Not now. Come back in five." His gaze returns to mine, and Hormones whack Brain with the back of a semi-automatic rifle and take over my mouth.

"One date." I cave in. Screw it. I need this interview.

"Say it like you mean it, Barbie."

*Pffffft.* He is so impossible. I never hated someone I like so much.

"Yes, Ty, I will go on a date with you." I'm slanting my gaze sideways to avoid the satisfaction in his face.

Ty grins and crushes his hard body into mine, pressing my back against the wall. He raises his left hand, his palm roaming my face. His hand is warm, the pads of his fingers rough and calloused, and he leaves a tingling trail wherever he touches. First stop is my cheek. Then he strokes across my jawline and to my mouth, a lazy smirk plastered on his face. He presses with his thumb against my primly clasped lips. And tugs.

I'm completely paralyzed.

"That'll do... for now." He brushes his nose against mine, his voice hoarse.

Hormones are clapping and whistling, and they make me do the stupidest thing. My hands travel downward to his shirt to lift it up. He is so ripped it's almost sinful not to take a look. My eyes are scorching and watery, and I try to blink back the heat. What am I doing? Just what the hell am I doing?

Ty takes half a step back and grins, holding his shirt up for me and doing a little twirl. I scan his stupid, prominent V-shaped waist, gulp a deep breath and close my eyes.

I don't want to force myself on him, but watching his perfect body just might drive me to do it.

"Don't feel embarrassed. Quality assurance. I get it." His dimples deepen with his mischievous grin. "Do you want me to kiss you, Barbie?" He is now fully pressed against me, his junk within dangerous proximity of my sex.

Fuck. Fuck, fuck.

Brain yells at Hormones, *But what about what's-her-face? And those three girls? And his tomcat reputation?* Hormones wave Brain off and order me to say yes.

I'm nodding my agreement. There is something liberating about admitting it. I want him to kiss me, even if I'll hate myself for it later.

I mentally prepare myself for a French kiss, taking a deep breath and parting my lips.

But Ty has other plans. Before I know it, he's disconnected our bodies completely. I almost fall forward, unprepared for his withdrawal.

"Told you, you'd be begging for it." He chuckles "Your ass will be mine for two hours. I won't touch you if you don't want me to and won't call afterwards unless you'd ask, but you're taking a chance on me, valley girl." He strolls out of the locker room before I have the chance to reply.

"I'm not a valley girl. I'm not a Barbie," I whisper, staring at the now closed door.

On TV, a very sweaty and bruised Ty is giving an interview to a hot girl who nods enthusiastically at him, holding a microphone to his lips:

*Mental foreplay is one of the most important things about this sport. I wanted to get into his head, and I did. I kept him on his toes throughout, and it paid off. Psychological preparation is half of my job, and I excelled today, as I always do...*

I'm pretty sure he only denied me this kiss because I asked him not to kiss me the last time I saw him.

And now I'm positive that if I'd let my guard down, he will crush me. Just like he does in the ring.

# CHAPTER 7

"Izzy."

"Sissy," she answers, but without her trademark squeal.

"Where's your skinny ass today?" I blow a cloud of soap bubbles I hold in my hand while in the bath. Izzy sounds tired and not her usual, cheerful self.

"New Zealand," she grumbles.

"What, no summary?" This is unlike my sister, who previously described Paris as "chic, beautiful and impossibly romantic," London as "gorgeously cultural and interesting" and New York as "the reason why foreigners still have faith in America."

"It looks like a sleepy Midwest town begging to be hit by a zombie apocalypse. Speaking of the apocalypse. Heard about Nana pulling a surprise wedding?"

"Yeah. Hopefully she isn't rushing into this because Simon knocked her up." I bite my lower lip, and Izzy oinks a laugh.

"Okay. My love life is in the toilet, along with a few of my last meals. Bad case of food poisoning. So let's hear what's up with Mr. Fight Club."

It's weird how Izzy never had much luck with men. In fact, guys don't even approach her that much. I'm probably getting hit on more than she does. Guess being frighteningly gorgeous comes with a price tag. She pays for her beauty with extreme solitude. No one thinks they stand a chance.

"Let's see. Tyler had the chance to kiss me in the lockers today... but didn't."

"So you're saying my chipped nail varnish is still seeing more action than your vayjay?"

"Well, he also asked me out and I said yes, but he is going all hot and cold on me. He didn't even take my number, and I have to get a move on with my assignment. Oh, which reminds me—Shane called you. You need to get back to him."

I step out of my bath and start preparing for bed.

"Ah... yeah, I saw." She sounds solemn all of a sudden.

"It's a school thing. Don't ignore him. You know he's a good friend of mine."

"Just tell me what he needs. I'll help him through you. I don't have time to talk to him."

"Bullshit." I start playing with all the moisturizers and beauty crap that's on our marble countertop while listening to my twin.

The peaks and perks of the Jack-and-Jill bathroom we share: Face mask. Botanical pore cleaner. Cheek refiner. Eye miracle cream. Lip miracle balm. By the time Izzy's done with these, she's applied enough skin care products to prep the Statue of Liberty. I try and use moisturizers in the summer but, alas, always end up neglecting the tedious routine. Izzy, however, is all about the beauty regimens.

"Just, please, I don't feel like talking to Shane. Let me know what he needs and I'll get it done. I promise. Now, back to Tyler. I Googled him. You hit the friggin' motherload, sissy," Izzy approves.

I squeeze toothpaste onto my toothbrush with slightly too much force. "Trust me, he is just an arrogant tool who shoves his you-know-what into anything he can squeeze it into."

"Sounds fun to me. Let me know if he has any single friends. Your twin sister is heading home soon and she's in desperate need of some action."

I laugh. Just as I slip into my blue Cookie Monster pajamas, the doorbell chimes, and I'm so startled by the visiting hour, I accidentally bump my head into my bathroom door. It's freaking 11 p.m.

I'm not expecting anyone. I hope it's not Shane.

Izzy is still on the line when I peer through the peephole.

"Holy hell. I gotta go." My heart flips, practicing its Cirque du Soleil moves in my chest. How did he get past security? Oh, right. Being a local celebrity, he was probably ushered straight to my floor.

"Who is it?" Izzy demands.

"It's him!" I squeak. All systems in my body clash simultaneously. Am I excited? Yes. Am I scared? Yes. Am I wearing my least sexy and inviting pair of pj's? Abso-fucking-lutely.

"Is it really him, or is it like the scene from *Taken*? Because I can totally call the cops. Cough twice if it's a kidnapper."

"Izz, it's him."

"So jealous. I'd cut a bitch for a steamy booty call right about now. Do him, Blaire. Do him for the both of us. I hear twins sometimes have a physical connection that allows them to feel the pain and pleasure of their sibling. Have a chain orgasm and teleport it to me, okay?"

I stare down my phone, half-disgusted, half-confused, and hang up on my sister.

Come on, it was a long time coming.

I open the door in my pj's and wet hair. Ty stands there, in tight black jeans and a matching leather jacket, looking like an advertisement for bad boys.

"What are you doing here?" I aim for a grunt, but my voice is smiling, betraying me completely with its high-pitched volume. I sound like Izzy.

"Taking you on that date." He drops his dark-eyed gaze to my unintentional cleavage, entertained. "Diggin' your outfit, by the way."

I'm wearing a blue onesie with huge Cookie Monster eyeballs on top of my blue hoodie. That's it. I'm never going to live through this humiliation.

"Why didn't you call first?"

He shrugs, as if to say *what for?*

"You know, to ask if I was available," I clarify.

"I already told you, Barbie. I don't do question marks."

I crack a can of beer for him while I get dressed. I have no idea where we're going, nor do I care. He wants his two hours now? That's what he'll get. But I'll be milking my interview with him to thirty minutes, and he better give me great answers.

The thought of Nicole sneaks into my mind again, but I shake my head and make it disappear, exchanging the blonde bombshell with a picture of my fragile grandmother, who is probably sinning out of wedlock on a regular basis while I'm stuck here, price-matching new pocket rockets on the Internet.

Considering Ty's casualwear, I opt for a Grumpy Cat muscle tee, black leggings and my denim chucks. I have no time to fix my hair and makeup, so I quickly draw on thick, black feline eyeliner and squeeze nude lip gloss onto my lips. When I walk out of the bathroom, ready for my date, Tyler isn't there.

And I have no way to contact him, seeing as I don't have his number.

I blink twice to make sure I'm not hallucinating. Maybe he finally realized he isn't going to get some and gave up. Or maybe my peculiar onesie broke his spirit? I walk across the living room and pick up the half-empty Bud Light. It is still cold and leaves a ring on the oak coffee table. I lean back into the sofa and glare at it, my only real proof of Ty ever visiting this place. The beer can, and his scent—that hot-guy smell that's stuck in my nostrils days after I met him.

I fall back onto the sofa with a sigh, determined not to let this affect me. I pick up my phone and text Shane, blocking all the questions running through my head.

**I decided I'm staging an intervention for you and Izzy. You'll work out whatever this is that happened between you two, and boy, this is going to be fun to watch.**

My mouth curls in amusement, knowing how ticked off Shane's going to be.

Then I hear the doorbell chiming again.

This time, I sure as hell expect someone.

I open up without even checking who it is. (I know, I probably would be the first victim if this was a B-grade horror movie.) But it's not a guy with a chainsaw. It's Ty.

"What is wrong with you?" I seethe, visibly cross. I'm not

sure what kind of game we're playing, but I know I'm on the losing end.

"A ton of things, but I don't think we can cover it in two hours. Maybe a whole weekend? Anyway, I forgot something in my car. Here." He thrusts a black velvet box with gold letters on top at me.

He follows as I place it on my coffee table, right next to his beer, and eye it like it's a ticking bomb.

"This doesn't look like flowers." My tone is still hostile.

"Pretty *and* smart." His husky voice matches the devilish look that's on his face.

Seeing as he brought a gift, my pissed-off level shouldn't be plunging by the second. Gifts are not my thing. In fact, I hate to be on the receiving end. Izzy pays for my stuff, my parents pay for my stuff. Sometimes it feels like I'm being held hostage by my relatives' capability to offer me everything I can't get for myself. But with Tyler, I somehow feel like I don't owe him anything back. He doesn't know me, and I'm guessing by the nickname he's given me that he assumes I feel like I belong in this glitzy apartment.

Wrong, hottie. Very wrong.

I reach for the box and open it hesitantly. I take out a pair of pink-leather boxing gloves. Slick, new and glossy.

"I got you these babies when I was shooting the promotional video for the fight in San Francisco. Passed 'em by, did a U-turn and walked right into the store. They made me think of you because they're stupid-pink, like Barbie, but they hold a promise to something darker, raw... like you."

A grin slips through my frown.

"She's cracking. I can see a smile." He takes hold of the gloves and insists I try them. Once he's helped me push my hands inside, he kisses the thick material of one pink glove and pulls me to my feet, twirling me in my spot like I'm showing off one Izzy's designer dresses.

I'm caving in this moment. Hormones are on a break, and Brain is dead right now. But you know who is rocking it like a badass? Heart.

"Listen up," he says. "For this date, I want us to start over. Forget the parking lot, forget kickboxing class and forget the shower. This is just a boy-meets-girl scenario. No prejudgment or reading into shit, alright?"

I give him the eye-roll treatment, way too embarrassed to admit that I like his braveness and new no-bullshit policy.

"I'm Ty Wilder. I'm twenty-six. A Libra, if you're into this kind of crap. Favorite food is probably BBQ beef ribs. I'm a cage fighter. Fun fact: I had my tonsils removed when I was twelve, and I've been losing small bits of other body parts pretty much ever since in the ring. Your turn."

"I'm Blaire Stern. I'm twenty-three. I'm a Scorpio, and not into that kind of crap. I've been a vegetarian since I was eight for moral reasons. I'm a college student and a part-time bartender. Fun fact: My older sister is supermodel Isabelle Stern. And by 'older' I mean she is four minutes older, because we're twins."

Ty's mouth twitches like he's fighting one of his boyish smiles. "Hot damn, you mean I got myself a date with a supermodel?"

"With a sister of a supermodel, not really the same thing," I correct. "But I prefer not to talk about it."

"Talk about apples and oranges. Isn't she some sort of a style icon or something?"

Was that a dig at me?

"I like your style better, just for the record."

"I remotely recall saying that I don't like talking about this just a few seconds ago." I squint my eyes at him, and he laughs, a real, belly laugh.

"Fair enough. Let's go, Barbie."

Ty's Hummer lumbers up to the freeway toward Lafayette. I slouch down in my seat, praying no one I know will pass us and recognize me in the monstrous vehicle, with flame-shooting skulls painted on both sides and a huge self-promotional bumper sticker that says Mind The Zombie. His license plate reads XZOMBIEX.

His profile is glorious, even more so with his slightly crooked nose, ruddy pout and strong, devilish eyebrows. I'm getting lost in his face, like another one of his groupies, and I loathe it.

Gotta. Stop. Staring.

"You do you realize your ride looks ridiculous, right?" Conversation that includes criticism. The kiss of death to a guy's libido. Let's try and see if I can kill Ty's.

"You're one to talk." He smirks, still watching the road.

"That's different. You actually have a choice." I pick up the iPod lying next to the gear shift, flipping through his playlist connected by Bluetooth to his stereo. "Just like you have a choice not to listen to crappy music, but you still do. Oh my God! Eminem? Soulja Boy? Mos Def? What are you, eleven?"

We've left the freeway, and he takes a sharp right turn, heading into a narrow labyrinth winding through the woods. He is laughing again, a sound I'm growing to like more and more.

"Gimme your phone, you little music snob." Ty shifts into a lower gear but doesn't stop driving, flipping through my playlist, his lower lip pulled into a pout. "Neck Deep? Belle and Sebastian? I don't even know... no, wait, found one I recognize." He swipes the touch screen and "Easy Lover" by Phil Collins fills the air.

"It's a classic." I giggle and blush simultaneously.

Ty is singing to the lyrics loudly and bobs his head, pretending to be into it. It's ridiculously cute, so I duck my head, looking away.

"I feel like I've got enough ammo on you for a lifetime," he says. "One day, when you're this hot-shot journalist everyone knows about, I'll use this info against you. Just wait."

"Oh, you charmer." I grin, staring at the wooded area we're driving through, not even slightly uncomfortable at the isolation surrounding us. I wonder if he truly believes I can become something big. The butterflies in my stomach are fluttering in full force.

"I'll have you know, I can be charming when I want to be."

"I thought bad boys don't do romance."

"Me? A bad boy?" He pretends to look shocked, his mouth forming into an O while he stabs his chest with his finger, his gaze turning from the road and back to me. "That's just hateful. Besides, romance is my middle name."

"What *is* your middle name, actually?"

"Raymond. Close enough, no?"

"Rad name, dude." I chuckle as he pulls to a stop in the middle of nowhere.

"I admit, it's not as cool as a twenty-three-year-old listening to Phil Collins, but I can live with that. Unbuckle yourself, Miss Cool. We've arrived."

Ty holds my waist as I hop out of his Hummer, and then he turns on his iPhone's flashlight. The air is fresh and warm and it's pitch black. I should be scared, but for whatever fucked-up reason, I trust him. He leads the way, his fingers brushing mine in a semi hand-hold as we walk wordlessly.

We arrive at a timbered wooden cabin, about the size of my living room, located far from civilization. Outside, there's a stack of chopped logs and an old, beat-up truck. It looks like someone occasionally lives here, but rarely takes care of the place.

He opens the door and walks in, and I follow. The cabin is full of scratched and lumpy furniture, but I also see a huge flat-screen TV with XWL's fight night dancing on the screen. A few lit candles flicker next to a big fluffy rug centered between a faded sofa and an ash-filled fireplace. Right next to the rug there's an expensive bottle of 25-year-old scotch. The smell of old wood and fresh herbs wafts through my nostrils.

"What's your poison?" His eyes are roaming my body despite my best efforts to look casual, and I quickly glance at my watch. Twenty minutes have passed since we left my apartment. An hour and forty to go.

"Take a guess." I settle on the rug. The bartender in me is curious as to how he sees me.

"No cocktails or girlie shit for you, Miss Cool." He grins. "Beer, probably. Though you wouldn't mind something stronger from time to time."

He pours a generous glass of scotch, hands it to me and pivots to the little kitchenette behind him.

"And you like expensive scotch. Unless... you just got this to impress me, in which case, mission failed." I take a sip of my drink, making a point of telling him I hate this kind of flashy behavior.

Ty comes back with a tray full of sushi. Colorful,

delicious, perfectly rolled sushi. With wasabi and salmon and sweet potato, avocado, and black and red roe and asparagus.

My mouth falls open. "Where did this come from? It looks yummy."

"I made it."

"No you didn't."

"I don't lie." He eyes me with pure ferocity.

He did this all by himself? I've never known a guy who knows how to cook. In my family, even the females have pretty limited culinary skills, mainly the occasional burnt omelet.

"But I can't eat anything with fish," I say, "being vegetarian and all."

"Then stick to this side of the plate." He motions to the sweet potato and asparagus side, his hand briefly brushing my knuckles and sending a delicate shiver across my skin.

He joins me on the rug, getting in my personal space again. I inch away, trying to put some distance between us. He stirs something inside of me every time we're close. I don't need this right now. I just want to fulfill my part of this deal and walk away. No need to freaking snuggle.

"This is delicious. Do you bake, too?" I pop a sushi into my mouth.

"Now you're pushing it. No, I don't, and I never really eat sweets. Anyway, I'm cutting weight for my fight in June. Sushi is the guiltiest food I'm allowed to eat."

"You need to lose weight? That's insane. You're all muscle." I instantly turn crimson red.

Ty grins a *busted* beam at me and crashes his shoulder into mine. "I have to weigh in before every fight to prove I meet my weight class."

"And if you can't make it?" I ask.

He shrugs. "Then you can't fight. There's a penalty you have to pay, blah blah. But that rarely happens. Fighters know how to cut weight. If things get desperate, you sweat it out, running laps, wearing plastic bags."

"That's crazy."

"It is. And it makes you weak. I plan ahead and I don't go easy on my competitors who don't. Which reminds me... what's up with you and the blond guy?"

He can't possibly mean Charlie Hunnam, right?

"You mean Shane?" I wash the sushi down my throat with a big gulp of scotch. "We're just friends."

"And he's good with that, with you just being friends?" Ty's eyes are probing mine, looking for the truth.

Well, no...

"Well, yes." I lift a defiant chin. "We grew up together. We go to the same university. We hang out, but that's it."

"I don't like him," he says simply. Like he has the right to. Like he even knows the guy.

"That's okay. I doubt he'll be asking you on a boys' night out anytime soon."

"His motives aren't pure. He wants you." Ty takes a small sip from his scotch, throwing a piece of gum into his mouth. I continue munching the sushi. He hasn't touched it, and after our little conversation, I doubt that he will.

"And you took me out on a date purely for my intellectual abilities," I drawl.

"No, I took you out on a date because I want to fuck your brains out, among other things, and I know that the feeling is mutual. Unlike your buddy Shane, I don't sugarcoat my intentions. I don't want to be your friend. I have no interest in hanging out with you at the mall or choosing outfits with you or crap like that. I crave you. I want all of you, every single inch of you. And call it an only-child syndrome, but I. DO. NOT. FUCKING. SHARE."

The scotch glass slips through my fingers. He doesn't even acknowledge my clumsiness. I pick up the glass and dab at the spilled scotch with a napkin from the sushi tray while he just continues to glare.

A part of me wants to knock the rest of the bottle of scotch down my throat, then jump on his body and tear every single item of clothing off of his unbelievably muscular physique. A different part of me wants to slap him hard for being so rude. A third part of me wants to hug him for making my heart swell inside my chest, telling me what I wanted to hear ever since I laid eyes on him.

Bottom line? Every single part of me wants to touch Ty Wilder. Bad.

"You're rude."

"I'm direct." His eyes wander to my lips, and something shifts in the atmosphere, making the room incredibly hot all of a sudden. I look away quickly.

I have to change the subject.

"My turn to cross-examine you. So who is Nicole, and how many Nicoles are there? I overheard her talking about you the other night at Ned's, and let's just say your female fan base will be thinning out pretty quickly if you keep fucking it up. Literally."

He looks impressed by my assertiveness, but his jaw tenses. "Any chance we can change the subject back to you being a vegetarian?"

"No chance in hell," I retort.

He sighs. "You're not going to like it."

I take a big gulp. What happened to Mr. Fuck-Your-Brains-Out? "Try me."

He shrugs and runs a hand over his head, an it's-your-funeral look plastered on his face. "There are countless Nicoles. I'm not even sure who the Nicole you're referring to is. It's all just a bunch of sloppy one-night stands. Though sometimes they stretch into a few weeks of fuck-buddy-ism."

"So these women just have sex with you and want nothing more?" I snort my condemnation. I shouldn't be judging. Sleeping with a guy without emotional attachment doesn't make you a whore. It can even make you a feminist.

Ty gets into my face, gathers my hair into a ponytail and grazes his five o'clock stubble near the sensitive area at the back of my neck. "Jealous, Barbie?"

I snort my amusement. "Please. It's just that I heard Nicole saying that you were with three girls at once. Is it true?" I not try to choke on my words, to look indifferent.

Please deny this. Please say it isn't true. Pretty, pretty please.

I mean, really? A foursome? A threesome is a stretch. A foursome is a *Bourne Ultimatum* mission.

Ty drops his hands from my face and bites his inner cheek, looking away. "This is not a good first date topic," he says evenly.

I have my answer.

I choke back my anger. "So what's all this crap?" I motion

around us with my hands.

"You're different," he replies.

"Bet you never used that one before." My legs push me upward. School assignment or not, this dude just told me in the middle of our first date that he's hooking up with a shitload of girls, sometimes four at a time, and Brain has had enough. It's getting ballsy.

"Sit down," Ty orders calmly.

"Take me home."

"You're mad because I told you I sleep with other girls?" He is mumbling to himself, almost as if it's the first time he's met a girl who isn't okay with this.

"Wow. You worked that out quickly. Are you sure you want to stay in the XWL and deprive the world of science of your incredible brain?"

I grab the scotch bottle by its neck and zigzag my way toward the door.

What the hell was I thinking? He is a famous, probably semi-rich, athlete. His whole reputation rests on the premise of his alpha maleness.

I push the door open and stride for the trees. I have no idea where I'm going, but I have to get away. Everywhere he touched me stings like fire, his skin infected with so many past girls who dirtied him up for me.

The black night swallows me, and the wooden cabin disappears from my sight. But worry is for calculated, levelheaded people. My head's a giant mess right now. I'm expecting him to storm out, to stop me, to explain himself. But with every step I take, I realize that this may not happen and that I'm ultimately screwed.

My chucks smack the ground, the decaying leaves, my body and face whacked with branches and mist. Brain shuts down, Hormones are gone, and Heart is pouting in the corner. Legs are the only ones who seem to work, and I have no freaking clue where they're taking me.

I stop dead when the earth curves into a hill, surrounded by nothing but blackness and chirping crickets.

My fingers wobble as I tug my cell out of my jacket pocket. The screen lights up before my eyes, but there's no service, seeing as I'm in the middle of nowhere. Worry converts to panic. I turn on the phone's flashlight and explore my surroundings.

Knee-high grass. Creamy fog. And the unmistakable scent of fear oozing from my pores.

I know there's a country road right in front of me, but even drunk I recognize that staggering onto the dark pavement is not the brightest idea. I take another sip of expensive scotch, squatting down and sitting on the damp grass beside the road. I polish off the rest of the bottle with a few gulps and pluck a blade of grass in frustration.

What am I doing? Who goes on a date with a scummy MMA fighter who has STD written all over him? Actually, this is probably one of the few things he hasn't inked on his body yet. I'd like to think I have more respect for myself than to become his flavor of the week, but thinking is not really my strong point right now.

I mentally bark at myself, *Hormones, you stupid idiots! Brain, you gutless nerd!*

I balance myself into a standing position. I need to try to find my way back to the cabin, despite the unsteadiness from the liquor. Then I feel a warm, strong hand on my waist. I turn around, surprised, and before I know it, two firm hands grab me by my midriff, swooping me up into a cradle hold.

"What the hell!" I scream, kicking my legs like a toddler.

"Shut up, Barbie. I'm taking you home. You were a bad first date." I hear Ty's familiar voice and let out a relieved groan.

"You aren't getting your own *Bachelor* season either," I sniff.

Ty laughs as he continues carrying me, striding briskly as if he is carrying a case of beer and not a 125-pound grown human being. I feel his iron-hard chest beneath the soft fabric of his shirt. His flexed biceps rub against my back; his defined six-pack presses against my waist.

But most of all... I feel drunk.

"Live by yourself?" I slur.

"Yeah. Why?"

"Your clothes smell too good. Someone else does your laundry, right?" I hiccup.

He offers me a You're-Crazy-but-Cute smirk.

I thrust my face directly into his chiseled face. "I love your dimples." Another hiccup. "But I'm not gonna date you, cause you're a man-whore. What kinda stupid name is Tyler Wilder, anyway? It rhymes!"

"You will date me," he states quietly, walking and looking straight ahead at the road. "But right now you need a bottle of water and an Advil. I recommend you stick to girlie cocktails from now on."

"Thanks, doc. Hey, did ya' read what they wrote about you online?" I nuzzle his neck brazenly. He smells damn good and even though I'm not drunk to the point I don't know what I'm doing, I take advantage of my own disastrous condition. Who knows if I'll ever get the chance to be so close to him again?

"Someone said she wanted to sit on your face," I announce. Ty kicks the door to the cabin open and places me carefully on the rug.

"Your point?" he asks.

*Hiccup.*

"Must be fun being you."

"Not so much right now."

*Hiccup.*

"You can kiss me now if you want." I close my eyes and relax backwards, resting my head on the arm of the old sofa that sits in front of the fireplace. I let out another hiccup, and this time pepper it with a sneeze.

"As much as I find you irresistible right now, and trust me, there's nothing sexier than a woman hiccupping her way to a drunken coma, I'm going to pass."

Wounded from his rejection, I pretend to fall asleep on the floor. It's late and I have enough alcohol in my blood stream to supply a frat party. Besides, anything else I say is bound to count against me. I've already been embarrassed— twice!—by asking him to kiss me and not getting kissed.

So I keep my eyes shut when he envelops me in a fleece blanket and picks me up again, as if I'm light as a feather. I keep my eyes shut as he places me in the backseat of his Hummer and drives me back to my apartment. I keep them shut when he lifts me up, opens my door with my keys, flops me down on my bed, removes my chucks, and pulls the comforter all the way up to my chin.

I peek for a second when I hear him rummaging through my bathroom drawers, but then I shut them again when he places a bottle of water and ibuprofen on the nightstand beside me and plugs my phone into its charger. I keep them shut as he kneels down and places his warm, full lips on the bridge of my nose and kisses it for a few long seconds.

And I keep them shut even when I hear the front door bang shut.

I keep my eyes shut, but I'm not at all blind to the magic that is Ty Wilder.

# CHAPTER 8

I'll never. Drink. Again.

My head feels like there's a rave party inside, the DJ is smashed, and everybody is wearing heels.

I wipe my eyes wearily and reach for the water bottle, taking a long sip before the pieces of last night's puzzle fall into place. When they do, horror surges through my veins, like ropes of pain chaining me to watch a slow-motion replay of the train wreck that was my last night's behavior.

He admitted to having a foursome and to participating in endless one-night stands.

I ran like a little idiot because he admitted to fooling around with other women while single.

I asked him to kiss me.

I hiccupped like a moron.

He rejected me.

I sneezed on his face.

He took me home and ran for his life.

I sneezed on his face!

Then I remember him taking care of me—the sweet way he tucked me in, the ibuprofen, the *kiss*—and that makes me feel even worse.

I bury my head under my pillow and burrow deeper into my sheets. If only I could disappear beneath my covers and pop back out with someone else's life (preferably Jenna Dewan Tatum's), all would be well. There is no point crying. I have an early class today and I promised Nana Marty I'd drop by and congratulate her about the wedding. I have no time for self-pity.

Reluctantly, I peel myself from my bed and sit up, holding my head in my hands so it won't explode all over the carpet (but only because that would ruin Izzy's chances of getting her deposit back). I see my cell phone on my nightstand beeping with light and check it.

Two missed calls from Shane.

One from Mom.

One text from an unknown number.

**You owe me that date.**

I don't recognize the number, but I sure as hell recognize the commanding tone. I want to punch myself in the face for the woozy sensation swelling in my stomach, but I can't help it. He actually took the time and effort to take my number and save his on my phone under the contact Ty Wilder. Even after my little drunken scene.

I type back too fast and too eagerly for my own good. **You owe me that interview.**

A moment later, I receive his reply. **I said I'd give it to you if we had a date. That wasn't a date. It was an open invitation for rape. At best.**

Ignoring his criticism, I text, **I need your interview. The assistant to the XWL president has already sent me some quotes. You're the only person I have left. Stop being a diva.**

**What are you doing tonight?**

**Just hangin'.** I hit send and then add, **With my grandma.**

**Sounds wild. I'll pick you up from her place.**

**So you can tell me more about your sexual conquests? No thanks.**

**You asked. And I've already told you, you're different. I'm waiting for granny's address.**

**Keep waiting,** I type and immediately erase. **You can keep asking me on dates. We'll never be a couple.** Erasing again and puffing out air aloud, I finally write, **Don't be late.**

*Oh, Blaire, you stupid little girl,* Heart reprimands.

Why am I going on a second date with this guy? His ego is the last thing I need right now. Then again, I must admit he was nothing but sweet to me.

My fingers move on the screen again. **Hey, thanks for being a gentleman**. I hit the send button before I can change my mind,

**Don't get used to it. Next time I won't be.**

ক্ষ৵

Shane and I are basking in the sun on our favorite red bench, drinking coffee.

He steals another sideways glance at me, messing with his phone and avoiding looking at me directly. He wears an "I Hate Being Bipolar. It's Awesome!" tee. I know I look like a hungover mess because my hair is wild and my eyes are bloodshot, but he doesn't ask what I was up to last night, and I don't bring the subject up either.

"Who are you texting?" I eye him suspiciously, taking a long sip from my double-shot espresso.

"No one."

"Hi, Bullshit, I'm Blaire. Nice to meet you." I smirk at him.

He looks embarrassed, pulling his hoodie all the way down his nose so I can't see his face.

"Shane Panty-Creamer Kinney! Tell me who you're texting right freaking now." My smirk widens. Maybe he's got a new dip. Maybe it's serious. Maybe I'm out of the doghouse.

He looks around. "I'm not texting anyone, I'm looking into reporting a crime. Someone slashed my tires and keyed my Mustang. And they did a hella good job."

"Shit." I jump up from the bench to face him. "You should definitely file a report. Show me what they did."

"Slashed tires, remember," he declares gravely. "I had to take the bus." His voice hints at something more serious, like *I have stage 4 cancer* or *World War III is coming.*

"You still lived to tell the tale." I pat his arm. "Instead of throwing a pity party, you can just go to the police."

"I think it's the MMA guy."

"Which one?"

"Wilder," he says, touching his cheeks absent-mindedly, as if he's contemplating this. "I think I saw his Hummer after my car alarm went off."

I'm tempted to say this could be any Hummer, but Ty's car is pretty unique, with the skulls, flames and all the other atrocities.

"Why would Ty do that to you?"

Shane shakes his head. "No clue. I know he had some beef with my roomie Josh, but that was a long time ago. Maybe he thought my Mustang was his."

I put my hands on his shoulders and look into his eyes. "Hey, buddy, trust me, it's probably some punk kids. Where you live in Oakland, you should be thankful it's just your tires they butchered. I'll give you a ride back home today."

This rewards me with a tight smile. It's not much, but I'll take it. I hate seeing Shane so down. It's unlike him.

"Oh, and good news. Izzy said she'd be thrilled to help you out." I bend the truth just a tad, babbling on. "She asked exactly what you need and promised she'll get you everything you ask for."

"Really?" He eyes me suspiciously, his nose wrinkling to disguise his gut-punched reaction.

I go out of my way to look enthusiastic, but I'm not exactly known for my convincing poker face. "Yeah. Whatever you need! Let me know and she'll pass it through me."

Shane offers me a knowing smile and we make our way back into the university building. "Of course you will. By the way, you never answered my text message."

What text message? *Oh, shit.*

I hurriedly tug my phone out of my pocket and scroll to my incoming messages. For some weird reason, the text under Shane's name looks like I've already opened it. It says, **Don't make me hurt you, B. You'll regret the day.**

I remember the last text I sent him. It was a futile threat saying I'd stage an intervention for him and Izzy, forcing them back in the same room to work out their issues.

Comprehension strikes me like a bolt of lightning. Did Ty see the text while I was snoring my way to Drunksville? He may have even interpreted this as some kind of a threat. But why slash Shane's tires? The only thing Ty seems interested in is his job.

And now me.

Why me?

A teeny, tiny part of me now wants to find out.

෴

I make a stop at the apartment to freshen up or, to put bluntly, attempt a makeover that transforms me from something that looks like it didn't crawled out of a sewer in a sci-fi film. Calling a truce in this war between Brain and Hormones, I've decided not to jump to any conclusions regarding Shane's vandalized car until I have the chance to run it by Ty.

I change my clothes and spray on enough perfume to stun a herd of buffalos. After which, I try three different lipsticks and apply my signature thick eyeliner. I shove a pack of mint gum into my jeans' pocket and head out. First stop: visiting Nana Marty. Final destination: date redemption with Ty Wilder.

For the interview, of course. Just for the interview.

Nana Marty lives in a high-end senior home in Oakland. It looks like a glitzy hotel inside and out. Martha Rosenbloom isn't just badass, she's purely lethal. She arrived in this country not long after World War II, straight to Ellis Island and told the officer her name was Miriam. He changed it to Martha and gave her candy: That's why she always told Izzy and me to "always take candy from strangers. It's yummy and sweet. Just make sure your parents are around when you do."

Nana Marty has a reputation for not giving a fuck about what people think. At eighteen, she headed west from her New York home and landed in San Francisco, where she bagged herself a job at Fisherman's Wharf selling spices and herbs. She knew every single sailor that passed by her store (in more than one way, if you ask me) and refused to settle down with any of them. Her behavior was unheard of. A single, young woman working and paying her way to independence. But she didn't want to get married. Until she met Grandpa Graham, that is.

Graham wasn't Jewish or a sailor. Actually, he was well off, coming from a family of liquor importers. Marty and Graham fell in love, but his parents weren't happy about her being uneducated, poor as hell and Jewish. Graham went ahead and married her anyway. Gran got pregnant with twins—my mother and her brother, Graham Junior—soon after. She continued working until the last day of her pregnancy and when the twins turned three, she and Graham managed to buy her store together.

Graham died seven years later of a heart attack.

Marty arranged the most beautiful funeral, held her chin up when she met his family, and got back to work the following day. She never asked for a penny from them, or from anyone else. Over the years, she had boyfriends here and there, but no one could fill a dead man's shoes. Especially when that dead man gave up his good life and fortune to be with you. Marty never forgot this.

Nanny Marty always tells me I'm a lot like her. Independent, stubborn and fundamentally batshit crazy. Izzy, on the other hand, is Graham through and through. A happy-go-lucky, well-mannered person. I always like visiting Nanna, and today, I'm especially eager to hear all the gossip. I take the train to Oakland, knowing Ty is going to pick me up when I'm done. I bring a banana bread with me, freshly baked from The Sweetest Affair.

I walk into the senior housing complex and glance around, struggling to believe Simon is among the sleepy crowd. I pass through the sage-green hallways until I reach her door and knock twice, trying to ignore the stale scent of mothballs, microwaved food and baby powder.

Old-people scent.

Gran opens the door wearing a pair of leather pants, matching black boots and a leopard top. Bleached hair, red lips—this woman is more of a pin-up girl than most of my twenty-something classmates.

"Hello, rascal. Oh, look at you, all dressed up and ready to impress. Who's the lucky boy?"

Nana Marty sure knows the drill.

She grabs me by my collar and pulls me into her apartment. Nana has a stylish condo, with floor to ceiling windows and abstract paintings hung throughout. The more it looks like someone threw up on the canvas, the more likely she'll hang it on her wall.

She pours us warm cider and munches on the banana bread straight from the tin foil. Signaling me to sit down with her red manicured fingernail, she clip-clops back and forth while opening a bottle of red wine to spike the cider.

"Is Simon here? I'd hate to barge in on something…" I bite back a smirk and take a sip of my alcoholic cider. It doesn't escape me that earlier today I promised to never drink again. But it's a whole different ball game now that I need to engage in yet another "date" with Tyler.

"He's at his place. We need our space or we go mad. You know your old gran."

I do, actually, since I'm much the same. I don't do needy, barely handle relationships, and even though I gave up my V-card when I was seventeen to my first serious boyfriend, it was mostly to get it out of the way and move on with my life as an adult.

"So getting married, huh?" I ask.

She slides a piece of banana bread onto a small plate for me, chuckling to herself. "What can I say? He's too sexy to say no to."

"Gross, Nana."

"Trust me, it's good news that your libido doesn't die before you do." She pats my forearm with her spotted, blue-veined hand, before sharing the story of her and Simon.

Simon arrived at the complex about a month ago. Reluctant would be an understatement to describe how he felt about changing his zip code. His sons forced him into moving here after he set his house on fire for the third time in two years when he hosted a romantic night with one of his lovers. (Yup. *One* of his lovers!) No longer willing to put up with his antics, his three sons pulled their widowed father by the ear and threw him into a retirement home.

Considering Simon spent his days on gambling, fine dining and working out, he soon found that he was bored out of his mind with the activities his senior building had to offer.

First, he tried his luck playing cards with all the oldies, spiking their tea with whiskey when they weren't looking and cheating his way into winning, until he convinced them to play for money. Management found out and banned him from playing, so he switched to working out.

Next, he got caught trying to bench press the weight of an elephant, so management revoked his gym privileges too.

The incidents just kept piling up like firewood. Everything Simon did made everyone cringe, until one day his neighbor Ruth saw him in the hallway and offered some advice. "You should really meet Marty. You two will either burn the place down or move in together and leave us in peace."

Figuring he'd already done enough burning for one lifetime, Simon opted for option number two. He knocked on my grandmother's door the very same day. He brought peanuts, beer and classic movies. When she opened the door and wordlessly ushered him in, he knew that she knew, too, that this was fate.

Soon, they started spending every other day together, playing cards (for cash!) and working out (military style!). When every other day became every single day, Simon went down on one knee and said, "Marty, I have no idea how much longer we'll live, but as long as we're still kicking, I want to make an honest woman outta you. Let's get married, move out of this shithole and show the world what we're made of."

Nana Marty said yes.

A tear rolls down my cheek when she finishes her story.

"Holy Moses, Blaire, stop being such a wuss." She knocks down the rest of her spiked drink in one long gulp.

"I'm not crying because of the ending," I sniff. "I'm just a tad emotional."

And what's stirring my emotions is the fact that I really am like my grandmother. I, too, take a shine to bad boys, apparently. The only difference is, I'm pretty sure my story won't have a happily ever after. I fight the impulse to wipe my snot with my sleeve.

Nana awards me with the widest smile she can anatomically pull. "Here, pat your eyes before your eyeliner ends up in your mouth." She hands me a tissue. "Now, tell me all about him."

It's funny how I'm able to tell my gran what I can't

imagine uttering in front of my own mother. My mother is the most motherly, don't-leave-home-without-a-sweater type of person. Mom would judge, then worry, then try and convince me to open an account on JDate.

But still, I tense when I tell Nana that I went on a date with a guy who cage fights for a living and thinks painting your car doors with flames and skulls is acceptable, even if you're not sixteen anymore. And that despite our disastrous first date, we're meeting again tonight. But I don't want to date him. Only, sometimes, I kind of do.

"I think you like him." Nana Marty leans forward, jabbing my ribcage with her manicured fingernail in accusation.

I nibble on my fingernails. "Maybe I do."

"Then go get him."

"Oh, no. I can't. Not now. I have this assignment—"

"Multitask. You're a woman. We're good at that."

"And he has this tomcat reputation—"

"He's single now, isn't he? And he made it clear he's interested in you."

"But—"

"No buts. Your mother and father will warm up to the idea eventually. Their other daughter is splashed on magazine covers, wearing nothing but a thong and two seashells to cover her modesty." Nana chuckles. "They'll get used to your guy too. Besides, you've always been the little rebel. You must feed the reputation. Like me." She wiggles her eyebrows.

God bless Nana. She really knows how to organize all the shelves in my messy head.

My phone vibrates in my pocket just as I begin to calm down.

It's a text from Ty. **I'm outside. Want me to come up and charm your old granny's elastic panties off? Or are you coming down?**

I smile and show Nana Marty his message. She toots, "Old granny, huh? I'll eat your boy alive and strangle him with my Elizabeth Passion undies if he dares to come up here."

A devilish spark makes me type her threat and press send. I watch as my cell screen darkens, and after two minutes of no reply, turn toward my gran.

"Maybe I pushed it a little too far. This is only our second date. Too soon to meet my grandmother."

"If he's as tough as he claims, the last thing he's afraid of is an eighty-two-year-old with a weak pelvic floor."

A firm rap on the door sends both our heads turning in the direction of the entrance.

Oh my God!

"Open up, Marty Rosenbloom." Ty's tone is amused, and I can't help but feel like someone is tickling the inside of my stomach with a thousand tiny feathers.

Gran slides from her chair, her eyebrows arching in surprise, and opens the door with a smile. "Exactly what I've ordered."

Her smile widens when she takes in the guy standing on her doorstep. She reaches for a handshake, but Ty takes her hand and kisses the back of it with a grin, not breaking their eye contact. He enters the apartment at complete ease, like they've known each other for centuries. He's wearing tight skinny jeans paired with a black tee shirt, his tattoos on full, unapologetic display.

He looks the handsomest I have seen him yet. Something about this style makes him painfully irresistible.

"What are you guys drinking?" He inhales the fruity aroma, leaning toward me and pressing his lips to my ear. "Barbie," he whispers into it.

I melt into my chair. Wait, am I seriously getting used to this stupid nickname?

"Sweet, alcoholic cider. Care for some?" Nana Marty dangles the nearly empty bottle in front of him.

"No thanks," he declines politely. "Water would be great. Need any help, ma'am?"

Nana elbows me, doing a onceover of his body. "Chivalry and tattoos. He's a keeper. Seriously, Tyler, what can I get you?"

"Water," he repeats. "I'm on a diet."

Nana sends me a shocked look.

I shrug helplessly. "True story."

She turns back to him. "But you mustn't lose any weight. Your body's perfect! Your butt is the cutest I've seen in twenty years, and boy, I've seen some cute butts in my lifetime."

I redden and try not to look completely horrified. What the hell was I thinking? My grandmother is the queen of TMI. This conversation could easily devolve into my obsession with wearing my diapers on top of my head when I was a baby. This is bad. Actually, forgetting your oven is still turned on is bad. Letting your date meet your crazy grandmother is disastrous.

I wanted to embarrass Ty and have him twist uncomfortably until he begged me to come downstairs. Instead, Ty rushed up to her apartment, and now they speak freely about everything. And I mean *everything*.

"Your ears look awful. Is it because of all the fighting? It looks like they collapsed inwards. Very unattractive." Nana Marty wrinkles her nose.

"Yeah, it's a souvenir from my very first XWL win. Vicious headlock, but I managed. The fighter ears definitely bring down my stock. It's a bitch, for sure. I constantly have to drain fluid from them with a syringe."

"That's disgusting, Tyler." This, from my nana, who has a green, double-headed dildo on her nightstand. My mom *still* thinks it's a decorative cactus.

"It's not for the fainthearted, but neither is the XWL," he says.

"So when are you fighting the guy?"

"June 13th, in Vegas. Should be an interesting weekend."

Nana offers me a meaningful look. "Yes, it will, sweetheart. That's the weekend when I'm getting married to my fiancé, Simon, in Sausalito. Right, the wedding!" She rushes to a sideboard and comes back with a crisp, creamy envelope. "Blaire, I need you to give this invitation to the Kinneys."

"Sure thing. I'll do it this week."

*Great.* Now please, just don't mention Shane's name. Please don't. Please don't. Please don't...

"And make sure to drag Shane with you to the wedding. Your mother said she walked in on you two the other day. I didn't know you were still in touch. I've missed that boy." She shakes her head, her smile nostalgic from all the times she saw us playing in my parents' yard and watching cartoons together as kids.

I turn my head toward Ty. Flared nostrils, clenched jaw, hands balled into fists, a vein throbbing in his neck.

Not happy.

On a scale of one to in-need-of-therapy, how fucked up is it that it's kind of turning me on that he is so worried about Shane?

"Hey Ty, let's wrap this up." I get up from my seat and tug on his sleeve, feeling the blood humming in my veins as I touch his hand.

"This was nice." Ty offers his devilish smile, but the flash of anger in his eyes begs to differ. I'm worried that he'll screw with my interview with him again.

"Tyler, come on." I tug his sleeve again, like a four-year-old.

"I don't know why you're so hell-bent on going so soon," Nana says. "He can't eat or drink alcohol, so your date is going to be challenging to say the least." She turns to Ty. "No offense."

"None taken." He flashes his dimples. "I can see where Blaire got her sass."

"It wasn't from her mother, that's for sure."

I'm now standing in the doorway, huffing. "Ty, I'm not joking. Get over here."

I can't take them together anymore. They make me feel like the responsible adult in the room. Me!

Ty finally drags himself to my spot and opens the door for me. His face is still fixed on my grandmother, and she awards him the same attention. These two are a dangerous combo.

"Have fun, you two, and don't forget to practice safe sex!" she calls over her shoulder, click-clacking her heels back toward her kitchen.

God, no filters with this one.

"Nana!" I roar as I push Ty out the door. I feel the unwanted pull when I touch him.

"What? I don't want my granddaughter catching STD's! No offense again, Tyler."

"None taken again, Marty." But this time he flinches. Or maybe it's a tick? Probably just a tick.

When we enter the elevator, I press the down button five times in a row and rest my head on the silver wall, wheezing like a woman who just escaped from a starving grizzly.

Ty stands to the far side of the elevator, his Adam's apple bobbing up and down, as he tries to keep his temper in check. The warmth of my humiliation melds with the burning sensation of my lust for him. I need to keep reminding myself this is for an interview. He has no right being mad at me. I owe him nothing.

"So, is Shane gonna be your wedding date?" he asks casually, stuffing his hands in his pockets and staring at his biker boots.

That's my chance. That's my getaway ride.

"Seems so, yeah." I blink twice and look the other way. That's it, Ty. Give it up. Give *me* up and let me move on with my miserable, action-free love life.

The elevator is slow, and the silence between us pains me. I regret those last few words as soon as they left my mouth. Tomcat or not, he is single, and I shouldn't want to hurt him like I do. My mouth falls open and I'm about to speak when the elevator pings and he walks out before I get the chance to say anything.

What the hell is going on with Heart? It's hurting.

# CHAPTER 9

"I'm sorry," I whisper when we arrive where he parked. He is just about to climb into his Hummer. It's barely audible, but he must've heard.

I watch his back when he turns around. I'm standing in the middle of the busy Oakland sidewalk, fiddling with my fingers, palms sweating, looking down at my chucks.

I pulled a dick move, time to own up to it. "Shane's not my wedding date. And we don't go on dates, period. We're friends. I didn't lie to you yesterday, and I'm not lying to you today. It's just that..."

I take a deep breath and close my eyes. Opening up to a stranger seems like an insane idea, but opening up to this hunky stranger—a guy who makes me feel so dazed, so hot, so bothered—in front of dozens of random bystanders, makes me feel downright nauseous. And still, his feelings matter, somehow.

"It's just that you kinda intimidate me. I'm sure you're a great guy. I just don't want to date you."

The few sexual encounters I've had were nothing to write home about. Sex was a way to be intimate with the two serious boyfriends I've had, not a tool for physical pleasure. They kneaded my breasts like it was cookie dough and drilled into me with the determination and grace of a drunken college kid jumping into a street fight.

I filed sex in my head as something rather underwhelming. Even if I could open up to the idea of dating a guy like Ty, I would embarrass myself no end the minute we stepped into the bedroom. He has the experience, the reputation and most probably really high expectations. I have nothing to offer him in this department.

He takes a step toward me, tilting my chin up with his finger and thumb. The hustle and bustle of the sidewalk blurs around me, the smell of food, body odor and pollution no longer wafts through my nostrils. His eyes shine with intensity. I want to break free from his gaze, but he is forcing me to stare at him, chaining me to this moment.

"You don't want to date me," he repeats evenly. No question mark.

I give him a quick nod, but my stomach is clenched, my body tight with anticipation. He takes another lazy step forward, his face unreadable.

"I'm going to kiss you now. If you don't want me to, turn away. Offer me your cheek. I won't be mad." There's a beat before he continues. "And you'll still get your interview."

My heart is crashing against my sternum when his forehead dips into mine. I'm swimming in a warm pool of honey.

Turn away, I tell myself. Don't do this. He's offered you an exit route. Move your feet and run.

But I don't. I close my eyes, my breath hitches, and I wait. And wait. Then wait some more, my skin itching for his touch. He's always chewing gum, and the minute I smell it— the minty sweet twist—I part my lips and let out a soft moan.

His lips find mine, brushing my mouth, leaving warm tingles wherever they touch. He's testing the waters. No tongue. No rage, just pure, surprising gentleness.

My toes curl when I feel him grasping my waist to bring me closer, body to body. He feels so firm and tight against my small frame. The only things separating us are a few pieces of clothing and my goddamn stubbornness. A stranger's shoulder bumps into mine by accident, and Ty is quick to shield me from the rest of the throng with his back, cornering me against a storefront, making sure that I'm safe.

His hand is in my hair and his body is pressed against mine, when he finally parts his lips, and not a moment too soon. His tongue explores my mouth eagerly, and I can't help but grin into his lips. He grins back, still kissing, so I allow myself to wrap my arms around his neck, my fingers trailing over his tattoo softly. I know that logically, we are not physically compatible. He is huge and I'm pretty small, but based on kissing him alone, it feels like we were created especially for one another.

We kiss for ten minutes, maybe a little more, but when we break away and I lift my eyes to his, my cheeks flushed, my heart stops completely.

The twinkle in his eyes is priceless. Different. Almost freaking vulnerable.

I want to remember this.

The surprise in his eyes, the tenderness of his touch, the sparks flying between us when I finally found out what he probably knew long ago—that I wanted him. Wanted *this*.

I touch my cheek self-consciously, so Ty lifts his hand to stroke my knuckles, his tone all business.

"Suffice to say you *do* want to date me."

I laugh into his chest, no longer afraid of his touch. I kissed him and survived. I kissed him and it was delicious. I kissed him and found out that despite his reputation, and the fears I failed to keep at bay, he was just a boy, kissing a girl, hoping she'd like it—and him—after all.

I stare at his face, not sure whose turn it is to speak. This is the first time I'm seriously toying with the idea of considering this as an actual date.

True, he is too hot to be mine. Hell, he is too hot to be anyone's. But weirder things have happened. I could probably name a few of them once I step out of the lusty mist I'm intoxicated with.

"So Shane...?" He leaves the question floating. This time I don't hesitate.

"Shane's just a friend. Honest to God, nothing less, but nothing more either."

Ty's eyes cling into mine, desperately seeking the truth.

"Good." He nods once and swivels, leading the way back to the Hummer. "Now, get into my car before I do something that'll get us both arrested."

⤳

Recipe for a successful second date with a hot MMA fighter you're equally scared of and lust after. Ingredients:

One girl who blocks away thoughts about other girls, particularly ones named Nicole.

One guy who blocks away suspicions about hunky, hetero BFFs, particularly ones named Shane.

One cozy Mexican restaurant.

A problematic trio: Brain, Hormones and Heart, who are surprisingly well behaved and in harmony, for a change.

The Mexican restaurant is on the outskirts of Concord, and we sit in a far corner, on a padded red bench, eating, laughing and teasing each other playfully.

Ty sticks to water, salad and chewing gum. "Don't worry," he laughs when I guiltily push and shove my veggie burrito around my plate. "You and I have a binge-eating date in an all-you-can-eat Mexican grill right after the fight."

We talk about Nana Marty and her life story, hold hands, gossip about the different characters coming to the XWL gym and confess what our dreams are.

"Let's say I retire when I'm around thirty-eight. I'm being optimistic here, because usually accumulated injuries mean you're lucky to make it to thirty-five." He rubs the back of his neck. My eyes flutter when I remember that's exactly where I wrapped my arms around just an hour ago when we kissed. "I hope I can save enough money to open up my own gym. But I'm more interested in kids."

I cock a surprised eyebrow.

Ty laughs. "In training kids, that is. I don't know, it seems more fulfilling. Lots of douchebags want to learn how to fight for all the wrong reasons."

"Like there's a right reason," I grumble, but drop the subject when I notice his expression is still warm and open.

"What's your dream, Barbie?"

"The immediate one is for you to stop calling me that." I bite my inner cheek, thinking about it. He deserves my honesty, but I'm not sure he'd make sense of it anyway. "I don't know what I want to do," I admit. "I want to travel the world, I want to learn how to speak French... I want to be happy."

God, this sounds so stupid. I cover my face, peeking through my fingers to watch his reaction. What kind of loser has no idea what they want to do with their life at twenty-three?

*Moi,* that's who. Well, at least that's one less word to learn in French.

Ty peels my hand from my face gently, enveloping it with his. "That's some deep shit," he says, and I allow myself to breathe again.

It is...?

"It is?"

"Yeah, like that John Lennon quote. When his school teacher once asked him what he wanted to be when he grew up, and he said happy, and she said that he didn't understand the question, and he answered that she didn't understand life." He paused, frowning. "I'm fucking this quote up, I think. Let's look it up on the Internet."

When he fishes for his phone, it's my turn to reach for him and hold his hand in mine. "No, you didn't fuck it up. I got it, and it's perfect. Thank you."

ༀ

Ty insists on paying for dinner, and after a long argument in front of a cringing waitress, who shamelessly checked him out, I finally agree. We leave the restaurant with our fingers entwined and walk to a nearby diner, where I consume a slice of chocolate fudge cake the size of a mature seal, and he chuckles into his closed fist at how cute I am.

It's weird how Ty shows me this different side of him, the sweetheart part, the kiss underneath the bleachers guy, who brings your mom flowers on her birthday and remembers shit like your first pet's name and when you get your period. I've never seen him so at ease. Usually, he avoids showing those cutie dimples at any cost. Tonight, he is flashing them like Miley Cyrus at a nudist beach.

When the date is over, we roll back to the busy street and he hugs me from behind. He enfolds me completely, tilts my chin up with his finger and locks his lips on mine. Every time we kiss a jolt of warmth flies straight down my spine. When he breaks away, he strokes my face softly.

"So, Miss Stern, where should we have this interview?"

"Your place. It would shed a lot of light about how you live," I answer.

He clicks his car open. "One honest interview and a side of first base make-out coming right up."

Ty lives in a rundown neighborhood in Concord. He has a chain link fence, and it's dotted with girlie mementos firmly tucked into its holes. There are thongs and bikini tops and love letters and phone numbers on the fence, all in different colors and sizes. I brush my fingers along the fence links as we walk to the locked gate and instinctively pluck out one pair of undies and examine it, only to discover that it's used and smells of the woman who wore it.

Christ on a cracker. I think I just totally lost my faith in humanity.

Fan letters are jamming his mailbox full and a huge American flag waves from his red-roofed, one-story house. A vintage, custom-made Harley-Davidson is parked on his wooden porch, and a black-lace bra rests on its leather seat. The image of Ty screwing a girl on his Harley in the middle of the exposed yard makes my fingers shake with fury. I feel whiplashed, sick and frustrated.

I can't believe I kissed the guy. What the hell was wrong with me?

Yes, I judge a book by its cover, and it's becoming apparent that the content matches the cover pretty perfectly.

We get in the house and Ty slams the door shut with his foot, but I'm still haunted by the sex shrine fencing his place.

There is something about the reaction Ty gets from girls that seriously pisses me off. It's the same reaction I have to him.

Complete. Lack. Of. Self. Control.

The letters. The underwear. The bra. Even if Ty were the nicest, most loyal guy on earth, it's too much to handle. We sit across from each other and he rests his head back against his armchair. His living room is slob-central, full of men's gadgets, books, Xbox games, three laptops, clothes and weightlifting equipment. I press my fingers to my eye sockets and try not to think about all the underwear I've just seen outside. The man is literally surrounded by pussy 24/7. How can I even concentrate on the interview?

His low voice soothes, "They're just fans, you know."

I drop my head into my hands. "And they're majorly supportive, in more than one way."

"Come on, that's bullshit. They don't even have the guts to come and see me face to face."

"Some of them do." I think about the bra hooked on the Harley.

"Yeah, some. And they're good for killing time. I think I'm done killing outside the cage. Now let's do this interview."

I place the recording device on a table between us in his living room and take out a notepad and a pen. I hate taking notes when I interview people, afraid to miss the flicker of emotion in their eyes when they say something important, scared they'll close up when I scribble something like a shrink and remind them that, ultimately, this is not a conversation, more like an interrogation. But busying myself with setting everything up allows me to gather my thoughts. Tyler really does seem to be genuine about his intentions toward me, but it's difficult to place my trust in his hands, because these hands have touched, caressed, pinched and stroked so many other women.

I turn the recorder on. "Start from the beginning. What made you become a MMA fighter?"

"Anger tantrums, mostly." He chuckles to himself, running a hand over his buzzed hair thoughtfully. He stares hard at the floor, not meeting my eyes. "I've always been physical, and as a kid, I was all over the place. Everyone knew how easy it was to get Tyler into a fight. I wouldn't back down, no matter how big, older or scary the other kid was. It wasn't bravery, it was rage."

I purse my lips, drawn to his sudden fragility. Tyler is always honest, but he isn't the brooding type.

"Let me guess, you always won?"

"Nope," he answers casually. He sends me a lazy smile,

shaking of his weird mood. "And it didn't matter. Still doesn't. I want to win... but I don't *need* to. I want everything else that comes with the fight. The anticipation, the head games, the thrill, the fear, the pain, the touch of my skin against someone else's. I need it like I need to breath. And if I manage to pay my bills by entertaining a bunch of people while doing what I love... well, it's a win-win situation."

He enjoys pain. Thrives on it. How sick is that?

"So you were a handful as a kid?" I steer the conversation back to the original subject. My body is inferno hot, and I feel a bead of sweat traveling down my spine.

"That's a nice way to put it. After I got into a lot of trouble and was suspended from school, my mom signed me up for this wrestling class for kids."

I smile. "You got hooked."

"Yeah, the rest is history."

"And the anger tantrums?"

He cocks his head to the side, a funny look plastered on his face. It's more of a personal question than a professional one. I clear my throat and straighten in my seat. "You're right. None of my business. Do you have any hobbies other than MMA?" "Sure. Krav Maga."

I roll my eyes. *Tomayto, tomahto.* Krav Maga is just an extension of MMA.

"You're called The Zombie in the XWL. Why?"

"People say my eyes look kind of dead when I enter the ring." He pauses. "And all the other cool names were already taken."

I laugh, and this makes him grin, like he's succeeded in doing something he wasn't sure he was capable of.

"Why do all MMA fighters have huge, dead-ugly, in-your-face tattoos?"

"Multiple blows to the head?" He scrunches his face, and I laugh again, and now his face practically radiates happiness. "Same reason the mob throws around body parts in neighborhoods—to spread fear."

I stare down at the next question on my notepad and fidget in my seat. That's an awkward one, but I had no problem running it with Jesse, so Ty needs to answer it too.

"You make sweet money—50k per fight, and another 75k

per win. Hey, dude, just reading your stats." I smile angelically as his face tenses. "What the hell are you still doing on the wrong side of Concord?"

"I like it here. It's close to the gym, to my friends..." He shrugs. "And it's not like I'm rich or anything. I get by, but I can't fight more than three or four times a year, I need time to recover, and paying for the gym, equipment, nutritionist, etc., drains your bank account." He lets this sink in before he finally adds. "Last but not least, I'm not money-driven, and neither are you, Blaire."

My chest tightens. I'm glad he picked up on that. I'm not sure how, but he did. It's one more step toward not being referred to as Barbie.

"What's the worst injury you've taken in a fight?"

"Broken nose, arms, legs. Cuts, blood loss. Hematoma right above my brow. I looked like the elephant man for two weeks." He touches the bridge of his nose, smiling, like the memory of it is sweet and laced with nostalgia. God, he is crazy. And sexy.

"Er... okay." I lose my balance, going through the pages without focusing on their content. It's still too hot for my liking, but I'm starting to think it might just be me.

"Are you nervous about your fight with Eoghan Doherty? June 13th is less than two months away."

"No, but he should be."

I continue the interview with a lump in my throat. The AC is on, and I know why I'm hot. I'm hot because I'm nervous. I'm nervous because I hated what I've seen outside his house, in his yard.

But I still can't hate him.

Frankly, sadly, I'm not even close to hating him right now. And that's just a crying shame for Heart and Brain.

# CHAPTER 10

I'm not ready to face Ty again yet, now that I've seen the fence, the bra, the letters.

After mentally falling apart.

I go to the I Prevail gig with Shane the next night, and he finds himself a shiny, new toy while I'm in the bathroom. A freshman, American history major named Gemma.

Well, at least he's off my back now.

Time drags painfully slowly all week. Izzy is still working abroad, and I spend my days lonely as a cloud. Everyone around me seems to be busy with life, with planning their summer, with living, while I go back to floating through life aimlessly, with only school to keep me going. If you really need a description of what my life looks like right now, I'll keep it short and simple: *meh.*

I study during the days and work at night. Ty calls once, the day after the interview while I was at the concert with Shane, but I didn't pick up. A pile of text messages he left remains unanswered.

Sunday: **Feel like catching a movie or something?**

Monday: **So I tried listening to Neck Deep, that band I saw on your playlist. What's their deal? They sound like Blink-182, but they're British.**

Tuesday: **Hey gorgeous, your music sucks**

Wednesday: **Have I been humped and dumped, Barbie? I'm shocked and hurt**

Thursday: **Okay, the shock and hurt just turned into anger. WTF, Blaire?**

Friday: **Fine.**

This was his last word. *Fine.* Only it isn't fine, because I keep thinking about him. I just can't give in and date him. Rottweilers don't turn into neutered Chihuahuas. I don't want to get hurt, but my days without him seem empty, boring, lacking. I'm desperate to stay away. I *need* to stay away. But I'm no longer sure which will hurt more—staying away or seeing him.

So on Saturday, when I know I'm ahead of my game with the MMA assignment and well prepared for an upcoming exam, have already finished scrubbing the apartment clean and have ticked every single to-do-list box I have hanging on my fridge, I text him back.

**Sorry, had a busy week. What's up?**

The ball is in his court, but what if he's already headed to a different court, playing with someone not as uptight?

He doesn't answer. I know for a fact that Saturday is not a busy day for him. I learned his training schedule by heart back when I hung around The Grind.

To make matters worse, I have the weekend off from Ned's. I booked it in advance long ago so I can concentrate on my assignment. Now I have nothing to do but sit around and think about the fact I might have lost him. Lost him because I'm a coward. The one guy I actually liked in a very long time.

I barely get any sleep between Saturday and Sunday.

In the morning, I wash my face, examine the dark circles underneath my eyes and throw on a red plaid shirt, black leggings and deep-red chucks to match my bloodshot eyes.

Before I have the time to regret it, I make my way to Ty's place in my pink Mini. Sunday is a relatively free day for him, with a sparring session at noon and nothing else. He may not be home—or worse, may be home with someone else—but something in me can't seem to stay away.

I pull to the curb in front of his house and slam my car door, still debating whether to do this or not.

I breathe hard, my chest hurting from excitement and fear, when I notice the fence. I blink the surprised sting out of my eyes.

The fan mementos? Gone. Everything, from undies to bikinis. The mailbox has been emptied. I rush forward, peeking through the slightly ajar gate, and I take it as an invitation to walk in.

The bra on the Harley is gone.

Everything I hated, vanished.

I can stand here for forever and study it in wonder. The fence, so clean, so pure, its gate so inviting for me to walk through. My feet hurry into his front yard, and I rap on his door twice.

"Yeah?" Ty opens the door and stares down at me, aloof. I expect his expression to defrost into one of those smiles he saves especially for me.

When it doesn't happen, I bounce on the balls of my feet nervously and look down. "Hey." I've missed his face. "Your fence looks nice."

His jaw is still tense. I get it. I get *him*. I disappeared for a week. So why can't he get how intimidating it is to date a guy like him when you're so used to being alone, so used to the nickname Boring Blaire? MMA fighters don't exactly have a reputation for being the best boyfriends.

"Guess I'm not the slob you thought I was, after all."

*Touché.*

"Wanna hang out or something?" I shoot him a hopeful glance.

He folds his arms on his chest, still unimpressed. "You want more stuff for your interview, huh?" he asks coldly.

Double touché. This is turning out to be more painful than I thought, but I guess I deserve this. "No."

"What *do* you want?"

I lift up my iPod with one hand and flash him an apologetic grin. "To educate you about good music. You badmouthing Neck Deep was seriously out of line, and I won't take this kind of attitude from a guy who listens to Soulja Boy."

And that's all it takes for him to fight that cute grin of his. Heart starts beating normally again.

"Unless you have other plans, of course," I say.

"My plans can wait." He doesn't budge from the door, though. I'm standing on the threshold, peeking inside, hoping that he'll get the hint.

"Can I come in?"

He clears the path for me. Was he just staring at me without talking or moving for ten seconds straight?

"*Mi casa, es su casa*, Barbie. Just don't bring any boys here if you want them to get outta here in one piece."

I order pizza while he eats steamed broccoli and salmon. I sit on his floor and browse through my YouTube playlists on his laptop. We've been doing this for nearly two hours, and so far, he hasn't kicked me out yet, even when I played him the really abstract stuff no one seems to like but me. Now I ease back into familiar territories to wrap up the session.

"And that was 'Jumpers' by Sleater-Kinney." I look up from the screen, awaiting his verdict.

He taps his chin with his finger, *hmmphing* with one arched brow. "Play the local band again, the one from Sacramento. I dig their stuff."

"'My Soul is Empty and Full of White Girls' by Slaves." I double click on the song. "Good choice."

"So you're serious about your music, then." He stands up, sauntering across the room to sit beside me after keeping his distance, both physically and mentally, for the past two hours. I immediately feel a flush of heat. Hot-Guy-Smell alert. Hormones are waking up from their week-long hibernation.

"Yeah, it's a huge thing for me. I listen to podcasts, follow music blogs, go to shitload of gigs, then of course there's the Warped tours every summer. I mean, Coachella is a freaking joke, you know..."

Tyler shifts closer to me, our knees almost touching. He reaches over, brushing a lock of hair from my collarbone, and by the intensity in his dark eyes, I gather we're done talking about music.

"What are you doing to me, Blaire?" His voice is gruff and throaty.

"I'm not sure, but you did it first to me." I'm unable to swallow the lump in my throat. "Why me?" I hear myself asking, and hate myself for it too, because why the hell not, you know? "It doesn't look like you're short on groupies and I don't exactly make things easy for you."

"I dig your cool." He leans forward, his lips almost touching mine, his breath on my skin.

Damn, I've missed those lips. My tummy dips.

"There's something real and unapologetic about you," he says. "You're funny and engaging. In other words, you have a fully human range. Sure, a hot girl can keep me busy for an hour. You? I want more of what you got. I'm not sure what exactly, but a whole lot more than just an hour of your time."

I let out a soft, unintentional moan when his unbelievably rough palm cups my cheek. Blood roars through my veins when his lips touch mine. This time, Ty shows zero patience and I have zero doubts. After a week of withdrawal symptoms, I just want to eat his face. We kiss passionately, gotta-have-you-now kisses while his hands move to the small of my back, pressing me harder against him.

I arch my back, my hips searching for his groin until they find what they were looking for. Just the thought of me being responsible for his hard-on makes my head spin. I fist his black tee until my knuckles go white and he takes the hint. Ty climbs on top of me, his legs straddling my waist and pinning me to his floor. And I'm gone. Completely, and utterly gone while our bodies grind together in perfect harmony.

I'm done resisting. I want this. Want him.

His hand cups my right boob and I immediately stiffen involuntarily. Cupping leads to touching other body parts, and I'm afraid I'll disappoint him if he finds out how unbelievably uneducated I am in bed.

"Is this okay?" He unglues his mouth from mine. It's ripping me apart emotionally, knowing that he really cares, that he notices every tiny reaction I have to him.

I nod, pressing my lips to his tattooed neck, and he groans his delight. His hand quickly disappears under my shirt and underneath my bra. He's tugging and teasing my nipple. This time he doesn't ask for permission. I think it's pretty clear that I'm minutes away from coming just from feeling his bulge against my groin.

In the middle of this make-out session, I feel his thumb

stroking my cheekbone intimately. He pulls away, catching my eyes while still on top of me. He leans on his elbows, careful not to crush me under his weight. I'm panting like crazy, while his athletic stamina allows him to stay collected and so much cooler than me in this situation.

"No more running, got it?"

I nod, breathless.

"No more running."

After we dry hump on the floor like two teenagers, he somehow convinces me to watch *Rocky* with him. Maybe it's because he let me talk about music for hours, because I feel privileged to return a favor. But something changes in me. I suddenly become more self-aware than I ever was around a guy. I'm super careful not to breath too loud, and I wonder if I still smell like citrus and coconut from the shower I took before getting here and what my hair looks like.

What the hell? I never pay attention to what my hair looks like.

I'm lying on top of him, my head pressed to his chest. He tickles my back as we watch the classic movie. I catch him mouthing the words, his eyes glued to the screen, like a five-year-old.

Heart aches like it's been broken, which is ironic, because for the first time in forever, I feel truly happy. With every kiss he plants on me, I taste more of his emotions and less of his rage. I'm shell-peeling a delicate soul, so I try to tiptoe my way into his heart. We end up falling asleep on the sofa, arms tangled, legs entwined. Tied.

♥♥

I think I have a boyfriend. I mean, I may have a boyfriend. We haven't discussed it yet, though. Tyler and I are always together. When we're not together, we text each other. When we're not texting and not together, I think about him. All the time.

Sometimes I ask him to help me out with my assignment. To read a new paragraph I wrote, to explain things I didn't quite get about the XWL or about the differences between the martial arts. What I adore about him is how he takes this so seriously. How he acts like my work and my school matter.

On the day I ask him to go over the first draft of the whole article I wrote, he shows up at Ned's unannounced, orders a Bud Light and takes out the article that he printed from his duffel bag.

"Can I get you anything else, cutie? It's on the house." I wink at him while he sits at the bar.

He lifts one finger, gesturing for me to wait, his eyes skimming through the text. "I'm reading this fascinating article a chick I know wrote. I think she may be talented on top of being seriously hot. Lethal combination."

"Tell me when you're done." I walk toward the other side of the bar so he won't see how incredibly pink my face is every time he gives me a compliment. What am I, like, five now?

Bree shoves a finger down her throat in amusement when I inch closer to her, far enough from Ty, and points at me with a superior smile. "Doomed, girl. You're doomed."

I offer her an exaggerated bow, confirming she is right. Maybe I am. Hell, maybe I want to be. Just because he looks like a bad boy, is rumored to be one and acted like one when we first met, doesn't mean that he is. He's been nothing but amazing so far, even when I wasn't, and I definitely wasn't anywhere near amazing to him when I ran away from that date and then proceeded to disappear for a week.

"You still think he's trouble?" I smirk, trying to look entertained by the conversation. Actually, I'm kind of hoping Bree will give me the green light.

"It's way too late for you to care about what I think." She squeezes my arm warmly, then wiggles her finger directly in my face. "Make him wear a rubber. No exceptions. Got it?"

"Yes, ma'am."

Ten minutes later, Ty slaps the paper on the wooden bar and announces loud enough for everyone around us to hear. "Perfect. Absolutely perfect."

Yeah, definitely boyfriend material.

৵৽

We watch his favorite movies (*The Terminator, The Bourne Ultimatum, First Blood, Mad Max*) and listen to my kick-ass music.

We go to The Grind together. He works out with Dawson and his teammates and I take classes.

We make healthy dinners together.

We accidentally make out in front of a kindergarten (no judging, remember?).

Three weeks in... we have sex.

It's actually pretty spontaneous. There's no set-up, and no candles, roses, dim lights or Champagne. We get back to his place after a night out and start out with a casual make-out session on the couch. I've had a few beers and he had one Bud Light and a soda, so the mood is right. Since I'm in charge of the music (damn right I am), I introduce him to Youth In Revolt. I think he appreciates the fast-paced music, because things get steamy within seconds of Ty kicking the door shut behind us.

We fool around as usual, only this time, he raises my shirt over my head at some point, leaning back down to unhook my bra. It's cool. I'm so freaking hot and ready for him right now I'm down with whatever it is he wants to do, and in-between kisses and little bites, I manage to strip him out of his shirt too.

Oh, Jesus Christ, his abs. And tattoos. Having this guy on top of me is like getting all my Christmas presents in one go. Almost too good to take.

He buries his face in my neck, biting, teasing and hitting all the right spots with his tongue, proving that he knows exactly what he's doing, that he mastered the art of pleasuring a woman long ago. Then it happens. His hand reaches down to my jeans, releasing two buttons and pulling them with his pointer fingers in one go.

I lay there in my underwear and nothing more, and I know exactly where this is going.

"I'm scared." I bite my lower lip, desperate to read his expression. I'm trying to downplay my nervousness, because I'm like, level eight hysterical right now. Normally I walk around a mellow two, even when I face stressful situations.

He flashes me a dimpled smile. "That's either the most flattering..." His gaze drops to his crotch. "Or disturbing..." He sends a slanted look toward his MMA gear at the far corner of the room. "Thing I've ever heard in bed. Why are you scared? You're not...?" He trails off.

I quickly backpedal. "Oh, no, no, no, no. No virgins in this room, unless you have a huge surprise for me." I feign laughter. "But I don't have a lot of experience and I..."

Ugh, this is so hard. Though it really shouldn't be, because Tyler is great. Scratch that—super-awesome, more like. He is so respectful and really, and I mean *really,* dragged it until the very last minute before he initiated sex.

I'm sure that if it were up to him, he wouldn't have spent our dates rearranging himself in restaurants, bars and movie theatre seats so that his junk wouldn't break his zipper. Dude is seriously rocking the sexual appetite of a seventeen-year-old with those constant hard-ons. I know he's been blue-balled to the max these last few weeks. But I think he knew I had my issues with going all the way, and I'm one hundred percent sure that he'd still be cool if we waited even longer.

"I don't need you to have experience. I just need... *you.*" He twists uncomfortably, as if this makes him feel vulnerable. "But this can wait."

Is he kidding me? It's not like I'm happy with our current arrangement. I'm a little hesitant, but I am also human, and he is also un-freaking-believably sexy.

"No, I'm good. Let's do this," I reassure. Great. Now I sound like a Girl Scout.

His shoulders shake. He's laughing at me, or with me, but either way, he is laughing, which is not something you're supposed to do during foreplay. Even *I* know that.

"Fuck sex, Barbie." His lips touch mine as he speaks. His breath sends a ball of heat straight to my groin. "We can watch a movie or something."

I pull away from him, so he can look me in the eye. "I really enjoy spending time with you, hottie, but I'm ready. Like, really ready." I shimmy my hips to make a point.

"You don't have to tell me twice." His hand dives directly into my underwear, and I don't even have time to digest the fact that his thumb presses my clit before he dips a finger in. "Yup. You're ready for me," he says.

I groan and roll my hips up to maximize his touch, but hell, he knows exactly what he's doing, and he is going for a slow buildup of playful strokes.

I feel him smiling into my neck, and my heart swells. Damn, I'm crushing on this guy so hard. Going into this with eyes wide open, and yet, somehow I feel completely blind. He takes my hand and slowly presses it against his crotch. I try not to freeze. I stroke him, knowing this could be so much better if he didn't have his jeans on, and he must be a mind reader because he stops the kissing and tugging to come up for a gulp of air and a plea.

"I really want out of these jeans." His voice is thick and full of lust.

"Go for it." I nod eagerly.

I've seen his boxers before on YouTube. Every time he goes on the scale during weigh-ins, he wears nothing but boxers. But hell if it isn't more exciting to watch him first hand. I want to reach down and literally do just that—touch the only part of him I didn't kiss or lick yet, but he's moved south, his mouth exploring my nipples with urgency. Every time he licks or bites them, my eyes glaze over and I feel closer to climaxing.

"Don't stop," I pant. "I'm close."

He doesn't. If anything, he speeds up the pace, his fingers working incredibly hard to make me come. And I do, I come on his fingers, swallowing back the loud moan that's tickling my throat.

Holy hell.

Ty kneels down for a few seconds, reaching for his jeans on the floor and plucking out his wallet, from which he produces a condom. He rips the wrapper with his teeth.

And just like that, all the pressure I thought I released earlier builds up again in my lower belly.

He pushes in slowly, testing the water, making eye contact the whole time.

"Does it hurt?" His voice sounds gruff and slightly concerned, like he is genuinely worried.

"It's amazing," I murmur. Because it *is* amazing, even if it does hurt a little. He thrusts deeper and deeper, faster and faster, and I shiver with pleasure, ready for the second wave of orgasm to wash over my body any minute now. We come together and I cover my mouth so I don't scream my ass off. I'm losing it. I can't even determine whether it was the best

TYED

sex that ever happened to me or if it simply was the best *thing* that ever happened to me.

He stays on top of me, his whole weight crushing me, and aside from the croaky groan coming out of his throat, he is completely motionless.

"Thank you," he says after a few seconds, leaving me puzzled and surprised. He doesn't budge, milking the last of his climax and the intimacy of just being close to me.

"Thank you?" I echo.

He nods into my collarbone. "Yeah, I kinda needed that. Thank you so fucking much."

ভ

My friendship with Shane may have taken a backseat, but I still feel guilty about his car. After class one day, while I send him to get us coffee, I slip an envelope with a few hundred dollars into his backpack. It's stupid, since this is pretty much confessing that Ty's to blame and because I, myself, don't have a penny to my name. But I do it anyway, to scrub off at least some of the guilt. I haven't asked Ty because I know the answer. He totally did it.

I hope Shane doesn't notice the money in there for a while. Luckily, he is busy with his assignment. The assignment I pretty much worked my ass off on, because he's transmitted all of his interview questions to Izzy through me. I guided her, pressed and pestered her until she came up with the good stuff. I also took it upon myself to gather all the phone numbers and e-mails for the PR agents, lingerie designers and other key players he wanted to interview.

In short, after giving him the money and doing his assignment for him, my conscience should be clear. And by clear, I mean spotless.

"Want some pot?" Shane enquires with a sinister grin as he hands me my coffee.

We sit on our red bench. It's a hectic day, full of classes, an exam, a study group and on top of things, a shift at Ned's.

I shake my head firmly. "No, dude, thanks. I'm done with that stuff. I started working out and I think the pot really messed with my body. I'm in bad shape."

Plus, Ty loathes the fact that I smoke, and as much as I'd

hate to admit it, his opinion matters to me.

Shane almost chokes on his laughter, but he still tucks the blunt back into his special cigarette pack. Good, he's put off too.

"Sure, okay. Don't want to be a bad influence."

"I take it Gemma doesn't mind?" I bump my thigh into his.

Shane wrinkles his nose, like he is trying to remember who the hell Gemma is. "She knows the score." He lifts his gaze back to my face. "What's up with you, B? Seeing anyone?"

This subject is explosive, but I don't want to lie to Shane. Whether he still wants me or not, lying will only make matters worse.

"I'm kind of dating someone, but I still don't know where it's going." Maybe I'm downplaying it, and maybe it's the truth. After all, Ty and I are not officially together. We haven't discussed it yet.

"Do I know him?"

I take a big gulp of my tasteless coffee, then clear my throat. "The MMA guy." I reduce Ty to what he does, and hate myself for it.

He is not the MMA guy. He's the guy who makes me laugh and giggle and see the world with more vivid colors. Oh, yeah, and come twice in twenty minutes, which no one has ever done before.

"Wilder?" Shane's eyebrows shoot up in surprise. Dawson is married and Jesse has a girlfriend, and Shane is freaking good at math, so he gets it quickly. He snorts. "Well, that's a random hookup."

Okay, that's good. He is taking it like it's a joke, not like he wants to kill me, or unfriend me, for that matter.

"I get what you're saying," I say. "We're pretty different."

Shane offers a grim smile. "Ain't that the fucking truth. So you chose him over me?"

I shake my head. "No. Never. You're my best friend." My voice is high-pitched as I hide behind my coffee cup.

There's an awkward silence before he gets to his feet, offering me his hand, which I take and jump up beside him.

"I don't like what I'm hearing here, at all. This conversation isn't over, Blaire. When is Izzy coming back?" he asks out of nowhere, his voice still laced with annoyance.

"Next Sunday. Why?"

Shane takes a few long strides, walking ahead of me. "Just wanna make sure I never bump into her when we hang out. Thanks for the heads up."

৽৵৶

It's five weeks into my relationship with Ty, and Izzy is due to come back from her world tour as an Elizabeth's Passion Fairy. She's even gotten her wings and is now one of the signature models of the lingerie label. She's as proud of her new wings as if she had won a Nobel Peace Prize.

I arrange to pick her up from the airport with Ty, because the drive into SFA is a bitch. I text her a few hours beforehand, warning her not to bring the volatile subject of Shane up.

**Hey. So, just so you know, Ty has a weird thing with Shane. He thinks he's hitting on me, and with Shane's weird-ass behavior lately, he's probably right too. So please don't mention Shane when we pick you up. It's bad enough to get groped by your BFF out of nowhere. Don't need to deal with more mess than necessary. Thanks, scrawny ass. x.**

Ty double-parks outside baggage claim and yanks me by the collar into an eager make-out session. Ever since we had sex, we've been going at it like bunnies. Sex is a new world to me, and I'm eager to explore it from all angles (and positions). It's epic, it's soothing, and it's absolutely mind-blowing. Ty must share my feelings about our sex life, because I almost lose my top, and only come to my senses when I realize his hand is rubbing my sweet spots and I'm about to climax.

"We need to stop before we get arrested." I let out a moan.

"Tinted windows." He raps one finger on his side window, his tongue swirling on my earlobe. "Remember?"

How can I forget? It's so mafia I feel like dying every time I drive in this shiny toy.

My phone rings, and I peel Ty off reluctantly. "Izzy."

"Babe!"

"Where's your skinny ass today?"

My sister's voice pipes triumphantly. "Home."

I bite back a smile.

"So where the hell are you?" Izzy brings me back to planet earth, showering me with a stream of shouts. "I'm freezing this ass in here! You know I'm too skinny to handle San Fran's summer drizzle!"

"Huh?" I guess my hearing is impaired since all my blood went straight to my crotch from that earlier make-out session. "What do you mean you can't see me? I'm right here."

Ty, who is sitting in the driver's seat, lifts one eyebrow, as if to say *Well, she is a model, so she ought to be dumb as dirt, right?*

"Hey Blaire, I'm pretty sure I would have seen you if you were out here. Our pink car stands out like a liberal in Mississippi."

I smack my forehead. "Sorry, Izz. Ty's ride is a black Hummer." I cringe as I give her further description. "With... skulls and flames and stuff."

"What the..." Her voice trails off. I spot my thinner, taller look-alike twin from the rearview mirror. She is wearing black leggings, an oversized gray sweater and a hat she stole either from Blake Lively or a seventeenth-century widow. She pushes her luggage fast, waving frantically at the car.

I flash her my widest smile, while wondering if I possess the same eccentric qualities that make her so quirky. Ty unlatches his seatbelt and reads my mind instantaneously.

"Clearly, I chose the hotter twin." He leans in to steal one last kiss before we have company, swirling his tongue seductively in my mouth and releasing my lower lip from his bite.

My mouth remains wide open and my horniness level is sky high as Ty gets out of the car nonchalantly and heads toward Izzy. He takes the mountain-sized suitcase from her hand and shoves it into the trunk. I catch a glimpse of her from the mirror watching his veiny, muscular arm as he flings the suitcase into the car like it's nothing more than a shoebox.

"Pleasure to meet you." She hurls herself at him and hooks her arms around his neck. My blood boils to an unhealthy temperature when I watch Ty returning the gesture and hugging my twin sister awkwardly, like a child posing with a giant snake in the zoo. He just wants out of the situation as fast as he can.

"God, Blaire wasn't kidding. Anyone told you you're yummy?" my sister purrs.

Can't blame her. From experience, I know seeing Ty for the first time is a groin-tickling experience.

"Missed you, sissy!" she squeals as I get out of the car to hug and kiss her. She pinches my ass, not in a friendly way but in a lay-off-the-mac-and-cheese way. "So, is he your boyfriend or can your cute sister have a go, too?"

"Yeah, this one is not for sharing, I guess." I try to keep it light, sliding back into my seat. I love my sister dearly, but I'm also self-conscious as hell around her. She's the successful, gorgeous one. I've had trouble believing Ty thinks I'm special in the first place, and the idea of a lust triangle with Isabelle is my biggest, scariest nightmare.

Izzy's eyes are glued to her cell phone, her face glowing from its screen. "Haven't seen your text yet, sissy. Reading it now."

Ty pulls away from the curb like a maniac, picking up speed and driving in his usual, guy-way. Elbow slung out the window, head against the headrest, he holds the steering wheel in one hand and distractingly runs his other hand over his head.

I watch Izzy intently from the rearview mirror. Her face falls when she reads my text, and when she lifts her face, her eyes meet mine in the reflection. My blood freezes. I don't know what those blue eyes say, but whatever it is, she's screaming it like a wounded animal.

"Everything okay?" I fish for a bottle of water and hand it to her. She reluctantly accepts, taking off her hat and tossing it angrily next to her.

"A lot has changed while I was gone," she spits. I'm not even sure why she's mad. Because I asked her not to talk about Shane? She's been avoiding him like the plague. I didn't think it'd be a problem.

"Not a lot," I correct her. "Maybe a little."

"Sucks to stay out of the loop. Right, Ty?" Izzy snaps.

"Sure." He puts his forefinger to his temple and pretends to shoot himself, eyes rolling.

Izzy can't see it, but I can, and it's making me wince. He

doesn't get her bitchy attitude. Frankly, neither do I. It's unlike her.

I fist my shirt's fabric into a ball, biting my lower lip so hard the salty taste of blood fills my mouth. Izzy and Ty are engaged in a semi-civil conversation, but I'm nowhere near focused enough to listen to what they're saying.

I hear Izzy's dangerously high-pitched voice slicing the air again. "So, Ty, have you noticed how Blaire looks a little like me?"

"That tends to happen when you're twins." Ty arches one eyebrow and, very casually, illegally passes the five cars ahead of us in a speed that would smoke a fighter jet. I need to kill this conversation before Ty kills us all. He is obviously struggling with my sister.

I steer the conversation to Nana Marty's wedding. That's when I discover that the owner of the venue they had booked cancelled their reservation at the last minute and refunded their deposit, after he realized the renovations on the venue wouldn't be completed in time for their wedding. This means a June 13th wedding is pretty much impossible and that we'll have to call everyone who received an invitation to notify them of the change of plans.

Only, there is no plan.

"I feel bad for Nana," I tell Izzy.

"I feel bad for me!" she retorts. She's not even slightly apologetic about her little, uncalled for tantrum. Though I have a strange feeling it has to do with my message about Shane.

I take a deep breath and let her pout. My only solace is that we are nearing our apartment complex and about to get rid of her ass faster than a dead body in a bad detective movie.

Other than hurling Izzy out of the tinted windows, Ty is doing everything he can to get rid of her. He drives so fast my eyeballs roll into my throat. The wheels squeal like Izzy as he comes to a full stop in front of our underground parking lot. He quickly darts out of the car to get her suitcase.

Izzy gets out of the car too, sulking into the night with her pissed-off face in full display.

"Dude," I say, pulling her into a forced hug, "are you

okay? What happened in the car?"

She waves her hand dismissively, refusing to make eye contact. "Nothing. It's just... has Shane really tried to hook up with you?"

My eyes widen in disbelief. Christ on a cracker, that's the one subject I asked her not to bring up in front of Ty... and sure enough, there he is, about two feet away from us, holding Izzy's suitcase and looking just about ready to destroy it.

"The fucking asshole." I hear his gruff voice behind me.

I shake my head. "He didn't try..."

"But you said so yourself." Izzy's voice sounds desperate and... is she crying? It's hard to tell in the dark, but she seems genuinely upset. All thoughts of Ty are thrown out the window once I realize that my sister is hurt.

"I said he groped me. Once!" Yup, that doesn't sound any better. "It was weeks ago. And I made it clear that I have no interest in him whatsoever. Anyway, he is dating a girl named Gemma nowadays, so..."

*Oh.* Oh shit. The writing was on the wall, but I refused to see it. Izzy and Shane. Shane and Izzy. Something happened between these two... a date? A kiss? A one-night stand? An affair?! Brain is just about ready to explode.

Wide eyed, I rush to my sister, who has already taken the suitcase from Ty and is now making her way to the entrance of the apartment complex.

"Izz, I didn't know..."

But she pivots on her heel and rests one flattened palm on my ribcage. "Sorry for doing this in front of Ty. I couldn't help it, sissy." She maintains the space between us like it would kill her if I got any closer, and hell if I even care anymore. She's so hurt, the only thing I care about is her.

"Let's go upstairs and talk about it."

She shakes her head violently. Ty's done being the good guy, obviously, since I can hear him behind me climbing back into the Hummer and slamming the door with force. I don't even blame him this time. Dude, I lied.

"Go with your boyfriend."

"No way, Izzy. I'm coming with. Come on, let's—"

"No." She practically pushes me in the car's direction. "I haven't been home in weeks. I want to take a bath, I want to have a glass of wine, I want to walk around naked and have my me-time. Shane's an old story. Go with your boyfriend. Have fun. I'll still be here when you get back."

I search her face to see if it's really okay. Izzy sees the doubt in my eyes and almost throws her suitcase at me.

"Oh my God, just go, sissy. Go!"

༺༻

We drive silently. After we roll onto the highway to Concord , Ty turns down the volume of the music playing out of the speakers. It's my playlist, and I bet you anything it's also one helluva statement.

"I'm sorry," I blurt into the deafening silence. I wish he'd say something, anything. "I didn't mean to lie to you. I thought Shane was just trying his luck with me. But now I see that he was just trying to hook up with me to get back at Izzy for whatever it is between them."

Ty arches one eyebrow, looking thoroughly pissed off. "You think your best friend is trying to tap you to get back at your sister?" He scowls.

"Yeah. Not that I'm mad or anything. I mean, she's gorgeous and successful and..."

"And lonely and detached and no matter what, she'll always be the less cool, less independent— and if you ask anyone with a dick—less sexy sister."

"Come on, Ty."

"Coming on, Blaire. You don't need an army of PR people coming out of your ass and million-dollar contracts to be awesome. Izzy can spread her legs in every magazine under the sun and she still won't be half the woman you are. The worst part is you have no clue. You really think you don't matter, that Izzy is better. But I see you." He parks in front of his place.

I rest my head on his shoulder and close my eyes.

"I see you," he repeats, whispering. "I see what you don't see about yourself, and it pisses me off that Shane sees it too."

I can't believe he doesn't give me shit for not telling him about Shane. Unless... is he is planning on paying another visit to Shane's place? No. That was a one off, I tell myself.

And besides, there's still a chance it wasn't Ty.

I listen to his heartbeat, slow and steady, and snuggle into his delicious, singular scent. No one else smells like him. I kind of like that.

"Whatever this thing between us is, I won't tolerate any lies." He growls.

"I swear to God," I answer, and I mean it.

But when the words come out, I realize that I don't actually believe that what we have is secrets-free. I may have nothing to hide, but Ty is full of mystery. He has a pretty bad reputation, judging from the Internet and The Grind, and he's never even mentioned his family around me. I have a nagging feeling his whole life is pretty much his work and teammates.

"This is the only tiny secret I had," I say. "Hey, question—you think your mom will like me?" It may sound random, but I hate that he already knows so much about my family, and I still don't know anything about his.

The only thing I do know is that Ty's dad isn't in the picture and that he has no siblings. I stumbled upon an interview of his a few years back and found out he was raised solely by his mother.

"I don't think my mom likes anyone, including me." He laughs bitterly. "Na, you got lucky. I have no family that you need to suck up to. Just Dawson and his wife and kids. Maybe Jesse, but that's it."

My mouth curves downwards as I run my index finger over his lips. If I show him pity, he'll hate me. Forever. "Thank you for not giving me shit about Shane. You're awesome."

He presses his warm, moist lips into my finger, staring into my eyes. "You bet your hot ass I am."

Heart's throbs are piercing my ears, Brain swirls in a pool of sticky goo, and Hormones are dry-humping Ty's leg. I take a deep breath and get out of the car, walking toward his house and stopping just as I reach his fence. One, new pair of underwear is tucked in the links. Oddly, I don't go ballistic this time. I placed my trust in his hands a few weeks ago, and he's yet to let me down.

Ty is by my side, and the next thing I know he's slamming

his body into mine and his hands are roaming my waist and thighs. It's late at night, but people are still walking past us, cars passing by. Ty doesn't care. He nudges my thighs apart, grabs my ass forcefully and raises me up. I knot my legs around his tight abdomen and we mold into each other.

My fingers curl into the holes of the fence when he fists my top into a ball behind my back. His warm tongue finds mine. Ty tastes good. Fresh and sweet and manly. He sends his free hand behind one of my knees, caressing the spot through my jeans. I didn't even know I was sensitive there. I'm about to explode into a loud scream, my core quivering against his body, and I dig my nails into his back to signal I'm ready for the homerun. He bites my neck, his teeth sending a shiver down my spine.

He whispers into my collarbone, "You are mine, and you better tell that to Shane, or I will. And I won't be nice."

It's a good thing I'm about half his size, because I'm tempted to punch him. I just nod my agreement. *Yeah, whatever.* I'll deliver the message. My fingers caress Ty's tight abs, exploring the hills and valleys of his six-pack.

"Fuck," he whispers into my mouth, tugging my head back. He sucks on my throat, my hair in his fist. His other hand, still clutching my top from behind, rips the fabric in one go. I hear the material tear and feel the chill of the metallic fence against my bare back.

Ladies and gents, I'm officially half-naked.

Quick recap to those of you who haven't paid attention: I'm in my bra, thighs wrapped around an XWL fighter, dry humping him in the middle of a city street.

Yes, I need to take a long, hard look at my life.

No, tonight is not the time for it.

"I should be mad at you, but I can't, and that annoys the hell outta me." He lowers his head, letting out a frustrated groan. His eyes are trained on my lips. They are dark, full of want, and holding dirty promises. "Come on, baby. Let's just get you inside."

I moan into his mouth. He holds me by my ass and carries me into his house swiftly. When he kicks the door open, it rattles on its hinges. He takes me to his bedroom and drops me right next to his bed. We stand in front of each other, panting like two marathon runners on their last few hundred yards. My knees are wobbly. There's a warm vortex in my pelvic region. I'm flushed, I'm devastated,

I fucking need him.

"I meant what I said. I'm sorry. I didn't mean to keep things from you." My voice is barely audible.

"I know." His fingers vanish in my hair, kneading my head, making me feel dizzy, drunk, crazy. "It's a weird-ass thing, though. I get mad so easily, but I can't stay mad at you, even for a minute."

His forehead collapses onto mine. Join the club, I want to tell him. I know I'm totally ignoring crucial things, like the fact that he had enough fuck-buddies for a lifetime. Countless Nicoles, remember? Or Shane's vandalized car. I'm a pathetic mess.

"We should probably talk about Shane," I suggest. But I'm hoping talking is not on his agenda right now.

"Okay. I just need one…" His lips crush mine hungrily. "Small…" He bites my lower lip. "Taste."

He stares down at me for a second before thrusting me with a gentle push back onto his mattress and rumpled sheets. We never spend enough time out of bed to find time to make it. He kneels before me. His mouth runs all over my stomach, his fingers unhooking my bra, and then his face dips lower.

"From one to ten, how much do you like these jeans?" His warm breath is tracing a path below my belly button... lower... lower... and melting every functional brain cell I still possess. And there aren't that many left after the last few weeks.

How the hell am I supposed to recall what pair of jeans I'm wearing? I can barely remember my own name.

"Minus eleven," I grunt, firming my grip on the sheets.

Plink, plink, plink. I hear what I think are the buttons of my jeans hitting the hardwood floor. Jesus Christ, he actually shredded my jeans from my body. I look down to confirm my suspicion.

My jeans are now a heap of fabric, resting near the foot of the bed, buttons nowhere to be seen. Ty inspects my underwear, a baby-blue cotton pair, nowhere near as interesting as the bimbo thongs that hung on his fence. He rips my panties from my body with his teeth. His mouth grazes my sex, making every hair on my body stand. He grabs the pillow next to my head and shoves it underneath my butt, tucking his huge shoulders between my thighs.

"Oh, God!" I yelp as his tongue runs over my entrance, top to bottom. My thighs are trembling and my core is about to explode. Ty sends one hand to stroke my nipples, and digs in, his mouth and tongue giving me no escape. He picks up intensity and speed gradually, sucking on my clit and using his fingers with his free hand.

"This is what I have on my mind twenty-four-fucking-seven, Barbie." His voice touches everything inside me.

My teeth are chattering. Everything, and I mean everything, tingles. I stifle a moan into my forearm, worried my screams will make his roof fly sky high. I feel high. I have zero control of my mouth, my legs, yet strangely I've never felt more connected to my body.

My orgasm comes crashing in waves. It washes over me from the top of my head to my curling toes. A scream escapes my mouth and Ty rushes back up to shut me up with a rapturous kiss before the neighbors call the cops on us. He forces me into tasting myself. I pant heavily as his weight crushes against me and he grazes my chin teasingly.

"Shhhhh." He plants feathery kisses over my lower face. "You'll wake the dead."

Well, for once, I'm actually speechless. Sex with Ty is like nothing I ever imagined. It keeps getting better and better. And it's made me realize some not-so-fun facts:

1. No matter what I previously thought, I never had an orgasm before I hooked up with him.

2. Every guy I dated previously had absolutely no idea what he was doing.

3. I, myself, had no idea what I was doing.

4. Selfishness aside, Ty Wilder should totally give out orgasms for a living.

He is lying on the other side of the bed, lips glistening sexily. I want all of him, so badly. There'll never be enough of him to keep me satisfied. I want to drink him in, to gorge on him, to have him every second of the day. Hell, I want to know that he is mine.

I shoot him a glance, digging up my courage. "You make me happy, Tyler. Which is weird, because you're not even my type!"

Ty smiles his blazing hot smile, half his face still smashed against the pillow. "Yet you're here."

"Yet I'm here," I agree. "Guess you had me at 'I won't hit you, but I'll hurt you'."

"You had me at 'Keep walking, cowboy,'" he rasps.

The room is so hot my eyes are burning like I'm standing too close to a bonfire that's about to get out of control. Beads of sweat glue my hair to my back and both our bodies shine under the yellow light in a caramel hue.

"Really?" I laugh, repositioning myself on his bed so I can lean and watch him closely.

He nods, picks up a bottle of water from underneath his bed and takes a swig. "When I first met you, I thought you were pointblank crazy. You're less than half my size. I could have killed you just by blowing air in your direction. But I liked how feisty you were. Also, you were pretty funny."

"Thank you."

"And sexy. I wanted you before I even knew your name."

"Buttering me up, are you?" I grin and crawl my way to his side of the bed, shamelessly nuzzling. "So, do we still need to have that talk about me not telling you about Shane?"

"No, but you really need to work on that honesty thing."

"Are you one hundred percent honest with me?" I ask. He exhales sharply, the mist of his body heat and luscious scent prickling my face.

To my surprise, he shakes his head. My heart plummets when he stops the caressing and straightens up against the headboard. "I need time to sort some shit out," he says. "I got myself into a sticky situation before I met you. I guess I need to share this... I just don't want to do it right this second."

I knew this was too good to be true. This is not a love story. This is a Blaire-story. Happiness doesn't live here.

Then he looks straight into my eyes. "I need to know that you'll stick around 'till shit blows over, that you won't bail on me."

Brain shuts down. Hormones have their backs against the wall, and Heart is taking over mouth before I have time to think it through.

"I love you, Ty," I hear myself saying, and feel the flow of panic pumping through my veins.

Shit. What the hell? What made me put myself in such a vulnerable position? I run my hand over my face, acting as if my confession was HIV positive related and not a love declaration. It's not even declaration, though. More of a fact. I just do. I love him.

He pulls me into his strong shoulder and kisses my forehead. No. No, no, no, no, no. I did not just say that after dating him for less than two months. This is crazy talk.

"So stick around." He shoots me a dimpled smile.

And he doesn't say it back. Why would he? He's had a longer relationship with his freaking mail lady.

"Yes," I say gruffly, deflated. "Yes, I will."

# CHAPTER 11

I get a text message notifying me the grade for my assignment has been posted online on my student page. I rush to check it on my laptop. I'm outside on the library steps. I've been studying for my last exam. My computer has been slow lately, but when I finally manage to log in, a yelp escapes my lips.

I got a freaking A.

I never shine academically. Scratch that—I never shine, period. It feels nice. Different, but nice. I busted my ass on this assignment, and for once I actually feel worthy of the good grade.

I want to yell, announce my grade to my parents on a helicopter banner or take a picture of the proof and post it online on social media so everyone can see. Then I remember that I have, like, eighty Facebook friends, so instead, I send a message to my loved ones: Ty, Izzy, Mom and Shane.

I text, **Guess who got an A?!**

Izzy is the first to reply. **OMG, sissy, great news! So proud!**

Shane, who I know is in the building right now, about to take his own exam, confirms, **This is epic, B. You're epic. Keep it real.**

Mom is less than encouraging with **Blaire, is this a joke? If**

121

**not, your father and I are very proud of your accomplishment, sweetie. We knew you had it in you. You just needed to apply yourself.**

I take a deep breath and force my lips into a smile. This may have hurt me a few months ago, and it's still a bitch to read, but the last weeks have taught me that if people don't believe in me, maybe it's their problem, not mine.

Ty doesn't reply. He is probably training, I tell myself. Don't be one of *those* girls. Think positive. I spend the rest of the hour hyperventilating over my good grade. Up until now I wasn't sure I cared much about this degree, but this journalism assignment kind of rocked.

I don't know if it was the topic, the time and place I was in my life, or the outcome of the research, but hell, overall, I really enjoyed it.

"What's up, brainy?" I hear a familiar voice. I don't know how Shane got to the library so quickly, but I'm grateful for his support. Too bad a part of me wants to strangle him, now that I know how much he hurt Izzy.

Yes, we talked about it. About all of it. But it's her story to tell, and I know I need to stay out of this.

I stand to face my BFF. "Being smart is exhausting." I pretend to wipe my forehead. "And I'm pretty sure my head has gotten significantly heavier since I saw that A on my screen."

Shane falls in step with me as we go down the stairs. "You do have a Mr. Garrison thing going right now." He chuckles at his *South Park* reference.

"What did you get?" I ask.

"You mean what did *you* get for your other assignment." He grins. "B+. Great job, brainy."

We walk in comfortable silence across campus, until Shane clears his throat. "How's your sister doing?"

"She got her Fairy wings," I reply.

"Very Disney. I'm glad to hear it. And your boyfriend?"

Goddammit.

"He's not my boyfriend." But this didn't stop me from confessing my love to him.

"Still on drugs and shit?"

"Excuse me?" I stop in the middle of the sidewalk. I

shouldn't be giving him the chance to poison me with lies, but my curiosity gets the better of me. Maybe it's the fact I know that Ty is hiding something from me, but instead of shutting this down, I look up at my best friend, waiting for an explanation.

Shane steps into my face, so close his cologne stings my nostrils and his clean-shaven cheek almost brushes mine. His backpack drops, his books spilling out on the ground. He doesn't even seem to notice.

"Shit, B, you don't even know, do you?" He looks at me with eyes so miserable, they almost outweigh my anger toward him. "Remember I told you my roommate Josh had his nose broken in a fight? Well, what I left out was that the person who broke his nose was Ty Wilder. And the worst thing about it is that it wasn't an accident. He actually hit Josh on purpose. Smashed his head into the bathroom wall. Know why he did it?"

"Why?" I demand, but my voice lacks force.

"Because Josh was at the wrong place at the wrong time. He walked into the locker room when Wilder was in the middle of a fishy exchange with a drug dealer. I'm guessing steroids because Wilder is way too self-centered to use anything that doesn't promote his career. Anyway, when Josh came in, Wilder told him to fuck off. When Josh insisted he wanted to take a shower because he was late for his night shift, Wilder punched his face and finished off by banging his head against the wall. Your precious Dawson covered for it, and Wilder and his buddy Jesse went to the hospital and threatened Josh, so he decided not to press charges. His membership at the gym was revoked soon after, and he's now banned from The Grind. This is the man you're getting in bed with, Blaire. Make no mistake. He's not a bad boy... he's just bad."

As much as I hate to admit it, Shane's story is believable. He is not a liar, not a gossip, and Ty admitted himself that he is more than happy to throw fists instead of settling things with a civil conversation.

But the drug deal? No way, Jose. Ty lives healthy, eats clean and hated it when I smoked pot, so much so that he's probably a big part of why I decided to quit. He's not a drug user. No freaking way.

"Why are you telling me this now?"

"At first I didn't want to make a fuss. I figured this guy would get the fuck out of your life before you even blinked. Then when I realized you were spending more and more time with him, I didn't want you to think I was saying something because I was jealous. But it's not about me. It's about you."

My phone starts buzzing in my hand, and I turn the sound off immediately. I know it's Ty. I recognize his ringtone—"My Soul Is Empty And Full of White Girls" by *Slaves*, his all-time favorite song that I introduced to him.

Shane shakes his head. The phone is still buzzing, but his eyes are screaming at me not to answer. And I don't. I just glance at Shane, my phone, and then Shane again.

"Ask him about it, okay, B? I care about you."

I know he does. Because he sees me. Like Ty said. They both do. I take a step back from Shane.

"Fine. And Shane? Please don't try to hit on me again." I rub my flushed cheeks.

That's it. I kept my promise to Ty, my loyalty to Izzy, and it feels... well, it sucks.

Shane looks up at the sky and sighs in frustration. "Talked to Izzy?"

I shrug. "You don't want me, dude. And that's fine, I don't do blonds who aren't Charlie Hunnam. But don't do anything just for the sake of crushing Izzy. I won't ever forgive you."

Shane looks tongue-tied. The tables have turned. Now I'm the one preaching to him.

He opens his mouth, his stormy-blue eyes laser-focused on mine. "I'm not—" he starts, but I learned a good trick from the master of mind-games.

I stop him mid-sentence, my hand on his heaving chest. "I'm going to kiss you now. If you truly want me—me and not my sister—give me your lips. If not, turn your cheek." I pause, biting at the corner of my lip as I contemplate my next sentence. "And I'll still be your friend."

I tiptoe to Shane, and I'm smiling, confident that he'll do the right thing. This is my best friend, here. He always does the right thing.

Third grade—Izzy and I got our hands on a pair of scissors and gave him the worst haircut in human history. He didn't rat, even when he got into so much trouble.

Sixth grade—he stood up to a bully at school, even though he didn't even know Liz Shudell, the girl who got victimized by the turd ass who wouldn't let her walk the hallways in peace.

Junior year—he turned down one of the hottest girls in high school because she was drunk when she tried getting it on with him.

Senior year—guess who he took to prom? That's right, Rhonda Chan, who was in a wheelchair at the time and crazy bummed about it.

Now, we're grown-ups (sort of) standing on a campus sidewalk and getting attention, for sure, but I still trust Shane like I did in third grade. I close my eyes, my lips reaching for his skin. I smile when I feel the one-day stubble on his cheek. He didn't act on it. He is not mine.

Well, he is, but now I know he is Izzy's too.

Shane looks all kinds of pissed off, his lips thin and his forehead wrinkled, when he picks up the content of his bag.

"Thank you for the money, by the way. You shouldn't have covered for him. But you did. You always do."

"It was a misunderstanding," I admit.

"Yeah, there seems to be a lot of those whenever Ty is around."

"Jesus, Shane," I look away, not really wanting to face him. Why does he always do this recently? Rain on my parade when all I want is to dance in the puddles.

"Talk to your boyfriend, B," he grunts in annoyance.

"He is not my boyfriend." I actually twirl when I walk toward my final exam, the last one before I'm done with my degree, and send him a cheerful smile.

"Whatever, dude. Just do it."

∽≪

After my test, I try my best to make a beeline out of the building and back to the Mini, but as it happens, I'm graceful as a blind elephant and manage to make a lot of noise stumbling in the hallway and dropping my phone on the floor. I hear Professor Penniman's voice from an open door down the hall.

"Ms. Stern, come in."

It sucks donkey balls to be me right now.

I wad my gum into a tissue and dump it in her trash can. Best to pretend I'm a half-decent human being. I smile to Penniman, who is a prim, New England-type in her early fifties, and wait for further instructions.

"Sit down," she orders without lifting her eyes from the papers on her desk. I flop down into the chair opposite her, lacing my fingers together and tapping my foot against the table. I dread to think why she called me in here. Maybe she thinks I plagiarized the article. Frankly, I wouldn't blame her. I usually suck.

"I want to talk to you about your assignment regarding... what was it about?" She lifts her chin and one eyebrow behind her reading glasses. "MMA. Yes. Well, to be honest, it was quite excellent."

Great, so why are you saying this in a tone implying I sexually abused a kitten?

I nod, waiting for a *but*...

"I think we both know you've exceeded every expectation I've had, and I believe I know why."

Jesus, did Shane arrange a press conference to let everyone know about me and Ty? I feel my pulse. Everywhere. My ears. My eyes. My neck. My arms. My heart. I'm so not used to being praised. There must be a catch somewhere here.

"The reason why you did so well is because journalism should have been your major. You poured so much passion into this article I couldn't help but notice. Now, I happen to know *Diablo Hill* magazine is looking for an intern in their sports section, and I've put forward your name."

Penniman slides a business card at me with *Diablo Hill*'s editor's name. "Give Cameron a call. He's expecting to hear from you."

My hands shake when I take the card, and I blink in disbelief. So that's how it feels, to be respected professionally. Butterflies flip inside my stomach like firecrackers. It's not Heart. It's not Brain. It's... Me.

"I don't know what to say," I admit, stammering, "I... thank you."

Professor Penniman goes back to her pile of papers and waves me off like I'm an irritating mosquito. "Don't make me regret this, Stern. It's a huge opportunity."

I stare at her, smiling like she's just informed me that I won the lottery.

Penniman lifts her head and blinks twice, seemingly annoyed that I'm still here. "That will be all. You're excused. And Ms. Stern, I'll be watching you."

# CHAPTER 12

"Surprise!"

I don't particularly like surprises. It stems from my need to be in control over what's happening in my life, which, granted, is not a whole lot of things most of the time, but at least I don't get blindsided by my crazy family members.

Like now.

"What have you done?" The smile is drained from my face as I close the apartment door behind me and stare down at Izzy, who is wearing a mud mask and sipping some green-colored juice. She's watching *E! News*, her long, tanned legs lazily stretched across the sofa.

Izzy nods with her chin toward her bedroom. The door's open, and I notice a huge suitcase lying on the floor, maxed out with her designer clothes and stiletto shoes, and I'm assuming by the amount of things she's packed that she's migrating from the planet. For good.

"Are you moving out?" I blink. I hope she's not moving to LA. She's been wanting to do this for a while now. I can't afford this apartment. What am I saying? I can't even afford the microwave in this apartment.

"Yes, Blaire, I'm moving out and giving you a two hours notice." She giggles. "No, I'm getting a head start on packing for my trip. I'm going to Vegas next weekend... and so are you!"

I unleash a sardonic eye roll her way. "Is that green juice spiked with anything? Whiskey? Vodka? Heroin?"

Izzy jumps from the couch and skips her way to me, bubbly like a glass of Champagne. "Nana Marty and I have decided to surprise you. We knew Boyfriend Dearest had a fight in Vegas on the same weekend as Nana's wedding was scheduled, and since she couldn't find another venue here on such a short notice..."

I slap my mouth with my hands, my eyes bulging out of their sockets like a cartoon character.

Izzy nods enthusiastically and jumps in circles around me. "We are going to Vegas! We are going to Vegas!" she chants in a sing-song voice.

I feel the smile spreading across my face. This is awesome. And surreal. And hell if it isn't exciting. Izzy and Nana thought about me. They knew how much I thought it sucked that my parents didn't even bother telling Nana that I would be graduating in June. Never mind that it worked out fine and my graduation ceremony wasn't actually until the weekend after the wedding. I thought I'd be busy with Nana, so I never even thought about going to Ty's fight.

I admit I don't care much about seeing Ty beating and getting beaten up by Eoghan Doherty, but I'm excited about the prospect of being around him during this event. I know how consumed and worked-up he's been about the fight.

My tears drip down my cheeks, and I ugly-cry, because, damn, I'm so touched by these two special women in my life.

Izzy wraps me into a hug. "Awwwww, Blaire's suffering from an emotional overdose. That's a first!"

I find the perfect spot between her neck and her shoulder blade and nuzzle into it, even though that sticky mud mask is totally touching my hair.

"Izz..." I take a deep breath, because I know I'm about to drag her into a subject I don't want to talk about, but I have no one else to turn to and I am, in fact, suffering from an emotional overload. "I think Ty is keeping something from me."

"D'uh, of course he is. Who wants their significant other to know everything about them? What is he, crazy?" Izzy heads for her bedroom and I follow her there and into our bathroom. She turns on the faucet and slowly wipes off her facial mask.

I sit on the edge of the bathtub. "I don't know what he got himself into, but I think it's serious and it pisses me off that he hasn't told me what it is."

Izzy puts her hand on my shoulder. I shut my eyes, exhaling.

"Maybe it's not because he's hiding something fishy. Maybe it's because he doesn't want you to carry his burden with him. He likes you, sissy. I can see it in his eyes that he's crazy about you."

I daren't tell her that he didn't tell me he loves me back last time we were together. I can't. It's too humiliating and, besides, I'm repressing it pretty skillfully. In fact, I'm not even sure he didn't say it back. Maybe he did. Maybe I didn't hear. Maybe…

*Oh, God.* I'm an idiot.

"I get lonely," Izzy blurts. Her voice comes from a faraway place inside her, the place Izzy doesn't usually share with the world. "You have someone that makes you feel very seen, and not just in the obvious, sexual way." She swallows a lump of self-pity. "Don't give it up too quickly. I can bet good money Ty is all kinds of fucked-up, but don't forget—so are you."

❧

"Surprise."

This dangerous word floats in the air for the second time in one day, but this time it's coming out of Ty's mouth. I slide from behind the counter at Ned's the minute he walks in and invites me with his crooked smile to the seat next to him in a tiny booth, curling his finger seductively.

He is so breathtaking. It's not even his beauty. It's something far more powerful than that. And the fact that he took time to come say hi during his final push of training is amazing. He's been holed up in training camp for the last couple of days.

"Hey, smartass." He plants a kiss on my forehead and tucks his hand into his pocket, searching for something while making a funny face. "I got you a little something to celebrate your grade." He hands me an envelope. I take it in both hands, and before I even manage to tear it open, he announces, "It's kinda dorky, but I figured your schedule's cleared up with school over and everything."

I pull out a voucher from the envelope and grin, completely mesmerized by its content.

"You enrolled me in a French class?" I can't help but laugh uncontrollably, because really, Ty's gifts are the weirdest. He cups my cheeks and kisses me again, this time passionately, with tongue and everything, before I break free.

"One step closer to your happiness, Barbie. This one is for rocking it in your assignment. I'm proud of you."

My grin fades quickly when I remember what I need to ask him. I decided not to tell him about Vegas after all, to keep it as a surprise for when he sees my face for the first time.

But I still need to run Shane's accusation past him.

"Thank you so much." I wave the voucher in the air. "Hey, listen, I need to ask you something."

I must look serious, because he frowns almost immediately. "What's up?"

"There's a rumor going around that you're... using steroids." I almost whisper the last word, feeling self-conscious. "I told Shane there's no way..."

"Whoa, whoa, whoa, rewind." He is brooding, and he looks like he's about to tear this place down judging by his face. "What business does Shane have talking about me? He doesn't know me. And even if he did, why the hell would you believe some gossip he's spreading about me?"

He feels betrayed. His eyes are so dark and stormy, I can almost see my own reflection in them. And I'm glad I can't, because I know I'm very close to crumbling like a stale cookie.

"Ty, it's just a rumor. I wanted to address it, make sure there was no truth to it."

He stands up and eyes me with disapproval mixed with disappointment. I recognize the look immediately. After all, my parents perfected that look. I stand up too, looking around to make sure Mikey and Bree aren't witnessing this. I wish the song that was playing in the background wasn't framing this awful moment. I'll never be able to listen to "I Always Knew" by The Vaccines again and not feel a pang of pain.

"You want me to address this?" he drawls, his lips curve downwards in disgust. "Fine, I will. Off the fucking record, it was Jesse who bought the 'roids. Josh was threatening to expose Jesse when he said he was done buying from him. I didn't want to see my best friend getting screwed now that he's clean. The XWL has been making us take PED tests after every fight for a while. Great fucking research you did there, huh?" He starts walking toward the door and pushes it with force.

"And it's the last time I want to hear Shane's name. I swear to God, Barbie. Next time he pulls something like this, I'll kill him."

෨ඓ

Jane and Michael Stern booked two suites in the Las Vegas hotel we are staying, making sure their room is conveniently close to me and Izzy, just in case we need them. Don't ask me why. We're twenty-three and Izzy has seen more of the world than the two of them combined.

The minute I open the door to our Vegas room, the smell of fresh pastries makes my mouth water. It's like walking into the best bakery in the world. The bright side of rooming with a supermodel sister. Stuff is on the house, and there's a lot of it too.

Baskets of yummy food, cupcakes, and complimentary robes, soaps and whatnot are displayed on the blonde-wood credenza. A note welcomes Izzy to the hotel and she reads it with a mixture of boredom and mild irritation.

She opens a second card with this annoyed expression, until her eyebrows shoot up and the frown is replaced with a smile.

"What?" I ask.

"It's from Elizabeth's Passion. They sent me a gift."

"Wow," is all I manage. I'm seriously not in the mood for stroking my sister's ego. I usually don't mind, it's just that Ty and I have barely spoken to each other this past week and we haven't seen each other at all.

I get it. He's been holed up at his training camp, with his coaches and sparring partners, working out the best strategy to beat Doherty. From my research, I know it's common practice for a MMA fighter to isolate for a few weeks before a fight and focus on it entirely, eliminating things like family, friends and other distractions. But seeing as the last time we were in the same room he stormed out wearing his I'm-going-to-kill-someone face, I doubt the only reason he doesn't want to see me is his upcoming fight.

Then again, should I want to see him? Shane's vandalized Mustang. Ty punching Josh in the nose. Him covering up for Jesse, who cheated with steroids. I find myself torn between the loving, incredible and sexy as hell guy I am dating, and the mysterious (but not in a good, hot way), dicey guy that occasionally pays me a visit.

"The lead Fairy gets to wear this," Izzy gushes in the background, holding up a lingerie item that looks suspiciously like a chandelier. "It costs a freaking fortune. The diamonds are real."

I shrug and fall onto the king-size bed that we will be sharing this weekend. Jesus Christ. I can't believe they left this for her. It's kinda creepy.

"I'm going to try this on and take a few selfies, I'll be right back." She disappears into the bathroom, leaving me to chew on my fingernails and turn on the TV in a quest for a distraction.

Flipping the channels grumpily, I mouth "no" every time I bump into a crappy talk show or a mind-numbing reality show. I reluctantly watch the local news.

"Oh! My! God!" Izzy sings from the bathroom. "I'm smokin' hot in this! This selfie goes straight to my Instagram account. Jesus, all those squats paid off."

I shake my head, a thin smile on my lips, and summon the will to pretend to be in awe of how hot my sister is. Izzy stands in front of me wearing the uniform of a day-shift stripper. She twirls around while punching in a caption for the picture she just shared with her Instagram followers on her phone.

I rub my face using the back of my hand. "You need therapy."

We hear a knock on the door.

"The only thing I need is for the man of my dreams to walk straight into this room right now so I can win him over. Get the door."

Tired of being ordered around, I dive into the bed, head-to-pillow, and groan into the sheets. "Izz, please. Give me a break."

Izzy walks to the door in her stripper heels, tossing her hair to look pretty. She props the door open. Then I hear the worst possible thing to come out of Izzy's mouth: nothing. She is speechless, and that never happens.

I'm worried. I raise my head up to see the figure entering our suite. It's not Dad. It's not Mom. It's not Nana.

It's Shane. And he is wearing his usual uniform of a funny tee ("When Life Knocks Me down I Usually Lie There and Take a Nap"), fitted jeans and angst-filled expression. Actually, the expression is new. His face changes the moment his eyes land on Izzy. She rewards him with the same stunned reaction, maybe even worse, her chin quivering while she suddenly hugs her chest, protecting her modesty.

"Shane." I leap out of bed and dart between them.

Of course he came to Vegas for the wedding. I just didn't think we'd see him before the ceremony.

Shane takes a step forward, his chest going up and down like he is breathing short, desperate breaths. His lips flatten anxiously.

"My parents are a few doors down, unpacking. I have my own room on a different floor." He answers one of the questions whirling in my head. "I had to see you. Talk to you after you-know-what... and give you a little update." He runs his hand over his neck and hair.

Izzy winces when she catches this little gesture. And I'm not surprised, now that I know what happened between them.

"Christ, Blaire! Shane too? Is your pussy made of Cinnabon? What is up with you?" I hear my twin, who apparently recovered quickly.

For the first time in my life, I second Izzy. From a girl who wasted her days daydreaming about Charlie Hunnam and considered eye-humping a hot dude at the gym a sufficient sexual accomplishment, I turned into *that* girl, the one who has two hot guys fighting about her. I used to hate *that* girl when I wasn't her. But honestly? Being that girl turned out to be a headache.

Izzy and Shane are keeping their distance, but it's obvious that there's enough heat in the room to boil an egg.

"Play nice. Say hi," I instruct them both, taking both their palms in my own hands and forcing them into a handshake.

"Yay, look at us, one big happy family." I offer a toothy smile when they reluctantly obey.

"Last time I saw Shane we did things that normal family members don't do to each other." Izzy bites her inner cheek, staring at Shane accusingly.

I want to bark at her that this isn't helping, but Izzy is the least of my worries right now. For all I care, she can walk around the hotel lobby in a crotch-revealing Cher outfit, using two dildos as dangling earrings and singing "Copacabana" into a lipstick tube. I'm one hundred percent consumed by my love life, and the baffling thing about all this is that this love life is real.

Shane's blush deepens with every glance at Izzy. He's in danger of poking someone's eye out with his raging boner.

"Can we talk?" he asks me wide eyed. He may hate her, but he is still a man.

"Let's take it outside for one of those weird cocktails, cool?" I jerk my chin toward the door.

Izzy sulks in her lingerie, twisting in her spot like a five-year-old throwing a hissy fit. "You're seriously leaving me to have a drink with him?"

I pause, thinking about it while I find my shoes. Am I overstepping my bounds here? Nope, this has nothing to do with Izzy and Shane. It has everything to do with Blaire and Ty.

I tie my shoes and stand up quickly. "I'll be back before you know it." I bang my fist twice against my chest and point my finger at her. "Now put your big girl panties on and get over yourself. Actually, just put any panties on, because this is getting pretty annoying."

I slam the door behind me and pray to God she's dressed by the time I get back.

Shane and I take our conversation outside, standing in front of a tattoo parlor and sharing a fifty-ounce Coco Loco. Neither one of us like cocktails, let alone frozen cocktails, and the bartender in me is ashamed of what I'm doing right now, but I need the liquid courage to get through this convo and then surprise Ty later on today.

Shane leans his head back against a brick wall and closes his eyes, looking thoughtful. A bride and groom cross the road about a block away from us, and a bunch of drunk undergraduates raise their cups and holler a woo hoo! to the two of them. And it's only three p.m.

God, I love Vegas. I hate hating on it right now.

"It wasn't him," I say baldly, staring at the busy street without really registering any of it. "Ty wasn't the one who used the steroids."

"You believe him, B?"

I nod. I do. I really do. Not because I want to, but because this is not Ty. He wouldn't take drugs. He's probably done something else, something worse, but drugs? Not his style.

Shane is looking at me with eyes full of misery. It's a should-I-tell-her-or-should-I-not look, and I hate it. Brain is dying to know what else he heard, but Heart wants to punch the idea in the throat. What on earth is wrong with me? The last gossip I heard about Ty from Shane strained our relationship. Why would I put myself through that again?

*He was wrong the first time*, Heart yells at me, stomping its foot.

*Yeah, dumbass,* Brain retorts, *but Ty has a secret, and Shane's accusation had a seed of truth.*

I feel the bile climbing up my throat. Beads of cold sweat are running down my spine.

"Help me out here, B. I don't want to screw things up for you, but I don't want to keep you in the dark either. The only guy I do know that knows Ty well—Josh—has been saying some pretty serious stuff about him that I thought you should know."

I exhale sharply, shaking my head no. I'll be betraying Ty if I'll ask Shane for this information.

But Ty has been keeping me in the dark for weeks now, and I don't know what to think anymore.

Screw this. I need the truth.

"Just say it, dude." I throw my head back in defeat, rubbing my eyes with my fists.

"He's a male prostitute. And I don't mean it in a screw-around-for-fun way. He is bribing the assistant to the XWL chairman, Ray Holloway, by giving sex services to women who pay a lot of dough for him. They split the charge, fifty/fifty, but what he really gets from it, according to my source... is great fights. They hook him up with the toughest guys in his division. That's why he managed to climb up to where he is in only four years."

I turn to the planter behind me and throw up in the middle of the bushes. Shane jumps from where he stands to avoid the stream of vomit, and I rest my hands on my legs to support myself from falling. My head is spinning and my arms are shaking. I look at everything I've eaten in the last sixteen hours. Mac 'n cheese. Veggie soup. Diet Coke. They all float underneath my chucks. Shane flattens his palm on my back, his other hand running through his hair.

"Fuck, sorry, B," he whispers.

I raise my head slowly, smiling weakly through my bloodshot eyes and the rancid taste of bile. "Not your fault. Are you sure this is legit?"

But I know it's legit. The writing was on the wall.

Is that why Ty flinched when my grandmother taunted him about STDs? Because goddammit, he slept with me. We used protection, but yeah, I don't want to take a chance. It all adds up.

This is the dark secret he told me about.

The dark secret Dawson was talking about.

Stupid. I'm just stupid, stupid, stupid.

The journey back to the room is the worst. I don't want to be with Shane, so I'm more than happy to leave him to make a phone call outside the hotel, but I don't want to be by myself either. I hate to be alone with all the thoughts swirling in my head. People pass me by, drinking, laughing and talking.

"Hey gorgeous, you dropped your smile, want me to pick

it up for ya'?" A guy winks as he walks past me. My head is spinning and I feel faint.

Ty's known for fighting dirty. He always pushes people's buttons, and he can be an arrogant prick. But a male prostitute? That's difficult to swallow.

I drag myself to my room and find Izzy still in her lingerie, sitting in front of the mirror, staring at herself thoughtfully.

When she spots me, her mouth opens in shock. "Holy hell, Blaire. You look like you went down on that giant from *Harry Potter*. What happened to you?"

After an emergency sisterly meeting, Izzy and I decide to give Ty a chance to explain himself. Izzy gives me the brief about how rumors can sometimes be just that—rumors. She knows it first hand, since her name has been linked in the tabloids to half the males on the planet.

I fight my instincts, which tell me that every word that came out of Shane's mouth this time was true, and call Ty a few times, but he doesn't pick up. I pace the room, taking big gulps of the water Izzy has handed me.

"He's probably training at The Heat," I venture.

"Honey, this is Las Vegas, he won't be training in the cold." Izzy gives me a concerned look.

I roll my eyes. "The Heat is an MMA gym. His training camp in Vegas is there. He'll be there all day."

"So go see him."

I stop dead, mid-pace. Am I capable of crashing his training camp? I've never showed up anywhere uninvited. Hell, I've never even had the courage to come as someone's plus one. That's how socially insecure I am. And the place is going to be packed with fans, fighters and trainers. I planned on surprising Ty, yes, *after* the fight. When he is not on edge. When he is ready for a distraction. Crashing his training camp the evening before his fight, however, is the mother of all distractions.

Izzy levels her gaze on me, clasps both my shoulders and instructs, "Listen to me, sissy. We're going to The Heat. You'll talk to him, confront him, and drag your ass to Nana Marty and Simon's wedding without this shitty cloud over your cute head. Got it?"

Whether I get it or not, by the time I scrape up the energy to protest, I'm already inside a rental car, sitting next to Izzy, who thankfully dressed for the occasion in more than a piece of silk to hide her ass crack. I'm going to chase the truth on the streets of Las Vegas.

I have to admit, this is one hell of a surprise that I've set up for Ty. Not the one I wanted to pull, but surprising nonetheless. Have I already mentioned that I hate surprises?

# CHAPTER 13

There's a saying that when you're dead, you don't know that you're dead.

It's the same way when you're acting stupid.

Right now, I feel both dead and stupid.

Dead, because the idea that my relationship with Ty may be a major mistake makes me feel cold all over. Stupid because my gut tells me that I'm in for a terrible surprise, and my gut is never wrong.

Izzy is babbling to distract me so I don't overthink. My sister, despite disguising her own problems with superficiality, is actually one of the most compassionate human beings I've ever met. She doesn't want me to think about Ty when I'm sad. She'll never kick me when I'm down.

"I was like, I can't believe I'm eating carbs after six! But Blaire, you had to see the catering in that place..."

I watch her talking with her dramatic hand gestures. She has tons of rings and bracelets on both hands and she mimics other voices as she tells a story about Singapore.

I mumble responses at her on auto-pilot as we slide into the huge parking lot of The Heat. The lot is at the side of the peeling yellow-stucco building and is packed with cars. Why, I don't know. The gym is as depressing as being cornered by your oversharing aunt at an open-bar wedding. Decaying walls, half-torn fences and garbage baking in open dumpsters.

Nothing good is going to come out of a place like this.

Izzy has stopped talking, and she now has my hand in hers. I didn't even feel her taking it, but I'm grateful for the human touch. If it's true and Ty really is a male prostitute, whatever reason he may have (I know he isn't driven by money, but he is one hundred percent addicted to his job), I will need a lot more than a hand to get me through this.

I dread the idea of walking into what fate has in store for me, but I'm also eager to step out of the dark.

I squeeze Izzy's hand with a grateful nod and slide out of the car, weaving through the parking lot to find the nearest entrance. I decide to try the back, hoping to sneak in, unnoticed until I gather my nerve. I suddenly feel like I'm spying on Ty, which, of course, is totally untrue, because spying is mysterious and sexy, and I'm sweating my pants off here. I'm guessing throwing up my guts earlier today didn't actually send me on a brisk walk down Hotsville either.

As I get ready to turn the corner to the rear of the gym, I look over my shoulder and see Izzy sitting in the idling car, AC on full blast no doubt, as she messes with her phone. She's my getaway ride if things go south. I'm completely shaken by the prospect things will go south.

I hurry toward the entrance, constantly glancing sideways to see if Ty is among the fighters practicing in the venue. Then I spot his Jeep. His unmistakable ride. Even though I knew he was here, my heart beats wildly in my chest. My eyes are trained on his vehicle when I take more and more steps toward the door. Then I hear someone pushing the door open and a dark, muscular man steps out, laughing and sucking on a protein shaker.

Jesse.

I crouch down immediately, surprised by my own instincts, and crawl underneath Ty's Hummer. Thankfully, it is huge. Wait, thankfully? Why am I even hiding? Ty is the one who has some explaining to do, yet I'm the one tucked underneath his car.

Shane is right, I'm way different whenever Ty is around.

"Shit, man, Doherty's going down!" I hear Jesse's hearty laugh. Then I hear Ty's throaty chuckle. He is out here, too.

They both sound so close to me, *too* close to me.

I try to breathe as silently as I can. *Shhhhh, Blaire. Oxygen is overrated.*

"Let's see these bad boys in action." Jesse is jumping up and down beside the Hummer, like he is warming up.

I shrink lower and peer under the car, praying they'd walk away.

"Guy's as good as dead," Ty says, laughing.

God, I've missed his laugh.

They seem in good spirit, and I find myself easing a little. He didn't answer my calls because he was practicing. There are no girls here. No funny business. Just work.

"I saw him with his trainer earlier," Jesse says. "He looks jittery, unfocused. You've got this, bro."

My heart is beating like a motherfucker. It's not like I can't just stand up now and yell *surprise!*

Damn. I can't get caught. Eavesdropping is a complete breach of faith, and although slashing my best friend's tires and keying his Mustang doesn't precisely scream boyfriend material, I know Ty has more style than to hide and listen to my conversations. I have no way to explain this situation. And I already demonstrated a healthy dose of nuttiness in front of Ty without adding stalker to my list of personality faults.

I hear a car squeal into the parking lot. It's obviously being driven by someone with a ballistic missile shoved up their ass. A stray cat shoots in my direction before the car— Mercedes actually, I now see—screeches to a stop in front of the Hummer.

"What the fuck, man," I hear Ty say. "He almost flattened that cat.'"

If the driver was driving like a human being, and not like a NASCAR driver on steroids, Ty might have spotted me, but the distraction gives me time to dart from the Hummer to behind the truck in the next parking space.

I crouch down behind the huge tires of the jacked-up Ram truck. For once, reckless driving is not a liability.

NASCAR Wannabe's car door slams. I peer under the Hummer and see a pair of shiny snakeskin boots. "Gentlemen! Good to see you, Ty. I wanted to talk to you."

By the guy's voice, I'm guessing he's at least in his forties. He's got a slight Southern drawl. I peek between the truck and the Hummer and see him hitching up his pants, walking toward Ty, his legs spread, like his balls are made of titanium.

I don't recognize him, yet I find myself disliking him immediately.

"Cut to the chase, Ray. I'm busy." Ty steps into his face.

"A little birdie told me you're a little hard up for cash with all the money you've spent getting yourself ready to fight. I figured you might appreciate a side gig, maybe a little encore for old time's sake. Dina's in town, you know."

Ty, who usually reeks of blasé, Ty, who would probably roll his eyes in boredom at the announcement of the zombie apocalypse is letting out an exasperated growl.

Ray shuffles back to Jesse and flicks something. I smell the stink of a cigar.

"Seriously, Ray?" Ty barks, tone annoyed. "I told you I was done. It's been months. Stop bringing this shit up now,"

"Jesse, how about you give us a minute," Ray says. "Run along now. Shoo."

I'm expecting to hear Jesse's fist hitting bone. I'm stunned when I realize he's just walked away.

"So Ty, what'd you say?" Ray says. "One last gig, plenty of cash. Dina's always been your biggest fan."

My blood freezes in my veins. Please, don't tell me it's true.

"Ray, man, you're just not getting it, are you?" Ty sounds frustrated. "I'm done. I was done six months ago. I won't get back into this, ever. For any money, anytime, anywhere. I hated every second of it. I did it because I had to. I had to because I was getting shit fights and couldn't afford the freaking gym membership when I first started."

Oh, damn. This went on for a while, then. Ty started fighting for XWL four years ago.

"Last fight was the last time, and that's final," Ty spits. "Tell Dina I'm sorry... you know what? Don't. Don't apologize. Paying for sex is sick, whether it's a man or a woman."

I want to hug him so bad right now. I press my palms

against the hot asphalt to resist the urge. Ty's doing the right thing, and there isn't a trace of doubt in his voice.

And yet, I know that he's ruined for me. Shane was right. He is not a bad boy... he is just bad. For me.

"I pulled a lot of favors to make you happen," Ray says. "You can't just brush me off with a no thank you."

"Watch me." Ty's takes a few steps toward the gym.

"Don't walk away from me." Ray slams a fist on the hood of the Hummer. "Goddammit, what makes you think you're better than you were six months ago? You're not. Same guy, same thing. You've slept with hundreds of women but you can't even do this one favor for me?"

"I was young and fucking stupid. I'm older now and would like to think of myself as slightly less of an idiot. I'm done. Sorry, Ray, I'm forever out."

And that's it. Ty's feet disappear, and a minute later I hear the back door of the gym slam. I shut my eyes, waiting until Ray's engine roars. Once he finally drives away, I stand and fish my phone out of my pocket.

Should I call him?

Should I confront him?

Should I spare myself the drama and just slink away to wallow in my pain? Because there's seriously no way I'll ever get over this in this lifetime.

I smash my phone against his Hummer and watch as the hardware flies to all directions. Much like my soul, there's nothing left of the phone.

Now he can't contact me either.

Shit, I realize that his favorite song—the freaking ringtone I put him under on my phone—was a song called "My Soul is Empty and Full of White Girls." The writing wasn't only on the wall, it was on a giant billboard in Times Square.

God, this hurts.

Izzy doesn't ask me how it went. She takes one look at me and gets the full picture. My face tripled its size in a matter of minutes. I'm not just crying, I'm shooting fluids from every hole in my face. My eyes are streaming tears, my nose is leaking gooey snot, and my mouth is dripping drool. This is the ugliest of the ugly-crying faces known to mankind.

"What a prick," Izzy declares, not even knowing what

he's done. She reaches for her bag in the backseat and hands me some tissue.

I blow my nose loudly and pat my damp eyes with the same wet tissue. "Take me back to the hotel, please."

My sister is driving as fast as Ray, weaving through traffic with no thoughts of caution. She is not asking any questions, though, which I'm grateful for. When we pass a giant accident, with two very smashed cars and three ambulances lining on the shoulder of the road, she shoves more tissues at me and says, "And you thought you were having a bad day, huh?"

As weird as it sounds, she is right. I've just found out my boyfriend was a man-whore for a few years and that he has only recently stopped after screwing hundreds of girls. Brain reminds me I'm still alive. Still in one piece. It's Heart that's in pain.

We get back to the hotel and Izzy throws the rental car keys to the valet. I unfasten my seatbelt as she opens the door for me and offers her hand.

"Come on, sissy. Let's get minibar-drunk and hate on Ty in detail."

I let her swoop me out of the car, nuzzling into her hair so no one will see just how messed up my face is. I hear Izzy's cell pinging with a text, followed by another one.

Then another. Now it rings—and we're not even halfway to the foyer. Izzy stops to inspect the number flashing on her screen with a frown.

"Should I answer?"

"Don't answer any unknown numbers until we leave Vegas," I plead quietly.

"Bitch, I'm a supermodel. I don't do unknown numbers, in or outside of Vegas."

I force my lips into a smile and let my twin usher me to the elevators.

"Nana Marty, brace yourself. The Stern sisters are coming to your wedding." She presses her lips into my ear, her arm hooked around my shoulders. "And we're going to be oh so drunk."

৩∼৩

Dearly beloved, we're gathered here today to pay our final tribute of respect to my deceased Heart. Heart started off as a casual dude not ready for commitment. It was often bullied by Hormones and pushed aside by Brain. But once Ty took over it, I knew we were both fucked.

A flashback of Ty standing in the empty XWL classroom, telling me he's not going to hit me, but still going to hurt me, gives me goose bumps.

I drain another plastic cup of whatever-the-heck alcohol Izzy has placed in my hand. Nana Marty is getting married tomorrow evening, and I'm getting shitfaced in my hotel room, crying uncontrollably like I just found out my family died in a grotesque plane crash.

Izzy tries to lift my spirits by playing wedding dress-up. She puts me into a vintage Valentino peacock-green dress, with a sweetheart neckline top and matching, emerald heels, and arranges my hair in a French twist. I should feel like Beyonce, but instead, I feel like St. Paddy's Day.

"How many messages and missed calls?" I sniff afterward, lying on the king-size bed in my Valentino and clutching my empty Solo cup, teary-eyed. Ty is wondering what the hell is up, and he's been calling Izzy pretty much nonstop since he realized my phone is dead. Though seeing as I smashed it against his precious car, I'm guessing he already knows I'm here, and that I am clearly ten shades of pissed off with him.

"Eight messages, four missed calls." She glances at her phone, sitting in front of the vanity table and straightening her perfect hair. "Do you want me to answer it next time and tell him to piss off?"

"No. Let him squirm."

I hear a firm rap on the door and cover my face with my forearms. Izzy shoves her chair as she gets up to answer.

"Who is it?" Izzy sing-songs.

"It's Tyler. Get Blaire."

I put the pillow over my head and hear Izzy's heels clicking in my direction. He found out. How did he find out where I stay?

"No," I say flatly underneath the pillow.

"He sounds crazy worried," Izzy says carefully.

"Well, I'd be even crazier if I decide to listen to his excuses. No, Izz."

The banging on the door becomes louder and firmer, and it's distracting me from wallowing in self-pity.

"Blaire, open the fuck up. Let me in." The urgency in his voice makes the hair on my skin stand up. I've never heard him so... panicked?

"He sounds desperate. I should open the door." Izzy chews on the corner of her lip, going back and forth. She is wearing a canary yellow Vera Wang.

"Don't open the door. He won't strangle you. I will," I warn.

"Fuck, Blaire, fuck!" He punches the door hard.

I hear a door open down the hallway. I hope it's not my parents. Maybe it's not them. Maybe it's someone else. Just because someone is yelling their daughter's name, doesn't mean it's them. *Have faith, Blaire.*

"Excuse me?" I hear my mother asking Ty, and by the low, throaty coughs, my father is by her side.

Screw you life, we're done.

Izzy yanks me by the elbow and we both shoot to the door, she is placing her ear against the cool wood to hear how this one plays out. I wince, hoping he isn't going to make more of a jackass of himself.

"Mr. and Mrs. Stern, right?" Ty's tone goes down a notch. "Not the kind of introduction I wanted to have with Blaire's parents. I'm her boyfriend, Ty." He presents himself assertively. "What I'm about to do here is going to get you worked up, so let me start by promising I'll try and change your mind about me after this crisis is over. Obviously, I'll pay for the damage too."

I can feel his presence on the other side of the door. The heat. The passion. But also the man who fucked me over and kept me in the dark about him humping HUNDREDS OF WOMEN FOR CASH AND CAREER OPPORTUNITIES.

"Blaire, Izzy, open up in five seconds or I'm breaking this shit down. Five."

Izzy's eyes bug out at me, and I shake my head no.

"Four."

Izzy takes a step back, and I roll my eyes at her. As if... right?

"Three."

Izzy grips me by the midriff and tugs me away from the door.

"Two."

Her eyes are pleading for me to give him a chance to explain himself. That I should at least open the door. I can't. The guy did enough damage already. Why are we even having this eye conversation?

"One."

Silence. I huff and shoot her an "I told you he won't do anything" sneer, when the sound of shattering wood fills the air. I gape as I see Ty's foot in the air. His kick has sent the door flying open and cracked its frame.

Holy Moly Guacamole.

Ty storms into the room and picks me up like a caveman, draping me over his shoulder in a fireman's carry. He pivots back to the door and marches out wordlessly. I notice my parents standing in the hallway, downright stunned. Shouldn't Dad be fighting him off? Well, he doesn't.

Izzy follows us while Mom follows Izzy. Then Dad snaps out of his stupor, rushing furiously after all of us. We're a chain of crazy people running down the hallway of a Vegas hotel, and we stumble upon half-eaten room service trays and the bewildered stares of other guests.

"Is he really her boyfriend?" I hear Mom panting to Izzy as they try to catch up with Ty's long stride.

"Yes. But she's not talking to him!"

I can barely see any of them from my angle, as most of the view I get is of Ty's tight ass and shoulder tattoos. He is not wearing much. Black sports shorts and a sleeveless top. Is it wrong that I love the scent of his sweat, especially now, after everything that happened? I know it is, no need to answer that.

"Should I call the police?" Mom asks.

"No, he's not going to do anything to her. If anything, she's the one who is in bitch-slap mode," Izzy says. "Where are you taking her, Ty? She's wearing a vintage Valentino. Can't you kidnap her in one of her signature Target sweatpants or something?"

"Thanks, Izzy." I send her two thumbs up, because lifting

my head after all the alcohol is a bad idea.

"Sorry, sissy."

Ty stops at the end of the hallway, puts me down in front of the elevator and presses the button.

He palms my cheeks, storm in his black eyes.

"Take me to Shane's room before I kick open every door in this place," he demands. I've never seen Ty so agitated.

Is that what this douchebag cares about? Retaliation?

I put on an indifferent mask. "How did you figure out I was in Vegas?"

He reaches for his pocket, taking out my iPhone cover—a hipster cat with a trendy hat and Harry Potter glasses. Pointing the cover at me, he arches one brow. Yeah, I kind of gave myself away the minute I threw my phone in the parking lot of The Heat.

"Shane didn't tell me anything about you," I say. It's a lie, but I'm done playing fair. He fed me enough lies to last for a decade. "I heard you talking with that Ray guy."

Ty throws his head back, looking both pained and frustrated. "Stop covering for him, Barbie,"

I squint my eyes in annoyance, turning back toward the hallway and marching my way back to my room. He grabs my wrist, pulling me into his chest.

"Please get mad at me, Blaire. Kick me, punch me, curse at me, break shit. Throw me in the fucking doghouse and let me pay for what I've done. But please don't walk out on me. I can't change my past, but *we* can change my future." He closes his eyes, sighing in despair.

My family is still watching us like it's a Broadway show.

My ego is wounded. My heart is smashed. This has got to be the worst thing I'll ever have to do. I shrug and purse me lips. "Sorry, Ty. Shane was right. You and I are just too different to be together."

Ty's facial expression shifts back to frustration as the elevator arrives and two seniors smile in our direction from inside.

"Going down?" the woman asks.

"Yep." Ty pulls me inside with him.

The silver-haired couple exchanges knowing glares. They know who Ty is.

"Wilder! We bought tickets for your fi—" the man starts.

Ty cuts him off, completely focused on me. "I'm done hearing about this guy filling your head with bullshit about me. He has an agenda, and I'm going to make him admit it. You're going to see it now."

"Don't shoot the messenger, lover boy. We both know that what Ray said was true." I refuse to spell it out with a pair of avid fans listening. The old couple are staring from him to me, wide-eyed. "Anyway, good luck with your plan. I don't even know what room Shane is staying in."

Ty's phone beeps with a text message. He frowns at it briefly. The elevator door pings open.

"Oh, but I do."

Ty is racing down the hallway and I follow him, wishing I wasn't in a vintage cocktail dress so I could run faster and that I didn't kill my phone earlier today so I could warn Shane. Ty will crush him if he gets the chance.

I'm frantic and when I see a maid pushing her cart in our direction, I stop her and beg her to call security.

Tyler kicks another door open and walks straight into one of the rooms. I don't know who told him Shane's room number, but whoever it was had good intel. I see Shane sitting on the edge of the bed, fiddling with his phone.

"What the—" He stares at Ty in bewilderment, but regains composure fast. "You have a lot of nerve coming here, Wilder. You slashed my tires. You beat up my roommate. You hurt Blaire bad. No offense, but you're kind of a mess, dude. People don't pull shit like that."

Ty grabs Shane by the neck of his I Can Give a Headache to an Aspirin tee shirt, but he doesn't hit him. I know he wants to prove a point to me, but he is struggling, still fighting his demons, his anger fits. And that's what I'm afraid of. That he is still the kid who can be lured into a fight the minute things go south.

"You…" Ty shoves a finger into Shane's chest. "Always wanted her for yourself. Just take the damn hint. She doesn't want you. You lost. I won. She's mine."

Shane jerks loose of his hold. "Dude, you only won *momentarily.* And as usual, that's only because you cheated. She didn't know what kind of guy you are, what kind of stuff you do. Blaire's not yours. She'd never willingly get it on with a male prostitute."

Ty's eyes flare, his jaw clenching, and he takes a step closer to Shane. I know I shouldn't be standing here like an idiot, but things haven't gotten physical yet, thank God, and maybe there's a chance Ty will shed some light on his reasons for what he's done.

"You. Know. Nothing." Ty utters every word like a separate sentence. "You told Blaire I use steroids. I never touched them. You took half-truths from your junkie roommate and pieced them into a web of lies." Ty's low voice sounds like a constant threat.

Shane's not intimidated. He thrusts out his chin. "You put my roommate in the hospital because he somehow ended up on your and Jesse's shit list. And that's the truth. The whole, messy, inconvenient truth."

"Your roommate is the one who screwed up. Josh is not a stable guy. He needs rehab."

"And you need a new set of morals." Shane kicks his suitcase in frustration. "You can make excuses for nearly killing the guy, but what's your excuse for tapping hundreds of women to get fights and money? Let's hear that one." Shane folds his arms and narrows his eyes. "I bet it's good."

Ty's own eyes are furious now, and I know he's been pushed too far. I rush between them, resting one hand on each of their chests. Ty's heartbeat says it all. He's already in his own imaginary ring. I just hope it's not too late to drag him out, kicking and screaming, before he hurts my best friend.

"Okay, party's over. Ty, you have no business talking smack about Shane. He just wanted to warn me, as a friend. I could have heard the same stuff from anybody."

"Yeah, it just happened to be the guy who's probably wanted in your pants from the moment he met you."

I roll my eyes. "We met in third grade."

Ty looks momentarily stumped, but Shane isn't helping.

"Get the hell out of my room, Wilder."

"Not before you admit to Blaire you don't know shit about what I did or do, past or present."

Shane's fists clench. "Get. The hell. Out. Of my room."

"Or...?" Ty taunts.

Shane zones in on Ty's face, his blue eyes narrowing. He is not a violent guy, never has been. But he also never takes shit from anyone. He usually walks away when things get messy, but it's hard to walk away when a guy like Ty is blocking your way.

They stare each other down. Then Shane throws a sudden punch straight at Ty's face. Blood drips from his nose.

Ty smiles grimly, turning to me and offering me a wink. "Just for the record, baby, your right hook is so much meaner."

Shane throws a few wild punches, which Ty dodges easily. Shane is obviously pissed off, and maybe a little drunk. I spot some empty beer bottles next to the TV.

I can't move. I can't speak. I can barely breath.

When Shane launches himself at Ty, I know that Ty can't let this go. His fight reflex is stronger than him. Ty strikes back hard. The nauseating sound of his fists connecting with Shane's face and body jabs my ears.

"Stop it! Let go of him!" I sandwich myself between them, pushing Ty out of the room. "Get away from him." My voice cracks.

For a moment there, it looks like Ty gets his shit together. He looks down at me, his eyes tired.

Shane takes the opportunity to jet out the door, but Ty thrusts me aside and launches at Shane again. Panic rushes through me as he chases Shane down the hotel corridor. I race to catch them. Ty grabs the back of Shane's shirt and jerks him to a halt. I'm about to step between them and throw myself in the line of fire for Shane when I see Mom, Dad and Izzy spill from an elevator. A second later, Jesse and Dawson rush out of a second elevator. They're all sweaty and flushed, and other than Jesse, they all pant like they've just completed a triathlon. I suspect they've been running around hunting for me and Ty.

The men are tearing Ty apart from Shane before things get even messier for the XWL star. There are a lot of sins you can commit in Vegas, but sending a guy to the hospital is probably not one of them, especially if you're a professional athlete competing in a big televised fight. A quick look at

Shane reveals a busted lip, bruised cheeks and what will soon be a black eye. I'm too pissed off to examine Ty's face. Whatever injury Shane's given him, he'll survive.

Ty points his finger at Shane. "He twisted things to turn her against me."

Shane takes a seat on the floor and holds his head in his hands, trying to regulate his breathing. Ty is still blocked by Jesse and Dawson.

"Whatever he did," Jesse says, "you have to drop it now, bro. Get your shit together. You've got a fight tomorrow night. You can't afford to get arrested or hurt." He studies Ty's bloody nose and his arm, which sports a long, ugly scratch. His lips curl in disbelief. "Jesus, the guy scratched you?"

"No, that was my girlfriend."

"Does Shane need an ambulance?" someone interrupts. Maybe my mom. I'm not really present in this situation, everything feels like a bad dream, and like most dreams it's complete chaos. I wish someone would wake me up from this nightmare.

"I'm fine. No hospital," Shane says, but he groans into his hands.

Izzy hurries to his side. Her eyes are welling up, and she sits next to him, lifting his chin between her fingers. She examines the cuts and marks on his skin with furrowed brows, and my heart breaks in two to see just how much it kills her to see him hurt.

"You'll be okay. You're strong." Her voice is almost a whisper. "But we need some ice..."

"And a fucking whiskey to go with it," Shane snaps, and there are a few chuckles from my side of the family.

"Do I need to call my lawyer?" Dawson rubs Ty's back in circles, like a dad. "Will this douche press charges?" He is not even remotely annoyed with his fighter.

That confirms my worst fears about Ty. This isn't the first time something like this has happened. Ty is what he is. A violent, volatile guy who'll do anything to get what he wants, even if other people get screwed in the process.

"I'm not pressing charges," Shane blurts from the floor. Izzy is now running her fingers through his tousled blond hair.

"Are you sure that's wise?" my mom asks. "He's clearly dangerous."

It's like being punched in the face. I feel the tears and the pressure in my nose, like I'm going under water. I hate Tyler for what he did, but I also love him enough to know I'll never get over the fact that my parents will under no circumstances ever accept him after this.

"I can handle Wilder," Shane says. "I just want him out of my face."

"Fine by us. Let's move it." Dawson is only too happy to step out of the situation. I still haven't figured him out. Is he a sinner for putting up with Ty and Jesse's antics, or a saint for tolerating both of these boys?

"Blaire?" Ty asks. I shake my head, unable to look at him. I just can't. Not right now. Not after all he's done, and everything I found out.

"Please just go," I whisper, fat tears chasing each other down my cheeks. I can hear him taking a deep breath.

"She's right," Dawson says. "We need to get you cleaned up for the press conference." He pulls Ty toward the elevator, but Jesse lingers.

The other fighter leans close to my ear "Ty loves you. What do you need to prove it, a naked singing telegram? Don't crush him a day before a big fight."

My chest squeezes tight, but I don't waver. "I hope he's crushed. Serves him right for how he bagged this fight in the first place."

෴

I watch the XWL media day on TV from my room. I give myself a mental slap on the wrist for still being interested in Ty's fight—no, scratch that, in Ty in general— and a mental punch in the face for actually watching the press conference. It appears I have zero self-control, despite the fact that this dude totally kicked my best friend's butt. I don't care if Shane was the one to throw the first punch.

On TV, Ty is onstage sitting on a pair of barstools with his opponent, Eoghan Doherty. Behind them there's a wall of endorsements, and each fighter is circled by their own entourage. Ty holds the mic to his lips. He chews gum, wearing a black designer shirt, fitted cigar pants, high top sneakers and a black baseball cap.

He's so incredibly sexy I want to lick him head to toe, but then I remember a lot of other girls actually did do just that, and paid good money for it too. The thought makes me want to hurl.

It's killing me to see Ty still oozing charisma, while I'm falling apart, struggling to remember how to breathe.

Doherty looks extra douchey in a pair of sunglasses and a three-piece suit. There should be a special section in hell for people who wear sunglasses indoors. He smack talks Ty to oblivion and back. He pushes every single button, starting off by referring to Ty as an "inbred redneck." I get that they need to sell this fight, and that trash talk is a part of the game, but Doherty seems to have sold his soul, willing to do anything nasty as long as it's good for his career.

Oh, right. Ty did that too.

Ty gives his indifferent smirk, popping gum and blinking slowly in Doherty's direction. Dawson is sitting next to his star, his arms folded. Occasionally he whispers something in Ty's ear.

One of the reporters stands up with an anxious smile and directs a question at Ty, "I have a source that just texted me that you were in an altercation in a Vegas hotel earlier today. Something to do with your girlfriend. Care to elaborate?"

Ty bounces his leg and pinches the bridge of his nose with his thumb and forefinger. I notice that Shane didn't even leave a mark on his face.

"No comment."

Doherty gives a mean laugh. "Don't worry, Wilder, step into the ring with me tomorrow and your love life will be the least of your worries. I promise to smash your pretty-boy face."

The audience taunts with "Ohhhhhhhs!"

The crowd is eating this up, and the truth is, Doherty brought his A game to this press conference. He is shredding quiet Ty to pieces publicly. Doherty's a one-man show, and it's evident his opponent isn't up to it.

"Jesus, Blaire, can you change the channel?" Izzy bursts into the room. She's been helping Mom and Nana Marty with some last-minute shopping for the wedding. I was excused, obviously, seeing as my life is a circus of fatal mistakes and misunderstandings. Everyone just got a front-row glimpse at the show earlier today.

"I think I've had enough of Tyler Wilder," Izzy clarifies, as if there's any doubt what her complaint is about the TV.

I turn off the set and arch one brow. "You do realize that Shane threw the first punch, right?" And the second, and third, and fourth...

"You do realize that Tyler is a professional XWL fighter, right?" she mocks. She plops down on our king-size bed with a sigh. Her shopping bags frame her supermodel body. "Isn't there, like, a special oath they need to take, like doctors, so that they can't hit random, non-XWL people?"

"I'm not even going to dignify that with an answer." I bury my face in the pillow next to her. Everything hurts. My head, my eyes, my body, the thoughts swirling in my head like a tornado.

I can't believe he was a male prostitute.

I can't believe he cheated his way to the top.

I can't believe I slept with him.

*I can't believe I slept with him!*

My bad luck can't possibly up its game anymore, right?

Wrong.

Izzy clears her throat from her side of the bed, a clear sign that something awful is about to come out of her mouth. I lift my head from the pillow and, sure enough, she averts her gaze quickly and her cheeks flush. She is holding her cell phone in one hand. With her other hand, she reaches out to pat my head like I'm a three-year-old.

"What now?" I can't take more bad news. It's difficult enough coming to terms with the idea of not seeing Ty again, smelling his gorgeously manly scent, hearing his voice and laugh, or just watching one of his stupid guy-movies when he's next to me.

Izzy lets out a sharp breath. "I hate to do this to you..."

"Do what? There's more? Is this "let's crack Blaire in two" day? I hope it's not going to be an annual thing."

She chews on her lower lip. "Well, I was surfing the news on my phone and stumbled across something. Just to give you a heads up—your name and face are plastered all over a gossip website next to Ty's. And it's your prom picture. The really bad one."

Don't freak out. Do. Not. Freak. Out. Just don't freak out.

"I'm freaking out," I croak, sitting up on the bed.

Soon, my legs are criss-crossed, my computer in my lap. I don't understand. A week ago all was great in the land of Blaire Stern. Grades were high. Boyfriend was hot. Vegas was tempting. Brain, Hormones and Heart played nice, and everyone knows three's a crowd. What happened?

Izzy sits next to me, squeezing one of my shoulders, offering support yet pouting at the same time. She is so used to seeing *her* pictures on sites like this, I don't think she gets how awkward I feel right now.

Thank God Ty is not exactly Bradley Cooper. The item on his new girlfriend (ex-girlfriend, but they don't know that yet) is getting stale pretty quickly. I have to scroll down to see the story. There's a glorious picture of him smiling in a suit, the sexy twinkle in his eyes visible for all to admire, and an awful picture of me from my high school prom. I ended up wearing the dress Izzy decided to ditch at the last minute, and since I've always been a little curvier than my twin, the shiny-gold sequined, stretch fabric hugs all the wrong places. I look like a Twix bar.

*His Good Luck Charm?* the headline asks. A handful of comments follow, with one asking *Would you do Ty's chick?* and another answering *I'm guessing that he would. And did.*

Now I really, really need to throw up.

But there's no time to drown in self-pity, because I'm dealing with a clogged e-mail account and a buzzing Facebook profile, dozens of people I know (along with total strangers) wondering how come they didn't know Ty and I were a thing and sending me friend requests.

I don't answer any of them, and I'm so, so relieved that I destroyed my phone.

"You think you caught something when you slept with him?" Izzy rolls on her stomach on the bed and takes one more look at my hideous picture. She's really pissed that they outed me as her twin, seeing as I look like a nightmare in the prom dress.

"Huh?" I ask, and then her question registers. "Ick! I hope not." She's right. I need to get tested.

The irony hits me hard in the gut. If this guy, who is all about clean-eating and exercise and talking me into quitting weed ended up giving me something, I swear I'm going to lose it.

"I'll schedule an appointment when I get back home."

Izzy grabs my hand in hers and offers me a pity-smile. "I'll come with."

# CHAPTER 14

Izzy is standing right next to me in the Elvis Funky Chapel. We're both holding bouquets, but I'm not wearing the vintage Valentino I tried on before yesterday's disaster. I guess I've been metaphorically and physically stripped of my right to wear anything couture.

I'm back in the dark-red, mermaid-style dress I originally planned. I don't mind. What I do mind is being the center of freaking attention at the wedding. News has broken that Ty Wilder is (*was*!) my boyfriend. I try to look on the bright side—at least no one knows about his male-prostitution phase. The public and most of the guests all think he's just a violent jerk.

Shane, Izzy and I are the only people at this wedding who know the truth, and I'm planning to take this one to the grave with me. I may not have dated the most sought-after bachelors in the country before Ty barged into my life, but dating a former male prostitute is a new low, even for me.

Okay, maybe I'll just tell Nana Marty. Nana won't judge. She won't tell my parents. Nana can keep a secret. I'm pretty sure she's got a pile of 'em securely tucked deep inside her head.

I watch my grandmother in her very skimpy and age-inappropriate white dress, standing in front of her prince

159

charming, Simon.

Simon is pretty darn cool. He is handsome for his age—tall, with thick white hair and steely blue eyes. He is wearing a tux and looks better than my chunky, fifty-something father. My parents stand across from Izzy and me. It's obvious they are none too thrilled about the wedding. But unlike me, Nana isn't a person who gives a damn about what they think.

Mom keeps shifting and staring at her shoes, while Dad zones out. In his mind, he's at the golf course, talking politics with his friends and comparing golf clubs. The chapel looks like a deserted branch of Olive Garden, but the ceremony is lovely.

And me? I'm a hot mess. I'm trying to keep it together, but every thought I have is of Ty.

"Blaire, are you crying? Again?" Izzy whisper-yells at me as the Marilyn Monroe look-alike performs the service.

I feel so bad. Nana did all this so I could be in Vegas, and her plans backfired completely. I'll be dealing with the shock waves of the explosion for a long-ass time.

I shake my head. "Nope. Not crying. Just happy for Nana."

"You may kiss the bride." Marilyn beams at Simon. He looks at Nana Marty with eyes filled with happiness, but thankfully, keeps it clean and only gives Nana a peck on the lips. Mom and Dad smile tightly while Izzy and I jump on our fragile grandmother.

Izzy twerks around her, the flowers in her hand raining petals on the floor, while I cling to her shoulders like she's my only chance of being saved from a starving shark. An injured Shane is standing with his parents in an aisle, surrounded by a few more guests, golf-clapping. He is looking at Izzy. Not at me, not at the bride, just Izzy. She is his sun and his moon. The want in his eyes is unmistakable, even with the new, purple frames Ty has given him.

Nana pats me on the cheek and holds my chin firmly in one hand. "Oh, my darling Blaire," she murmurs into my nose. "Your mother told me what Tyler has been up to. Had I known you were going to bring enough drama for an HBO mini-series, I would have brought more vodka. I want all the gossip. Meet me in the lobby bar in an hour. Simon can pop my imaginary cherry tomorrow."

Hell, I'm going to need therapy after Vegas.

Back at the hotel, I tell Izzy I'm meeting Nana downstairs for drinks and ask her if she wants to tag along.

"Too tired." She slips out of her gown and walks around the room in her undies. That nasty Elizabeth's Passion thong she's wearing is glaring at me like a sweaty pervert in a raincoat, but other than that, there's no denying her body is damn near perfect. "I think I'm going to call it a night."

Izzy never turns down an excuse to drink, let alone in public, where she can be seen and fawned over by her fans.

"You sure?" I frown at my sister, perplexed.

She nods. "Seriously, go drown your sorrows, sissy. You totally earned it."

Nana and I opt to sit at the far corner of the bar. She is still wearing her wedding gown and the brightest, stupidest grin, and I'm tucked into a gray, loose-fitting garb I sometimes use as my period pajamas. No bra.

Like Izzy said, I deserve it after everything I've been through.

I knock down drink after drink in between chewing my swizzle stick. It's already approaching 10 o'clock, and I know Ty's fight should be starting right about now.

I don't want to think about it.

I can't stop thinking about it.

"This is so jacked up." I finally rest my head on the bar. The room spins around me and I feel nauseous.

"He's been pimping himself for... what? Four years now? Ever since he started doing this professionally. That could be a thousand women. How irresponsible can he be?"

"It's deplorable," Nana Marty agrees, wrinkling her nose, "but he didn't know you back then, and by the time he met you, he'd already changed his ways."

I scan her face in horror.

Maybe it's because I've punished myself and searched for pictures of him on the Internet again, this time with women. I can't see a picture of him with a woman without wondering... has she paid to sleep with him? Has she writhed underneath him like I did? How many times? What positions? When and

where? How much money? Who did Ty get to fight afterwards?
*Ugh.*

"Let's play the devil's advocate here, shall we?" Nana raps the bar loudly to snap me back to reality. Billows of cigarette smoke travel between us, and I cough in annoyance. I may have smoked the occasional blunt, but I absolutely hate cigarettes. How it's possible to smoke inside hotels here is beyond me, but I'm starting to realize that in Vegas, you could puff directly into a baby's face if you're willing to put some cash next to a blackjack dealer.

"He wanted to build his career. I agree that he was very young and unbelievably foolish to do what he's done. It's appalling, really, but is it your place to forgive him? He hasn't done anything to you, sweetheart. He just has baggage that is incredibly difficult to stomach."

Is Nana high?

"He. Was. A. Male. Prostitute," I pronounce slowly, hoping it'll drill into her brain. "And he messed up my best friend's car. And he kept this information from me, even though he knew it was one hell of a deal-breaker."

She watches me swirling the ice in my empty glass and hands me her drink. I guzzle it.

"I know how you feel, honey."

No you don't, I think. You have no idea.

"I'm just saying you may feel differently in a few months. You can close the door on your relationship with Tyler for now. Just don't lock it."

I rest my forehead on the bar counter and close my eyes. This is a nightmare. Ty loves sex. Even if I do change my mind about him (which I won't), there's no way he'll wait for me. Hell, he's probably already planning to either lick his wounds or celebrate his win with another, brand new girl tonight.

I should totally lock the door behind my relationship with Ty. I already slammed it hard enough for everyone around me to hear.

ڔۛڔ

I crawl back to my room and push the door open. The first thing I notice is that Izzy isn't here. Our huge bed is empty, sheets and bedtime mints still neatly in place. We've been moved to a different suite since yesterday, seeing as our previous room had its door kicked in by a violent, man-whore maniac. For a moment, I wonder whether I've actually entered the right room. But I did.

And it's still empty.

I stagger to the dresser and pick up a box with a card addressed *Barbie*. The box is white, sophisticated and inviting. I don't need to guess who it's from. I open the small box and find a fancy new cell phone inside. I turn on the phone and watch as the screen lights up. One new text message, the cell alerts. Checking it, I see Ty has already saved his contact number under the name "My Remorseful Boyfriend." His text says **Don't do this to us.**

It was sent way past midnight, a few hours after he was done fighting, and it clearly suggests there was no after-party on his agenda.

Not that I care. We're done.

I stay up most of the night, re-reading Ty's message over and over again. This is bad. I should not be left alone, with my feelings so confusing right now. Where the hell is Izzy? I mull over Ty's conversation with Ray.

Hundreds of women.

Hundreds of them.

Big, small, tall, short, brunettes, blondes, dumb, smart, good in bed, bad in bed, tongues, teeth, lips, fingers, positions we tried, positions we didn't. The list goes on.

I squeeze the new phone so hard I wince. I thought he saw me, but he didn't see shit.

I'm sitting in a chair next to the window, legs crossed, ignoring the view and facing the door, when I hear it creaking open. Izzy tiptoes barefoot into the room, holding her heels in her hand, not turning on the lights.

"Hope you enjoyed it," I rasp from the gloom.

Izzy jumps and lets out a small shriek. "You scared the hell outta me."

"Ditto. Where have you been?" I stand up and walk toward my sister, skimming her. Yeah. She definitely looks guilty. Flushed as hell.

"I went for a walk."

"Down Liarsville? How's the weather there?"

"Blaire."

"Izzy?"

She drops the heels on the floor and plops on the bed, rubbing her feet. "I'll tell you once you take a chill pill for real."

"Do I look like I need more lies and secrets in my life?"

"Fine. I went to see Shane in his room." She grabs a bottle of water from the minibar. Shaking her head. She takes a gulp and stares past me out the window.

The strip is still alive. Everyone else in this town seems to be enjoying it. She turns on the TV.

I snatch the remote, turning it off. "I don't want to know if he won or lost," I explain.

Izzy nods. "Shane broke up with Gemma before he came to Vegas." She smiles thinly. Not surprising, after what she told me about their little escapade abroad. These two will either kill each other or get married in the next few months, I'm sure.

"I'm sort of glad to hear it," I say, "even though Gemma doesn't deserve it. She seemed cool. He met her at an I Prevail gig."

"Who's side are you on?" She throws a pillow at me, but I duck in time.

My new phone bleeps again, making Izzy send a puzzled glance my way. It's 4 a.m. I peek at the new text.

My Remorseful Boyfriend says, **You're wasting your time, Barbie. I'm not giving you up.**

Shouldn't Ty be asleep? I'm sure he must be exhausted after the fight.

"Where the hell did this come from?" Izzy is ogling my new phone like it's a nuclear device.

"You weren't here when it arrived?" I pinch my eyebrows. "So who got it into our room?"

We both stare at the phone with dazed eyes.

"Hotel staff. Like, d'uh," Izzy blinks twice, trying to decipher why I'm so slow.

"He started sending me gifts," I mutter to myself.

"That's so nice of him," Izzy concludes. "But unnecessary. Not being a man-whore would have been more sufficient."

# CHAPTER 15

I drown myself with extra shifts at Ned's now that I'm not busy with school anymore. I'm functioning, which is great. I pour a beer with a perfect head for a middle-aged guy who always tips generously.

I lift my eyes to the flat screen TV that's mounted on the wall and catch a glimpse of a rerun of Ty's bout on ESPN. I don't want to look, but my eyes dart to the screen, betraying me completely.

There are only a handful of people sitting here, drinking beer. I wipe pint glasses with a dishcloth while watching the weigh-ins on screen. This is what Ty was starving himself for, for weeks.

The Invincible Eoghan Doherty is the first to step on the scale for the main event of the night, and after him, Tyler "The Zombie" Wilder follows. There are a bunch of ring girls in bikinis applauding behind them, and my heart tweaks in agony when I think about the close proximity of these babes to Ty.

The commentator is enthusing about Ty's newest addition to his tattoo collection. "Looks like Wilder got some new ink ahead of the fight. He's tattooed *Bmine* on his chest, above his heart. I wonder who the new girl is who he's asking to 'Be mine'?"

Jesus Christ, I think I'm hyperventilating again.

Ty and Eoghan launch at each other after going on the scale. Doherty has his fist balled up to Ty's face. They're yelling and pointing at each other, but you can't hear shit through the heavy metal music.

Back at Ned's, the men are watching the rerun intently, even though avid XWL fans already know how this fight ended last weekend. Everyone here is rooting for the Zombie from Concord. It's like cheering for your home team. You don't have a choice. That's your team and you stick to it.

"Such a great guy." The man who I just poured a beer tugs his baseball cap at the TV and beams at a very pissed off Ty. "Always nice to everyone in my shop whenever he drops by. Says hi and takes pictures with my boys. They're fans," he explains.

On screen, people are cheering and shouting and chanting for Ty, my Ty, the guy who used to snuggle with me every night underneath his comforter, his crooked nose in my neck, his tongue swirling and flicking my earlobe, his flexed muscles pressing against my skin. Now he's everyone's, and it makes me want to crawl into a cave and wait for a slow, painful death.

The fight is about to begin. Ty is coming out of the tunnel, wearing his signature black skull bandana, the one he wore the first time I saw him. His eyes are dead, completely turned off and indifferent to the chaos that surrounds him. I see a flicker of something flash for a second when they grease his face before he enters the cage. It's not exactly pain in his eyes, but... sadness? Anxiousness? If he is worried about something, I know it has nothing to do with Doherty.

It's about me. All me.

The place is bustling with hundreds of people, swinging their plastic cups in the air, cheering excitedly and waving both American and Irish flags.

*I see you* Ty signs to the camera, and I know that he's signing to me. I know that tattoo doesn't say "Be Mine." The B is for my name. *Blaire. Barbie.* I'm the girl he branded himself with, who he's claimed. *Blaire m*ine. *Barbie m*ine. The girl who doesn't want to hear from him ever again is his.

Me.

The minute both men step into the cage, my heart stops beating. I'm so anxious I find myself holding my breath. Mikey notices my expression as Ty and Eoghan circle each other, fists curled, throwing combinations at each other, but mostly missing one another.

"You know this fight is from last Saturday night, right? Both guys are still alive. Well, one of them barely..." He pats my arm, chuckling to himself.

I throw the towel over my shoulder and turn my back to the TV. "I know and don't care," I sniff.

Word got around fast at Ned's that Ty and I were together. Before the debacle in Vegas, he kept showing up every chance he got while I was working. The gossip site piece didn't help either. I'm not sure if Mikey has picked up on the fact that we are no longer an item, though.

"Blaire," Mikey says softly, as if he's reading my mind. "Come on, what's done is done. Watch it with us."

I turn around to watch the rest of the bout. Doherty may be good at hyping the fight, but Ty is an amazing fighter, who can spine-rip Doherty in seconds, *Mortal Combat* style.

He blocks Doherty's punches skillfully and has him on the mat in a matter of seconds. Then grounds and pounds him on the floor. He manages to take down Doherty in a minute and forty-five seconds. Months and months of preparations, endless hours of workouts and enough mental stress to rival a president at war, for less than two minutes of work.

*Ugh, men.*

It makes me giddy with emotion that he wins. Adrenaline pumps in my veins, making me dance behind the bar. The men at Ned's look pleased with the result, and I watch as both fighters pull their tees back on. Ty's is black with a white skull and says ZombieNation.

They bow to each other and shake hands politely, like they didn't just try to annihilate each other. The usual attractive woman reporter whisks Ty straight to the champion's interview, and I sneak to the back of the bar to stock up on some more Bud Light, and also to avoid watching him more.

He inked my initial. On his heart. He won the fight, despite being all messed up. This gives me hope, because if he can bury his feelings, so can I. And that's exactly what I intend to do.

Or, at the very least, I intend to try.

# CHAPTER 16

I decide to send the new phone that Ty got for me back to The Grind. I don't dare set foot in there, though. Not after how I had left things with Dawson, AKA the adoring coach, and Jesse, AKA the wingman. Both probably consider me public enemy number one now that I dumped their boy.

As for Ty, I would definitely never risk bumping into him.

No. I send the phone to The Grind via Izzy, who doesn't seem to share my disdain for the XWL. She returns home horny as hell and muttering about Shane. She's already replaced my old phone with a new one—her graduation gift. I purposely get a new number so I won't be tempted to text Ty when I get lonely, sad and teary-eyed at night.

I earned my degree, but I skip the commencement ceremony. I never really dug the whole college thing anyway. In hindsight, I may have been better off studying somewhere else, far away from home, but considering my lack of success in high school, there was no way my parents would have funded an out of state tuition fee.

Especially to major in communications studies.

Needless to say, my parents were *very* disappointed with my decision to keep the festivities to a minimum, even more so when they suggested we celebrate my graduation at a restaurant and invited me to a steakhouse.

Me. Their daughter. Who refused to eat meat since she was around nine.

I declined politely, Mom was angry, Izzy reminded her of my food preferences, Mom apologized, and now we're all good. And by "good" I mean the usual not-talking-about-it state or repressed anger and silent tension typical in my family.

But hey, I graduated.

I freaking graduated, and no one can take that away from me. They thought I wouldn't, but I proved them wrong. Hah. Take that, Mr. and Mrs. Skeptical.

Mikey and Bree throw me a little Sunday-afternoon graduation party at Ned's. It's nothing, really. Just a few beers and ice cream sandwiches with the staff. It's not even my shift, so I find myself sitting on one of the stools next to Bree, holding a root beer in one hand and an ice cream sandwich in another, grinning when Mikey goes on and on about how they're all so proud of me.

After his speech, Bree studies my face. "How are you holding up, honey?"

I'm not, I want to tell her, but instead take a big gulp of root beer, buying time.

"Yeah, not bad," I finally say. "Not bad at all." Jesus, even I don't buy this.

Bree cocks her head, a funny look plastered on her face. "Hey, are you and Ty back together?"

I snort loudly. "Not in this lifetime."

Bree purses her lips. She's awfully quiet when she excuses herself from the barstool next to me, grabbing her drink and joining one of our colleagues, Amy. She doesn't even like Amy.

I turn my head in the direction that made Bree change her mind about sitting next to me, and now it's my turn to purse my lips.

Oh, no he didn't.

Only he totally did.

Heart takes a nosedive and my shoulders tense.

"What are you doing here?" I say quietly, my voice almost a whisper. The unbearable emptiness I've been walking around with for the past week turns into an excruciating pain that slams into me with anger. I may feel hollow without him, but seeing him now only makes things worse.

"Can we please just talk? I'm running out of ideas about where and how to find you." His voice, that I missed so dearly, is pulling every emotional string in my body.

"Good." I try to keep my expression neutral. "That's the general idea."

But even after saying this, I know that I can't let him leave without hearing him out.

"It won't take long," Ty reassures.

I stride warily toward him, my quivering lower lip completely betraying whatever mask of cool I've been desperately trying to put on. Ty looks great, but not what I expected. Slightly thinner, not his bulky, usual self, and his eyes are tired. Usually, after a long-awaited fight, fighters go on binge-fests and rock a few days of relaxation, but Ty looks even worse than he did when he cut weight and trained like hell. He's beat.

"Let's take it outside." He nods at the door, and I follow him silently. He leans against the back wall outside, one foot and his back pressed against the bricks, his hands deep in his pockets. I fold my arms and wait for him to start.

"Well?" I ask, expecting him to apologize. But he doesn't, he just stares at me blankly.

"Well... what? I wanted to see you, see how you're doing, say congrats about you graduating. Have you gone to that job interview yet?"

Is he kidding me?

"Are you not going to apologize?"

"For what?" He wrinkles his forehead. I'm floored. Is this a joke?

"You were a male prostitute," I accuse.

"Before I knew of your existence, before we've even met. I've never even looked at a girl since our first date."

"You hid your past away from me. You had no right."

"I had every fucking right. It's my past, not my present, not my future. Besides, I remember pretty clearly I did promise to share my past with you at some point, when *I* was ready, not when your little BFF decided to throw another bash-fest for me."

"You put me at risk when you slept with me." I raise my voice, losing control over my emotions. My hands are shaking, but it doesn't stop me from waving them at Ty frantically. "I could've caught something. This is serious."

He looks away from my face, staring at nothing in particular. I know this strategy. I hit a nerve.

"I always used protection and I knew I was clean. Hell, you do realize we get tested before every fight to make sure we're all good, right? I'm sorry you were hurt, but I genuinely tried to up my game for you. It was never enough, though. You always kept running away every time things didn't fit into your perfect existence and listened to Shane instead of running things past me. But you know what? I don't remember giving you shit about it, Barbie."

What the hell? This is not what I was expecting to come out of this conversation. Why has he even bothered showing up here if he intended to lecture me about *my* behavior? Un-fucking-believable.

"How much did Nicole pay to sleep with you?" I taunt, feigning amusement. I can't seriously dignify his last accusation with an answer. I know I wasn't perfect, but I didn't hold a destructive secret either. "Tell me, so I can appreciate what you've given me for free."

He rests his head on the wall behind him and lets out a bitter laugh that makes my skin crawl. Frankly, he seems as pissed off as I am right now. More.

"Nicole was just for fun. I didn't charge her shit. She came along way after I wrapped things up with Ray. I've been out of the business for six months now. Happy?" His cheeks are flushed, his breathing heavy. "I didn't come here to talk about Nicole."

"So why did you come?" I'm grinding my teeth, annoyed with myself for even mentioning her name.

"I came here because I thought you might have calmed down. But I was wrong."

It's starting to seem like he's the one who isn't happy with me. I keep quiet, my eyes clinging to his face.

"Nothing to say, huh?" His sad smile fills the gap between us with more than words.

Ty pivots, and I have to do something more destructive. I

can't let him leave before I scar him deeper than he scarred me. And he got fucking deep.

"Ray's right. You're still the guy you were, you know," I spit after him. "You haven't changed."

He turns around slowly, squinting his eyes and zeroing on me. "This is your cue to run away, sweetheart. So run. I'm done chasing."

# CHAPTER 17

I suck at job interviews.

When Mikey interviewed me for the position at Ned's, I arrived half an hour late, broke the glass of water he had offered me and got caught lying about my experience as a bartender. So I'm keeping my expectations to the absolute minimum with the job interview as an intern at *Diablo Hill* magazine. In fact, if I manage not to break anything in the process, I'll declare victory.

The fact that I have absolutely nothing to offer—I didn't even major in journalism and my only connection to the school paper is that I once fooled around with a guy who wrote for the music section—doesn't help. But I'm eager to impress, and still on a high from graduating, so I'm hoping this will work in my favor.

The sports editor is named Cameron, and he's the guy I'm about to meet. I borrow an outfit from Izzy, because my wardrobe doesn't offer anything vaguely presentable. Fancy black pants with a white collared shirt and matching pumps. With my hippie, wavy hair and teenage posture, I look like I dressed up as a middle- aged bookkeeper for Halloween.

*Diablo Hill* magazine's headquarters is situated on the edge of Diablo Mountain in an architecturally dazzling loft with floor-to-ceiling windows. Beats me how a small, local publication can afford such lavish digs. I walk into the pristine white foyer, with blooming, fresh tulips carefully tucked into elegant vases and breathtaking pictures of the surrounding landscape hung on the walls. The receptionist greets me with a smile wider than the fields outside, her four-inch stilettos clicking against a pristine hardwood floor. She is insanely pretty and has the high-pitched voice of a toy dog, and I immediately know that I'm not good enough for a place like this. But I'm already here, so I might as well enjoy the ethically-sourced coffee.

Violet, the rail-thin receptionist, leads me to Cameron's office while engaging me in a casual chitchat, her huge grin both dazzling and scary. She knock on Cameron's door and announces I've arrived. Then she leaves me on a sleek white chair to wait. Everything around me is white and wood and fancy, and it makes me feel like I'm in a Reese Witherspoon rom-com. I didn't even know places like this existed in real life.

Cameron opens the door, and I'm instantly taken aback by his looks. He is hot. Hipster hot. He's got a messy, light brown hair, a dashing face and dreamboat blue eyes. He's wearing a denim button-down shirt, quirky glasses, tight skinny jeans and a sophisticated grin he obviously perfected over the years. Had I been emotionally available, Cameron would be the guy I'd crush on, for sure. Tall, lanky hipster, designed and molded to be unique and quirky and all *Oh, are those funky chucks personalized? Who-is-your-graffiti-artist?* and *Baby-Baby? Of course, I've heard of them. Great band.*

But I can't get myself to get even remotely excited about the idea of working closely with him when I am still so totally and completely hooked on Ty.

I shake his hand and flop into a chair opposite him while he sits behind his desk. Cameron is nice and cheery and asks me to call him Cam. His office window overlooks a postcard-worthy view of Diablo Mountain.

"So tell me about yourself." Cam knits his fingers together and gestures with his thumbs in my direction.

This one is difficult. I'm not good at selling myself. I could sing the praises of Izzy, Shane, Bree, Mikey and even Ty... but telling people about my strong points? Ain't happening. Still, I need to say something, so I do.

"I graduated from Diablo Hill School of Art recently. I majored in communications, and I'm very enthusiastic about my career. Professor Penniman was kind enough to recommend me after reading my assignment in journalistic reporting. I'm very grateful for the opportunity to be interviewed here."

Jesus. I just bored myself to sleep. I believe Cam has the same reaction, because he nods at an even pause, which means what he's really doing is thinking about what he should have for dinner tonight. He presses his knitted pointer fingers to his lips, probably thinking of a way to break the ice.

"What do you know about sports?"

"Very little. People usually sweat but not always." I downplay my knowledge so he won't have any expectations. A shout-out to all my underachiever peeps. High five!

"Follow any sport? NBA? NFL? XWL?"

So, editor Cam has not been reading gossip sites recently. Good.

"I follow the XWL whenever I can." I inwardly cringe when I say this out loud, because I really do condemn MMA as a sport, but I'm also aware that this is my strongest selling point at the moment.

"Yeah?" He scans me with an arched brow, obviously calling me out on my bullshit. "That's good, because we may have a local titleholder soon, and someone will need to cover that."

I gulp hard. "I think Ty Wilder stands a good chance of winning the championship."

Cam smiles, suggesting that I passed an unspoken test. He slaps his desk and straightens up quickly. "I think I need a caffeine fix. What about you?"

I think I need something stronger, like a shot of vodka or maybe crack cocaine.

"Sure, coffee sounds good." I follow him to the door, fidgeting with the hem of Izzy's designer shirt (too tight, as per usual).

Cam cocks his head to my outfit. "You do know that we don't really have a dress code here, right? You don't have to be all buttoned-down. We're a creative group."

I let out a relieved sigh. "Thank God, because I feel like

an accountant in this outfit."

Cam smiles. "Oh, and we have cool stuff like pizza Friday and a pool table and PlayStation and Xbox in the common room. We've even got Wii. And a terrific sound system, of course."

"I can work with that." I hitch one shoulder noncommittally. Cameron laughs and we roll out to the sunny afternoon. He immediately lights a cigarette and a pang of regret pierces through me. I would love to come home today and smoke a joint, take the edge off, but I know that I won't. Weed is no longer a part of my life, with or without Ty in the picture. We make our way to a local coffee shop and get our coffees, then Cam motions for me to follow him back to the office. We walk down the hallway but continue to talk. It's nice, knowing he can't examine my face while I answer his questions. It's less intimate, somehow.

"So when can you start?" Cam asks as he pushes his office door open. I curl my fingers around the hot paper cup, thinking about Ned's. I don't want to leave there. But I know I'd be stupid to turn down this opportunity.

"I'll need to check with my current employer, but I think a month's notice would be sufficient for them." My heart pounds in my ears.

"And what do you think about us hiring you?" He turns around to face me before we enter his office. His eyes sparkle behind his hipster glasses.

"I think you're doing the right thing. I'm kind of pleasantly surprised with my journalistic abilities." I feel the smile spreading across my face. I discovered that I'm good at something these past few months, and I can't wait to show it off to the world.

Cameron grins and motions for me to take a seat in front of him. We're back to square one. He is staring at me. I'm staring back. Baby, I got my staring lessons from a fighter. I will stare back at you right until my eyes bleed.

"You and I are going to get along just fine. And you'll meet a lot of awesome people here. My friend, Emilia, is the editor of the culture section, and I'm sure this one's right up your alley. You can contribute to the cultural section too. Your portfolio will pile up quickly." He seems to be at ease with our constant eye contact.

"Wow, I'd really like that." I don't know how much fun it's going to be working on sports items, but if I ever get anywhere near culture and music, I just know I'll thrive.

"Well, then, Blaire, tell your employer you're done serving drinks. Welcome to the *Diablo Hill* family." Cameron winks. And for the first time since Vegas, I'm actually smiling not just out of politeness but for real.

Cam wastes no time throwing me in the deep end. He ignores the fact that I still need to hand in a month's notice and fills me in on a piece he wants to publish this month—an editorial article about a new performance enhancing drug named Exo. He tells me Exo stimulates the production of red blood cells and is very popular among athletes, even though it's been proven that the medication, originally invented to treat cancer patients after chemo, increases the risk of death. In fact, Exo stimulates the growth of certain tumors, so by using Exo, a lot of athletes are risking their lives every day, just to get better, stronger and faster at what they do.

"The article is not about Exo itself. Exo is just the entry point. The article is about the psychological difference between competitive athletes and the rest of the population. We're interviewing a bunch of anthropologists and sport psychologists about this phenomenon. It's interesting how athletes will completely disregard their health for their sport. Sell their souls to the devil, so to speak."

You can say that again. I suppress a grunt. I'm guessing Cam would be head over heels to discover that Jesse Clement of XWL used steroids, and that Ty Wilder of the same MMA league pimped his body to get fights. But I'm afraid my loyalty lies firmly with the two fighters. I'm not even sure why, but the need to protect their secrets is way stronger than my need to impress my new boss.

"And I'm guessing there are plenty of examples," I say.

Cam nods excitedly. His blue eyes gleam. "Performance enhancing drugs are just the tip of the iceberg. People will go to great lengths to get to the top, and I mean bribery, blackmail, a ton of things that haven't been addressed yet. Athletes are a different breed. They don't think like us, they don't act like us. They make bigger sacrifices. It's just the way it is."

"Yup, the list could go on forever." I press my lips to the rim of my cup. Cam is pressing way too many sensitive buttons right now.

"So what's the argument of the piece?"

"That maybe it's time to cut athletes some slack, because, well, let's admit it, they seem to be wired entirely differently. Look, this is your brain." He opens the lid to his coffee cup. "And this is an athlete's brain." He takes my cup and opens it too. Both cups are nearly empty. Then he starts throwing candy bar wraps and an old piece of tissue he had tucked in his pocket.

"See the athlete's brain? It's cluttered with so much extra pressure. Elite athletes always score high on traits such as obsession, asceticism, the ability to focus on long-term goals. They're not as easily swayed by immediate gratification as most of us. Instead, they're able to push through pain, hunger and even social condemnation to get to their goal."

"I'm not sure I buy that athletes should get away with shit just because they can't help themselves."

Cam hurries to correct my conclusion. "I'm not saying they can do whatever they want. I'm just saying it's harder for them to resist cheating. No matter how great they are and how big the risk is, they feel compelled to win. Just look at Lance Armstrong."

"So if someone did something wrong, very wrong, let's say, to push their career forward..." I nibble my lip thoughtfully. "But then stopped because they felt it's morally wrong..."

"Then I'd say that they're displaying mental strength to take such a step. They deserve a second chance"

I blink my surprise.

"At their sport, of course," he clarifies.

Right. Of course.

We carry this conversation for a few more minutes, and even though I'm trying hard to concentrate on the actual conversation, I get a really weird feeling that Cam is... well, I wouldn't call it flirting, nothing feels too inappropriate, but let's just say that he seems overly interested in knowing more about me.

L. J. SHEN

And what I like.

And what I do.

And how I spend my free time.

By the time we walk back to the reception area and Cam drops me off at Violet's desk so she can show me to the HR department, I am sure of two things. One, if Cameron could (which I guess he couldn't, seeing as he'll be my boss), he would have totally asked me out. He checked me out thoroughly when we said our goodbyes. Two, if Cameron asked me out, I would have said no, because frankly, he may be perfect for me. Hell, Shane may be perfect for me. But the guy I want is perfectly imperfect, and I'm completely fine with it.

I'm not fine with what Ty did. I'm not fine with how he handled everything—us, his secret and his past mistakes. But yes, I'm fine with knowing that his actions are going to have some consequences, and I'm ready to shoulder some of the weight, some of the burden and even some of the pain that comes with it.

Too bad that after our last conversation, I'm starting to think that he might not be on board with that arrangement.

I've always been a late bloomer, and I have a nagging feeling that I may be late again.

*Shit.*

# CHAPTER 18

I officially have no social life. Nana Marty got whisked away to a month-long Hawaiian honeymoon. Mom and Dad are redecorating parts of their house, including the rooms that used to belong to me and Izzy. And Izzy is busy seeking out her next prestigious campaign and takes time off from Elizabeth's Passion to work her ass off at the gym five times a week. At least she's not working out at The Grind.

I spend my time trying to rebuild my relationship with Shane. A relationship that both literally and figuratively took a pretty serious blow.

Shane has started an internship at a new funky culture magazine based in San Francisco. It's called *Dazed* and it's supposed to be the American version of *Vice* magazine. A week into his internship, I take the train into San Fran and meet him for lunch in a hipster sushi place in Russian Hill. When I confess to the server, who has two sleeves of tattoos and a lip ring, that I'm a vegetarian, he doesn't even blink. In fact, he hands me the restaurant's raw vegan menu and points at the most recommended dishes.

God bless San Francisco.

Shane sits across from me, wearing his "TV Is Gooder Than Books" tee and a frown. His face has long ago healed and he is back to looking his normal self, but he doesn't look particularly happy. After the server takes our orders, he lets out a heavy sigh.

"Being an intern sucks ass," he says, and I take a sip from my Diet Coke and shake my head.

"You need to start somewhere," I point out. Shane and I have been incredibly lucky to bag paid internships. He shouldn't be sulking, especially considering the kick-ass magazine he is working for now.

But Shane leans forward and lowers his voice. "Wanna hear what I do all day? I go for coffee runs, transcribe boring interviews and serve as the official wingman for the PA's and secretaries of the fucking place."

"What did you expect? It's a trendy magazine. Everybody wants to work there. You need to work your way to the top. I, on the other hand..." I point my forefinger to my temple. "Am going to work for a local magazine that no one reads. I may get lucky and actually write articles, but the downside is that absolutely no one will read them. *Pow.* " I pretend to shoot myself.

Shane winces.

"It'll get better." He pats the back of my hand.

"Or worse." I manage a smile. "So what's up with you and Izzy? I know she paid you a visit in Vegas, but she wouldn't tell me what you guys were up to, and knowing you, it couldn't have been good."

Shane throws his body back into his chair and laughs whole-heartedly. "Why not? I broke up with Gemma before I saw her because I knew she'd kill me if she found out I was seeing a chick. No brownie points for that?"

"Not if she lost her virginity with you and you abandoned her... again. Wait, you can't lose you virginity twice, but you can still get hurt again."

Shane rubs his face. "That's not the whole story, and it's inaccurate as hell, Miss Soon-To-Be Journalist."

I shrug. "Answer my question. Are you guys involved in any way? Her sudden secrecy is freaking me out."

"No," he reassures. "Honest to God, the reason why she's not telling you anything is that there is nothing to tell. She was just checking up on me and got me some room service in Vegas. And when we came back home, she stopped answering my calls. Again."

"That's good," I say, and quickly backpedal. "I mean, not good, but at least I know that she's okay."

I wish I hadn't told Shane I know he took Izzy's V-card. I'm not sure he's supposed to know that I know. But here we are, staring at each other awkwardly, desperate to bury the thought of my best friend tapping my twin sister.

Good freaking thing we're not identical.

Shane clears his throat. "So any news from that nutjob?"

I stare at my hands. "Shane, I'm really sorry about what happened with him, but you have to at least try and see it from Ty's point of view." I can't believe this sentence just left my mouth, but it's too late to take it back, I guess. "First, he got some vibes about you wanting me. Then, he misinterpreted a text you sent me and thought you threatened me. Then, he found out you tried to hit on me. After which, you accused him of some serious stuff—twice."

"It's not an accusation if it's true," Shane huffs.

"One thing was true, but the other was a misunderstanding. And anyway..." I take a deep breath. "He wanted to clear things up between the three of us. You're the one who punched first. There's no excuse for his violence afterward, there really isn't, but him beating you up is not the whole story. There's more to it."

Shane is obviously annoyed with my case. "But you aren't taking him back," he says with conviction, and when I don't answer, he smacks a flattened palm on the table. "Jesus, tell me you're not taking him back. The guy was a fucking man-whore. No pun intended."

I squirm in my seat. "Please don't make a scene. Sit down."

Every muscle in his body is still tense. His eyes never leave mine. "You can't take him back," he says, more to himself than to me.

I nod, then shake my head, then nod again. *Ouch.* That was not a wise thing to do.

"I'm not saying I will. I mean, I may take him back. If he'll still have me. But I'm not sure he's my biggest fan right now. I pissed him off."

Shane pretends to look shocked, slapping a hand over his

mouth while his eyes bug out in disbelief. "No way. Are we still talking about the same Tyler Wilder? Because I clearly remember him being so stoic and composed."

Our food arrives and Shane still stares at me, while I tuck into my vegan tacos, pretending not to notice the way his pupils are boring holes in my face.

"You really love him," he says finally, and oh so very quietly. I nod without looking up, fighting back the tears.

"Dude." He runs his hand through his hair, rolling his eyes. "You really do love this loser."

Ty's a lot of things, but I'm pretty sure he isn't a loser. All the same, I confirm Shane's diagnosis with a hitched shoulder.

Then I hear him gritting his teeth. "Fine, but the next time I see him, I'll punch him again for what he did to me, just for good measure."

# CHAPTER 19

My routine is a source of security for me. I hang on to it and remind myself that I'm still alive. I work, go to sleep and repeat. Ty doesn't contact me, and even though that doesn't surprise me in the slightest—he's always been a man of his word—it's slicing my soul to tiny pieces. Has he touched another girl yet? Has he moved on? I want to know. I don't want to know.

Everything reminds me of him. Every smell, every face, every noise, everything that stimulates my senses. I'm living, but I'm not alive. And it's not like I'm losing grasp on reality—I'm losing interest. I can live like this for years. Thirty, forty, fifty, maybe sixty and more. Apparently, after the excruciating pain, comes the numb. I'm at my numb phase.

I'm heart-crushingly numb.

Izzy tries to convince me to talk to Ty several times, but I refuse. I know he needs the time. Hell, I need the time too.

Nana Marty calls me a few times from Hawaii to ask how I'm doing and I always put on a brave face, letting her know that I'm okay. Mom and Dad have been asking me what's up with my so-called boyfriend, but I think they're relieved to find out I cut my ties with him and that he made it clear he's done with me too.

Three weeks after Ty beat Eoghan Doherty, the XWL announces that he will face Brazilian Jesus Vasquez four months from now for the championship belt. They talk about the match-up in the local news, on the radio, and on the XWL and other MMA websites.

However, Ty is MIA in the media and my life, and I just have to deal with it.

A week after the news breaks, I lie in bed and binge-watch *True Detective*. Izzy is in LA, and I have the feeling she is going to move there by the end of the summer. I don't like it one bit. My internship is going to pay pretty much the same amount of nothing I earn at Ned's, and I have no idea where I'm going to live once she leaves.

When my doorbell chimes, I have no idea who could be at our door either. I drag myself out of bed and ask who it is. The answer makes my heart race.

"It's Jesse."

I open the door in my pj's, my hair in a messy bun, face sans makeup.

He checks me out head to toe and shakes his head. "You look like shit."

He is probably right. On a bad day like this (and I've recently had few of those), I'm very much the girl next door. Not the one you have a crush on—the one who spends her days playing with her dog in the backyard because she has zero friends.

"Can I come in?" His hands are on his waist. He's wearing his gym gear, and I wonder if Ty sent him to talk to me. I motion him inside while he scans my apartment looking for... what, exactly? A voodoo doll?

"What's up?" I choke on my heart. I'd started to fear that Ty had forgotten about me and moved on.

Maybe he hasn't. Maybe he's still stuck on me like I am on him.

"What's up?" Jesse challenges. "Nothing is up. Everything seems to be going to hell, baby girl."

"I hear accusation in your voice."

"What you hear in my voice is pure concern."

I offer him an annoyed pout and some coffee. I know he doesn't take his with sugar. Goddamned athletes and their clean-eating ways.

"Sit your ass down," he orders, and I perch on the barstool, sulking. Jesse is not as charismatic as Ty, but they both fall under the category of people who can tell you to do just about anything, including rimming a dead donkey, and you'd do it.

"Ty is a big boy," I say. "He can come up here himself if he has something to tell me."

"Tyler didn't ask me to come here, Blaire."

My stomach knots. Maybe he's moved on after all.

"Right. So are you here just to rattle my cage? Or is this a social call?" I take a sip of my coffee without even tasting it. All my senses are focused on figuring out what's new with Ty and why Jesse paid me a visit.

"I'm here because I need your help." Jesse leans forward and locks eyes with me. "Tyler is in bad shape. Really bad shape. He's drinking himself to death. Not showing up to the gym. Not eating—at all. He's losing muscle mass when he should be putting it on."

"The horror," I gasp sarcastically.

"At this rate, he'll have to cancel his match with Vasquez." His tone vibrates with worry. "If he doesn't get his shit together soon, he might as well tap out now."

Considering Ty is the most undramatic person I've ever met, this is news. He was all about issues with anger, not partying. I never pegged binge drinking to be his style.

But I was wrong.

"What the hell do you want me to do? Get back with him so he can win the championship?"

A part of me is hoping he'll say yes. That would be a great excuse to contact him. I know I should be devastated to hear Ty is falling apart, but the truth—the raw, rotten, disgraceful truth—is that it makes me happy to learn he's struggling like I am. I'm not drinking, but I'm dead inside. I don't go out. I don't smile. In some ways, it's even worse, because at least Ty is already dealing with our breakup.

"He has no one, Blaire."

"He has you." I rub my forehead.

"I have a fight coming up next month. I'm training and have a lot of hype to sell. Don't have time."

"He has Dawson."

"Dawson's wife is pregnant, and he's got three kids, his plate is full."

"He has his mom."

Jesse lets out a hostile laugh. "That's who I wanted to talk to you about. There's no way in hell Mary will ever talk to me. Last time I saw her, I helped Tyler box up shit from her house and she almost called the cops on me just for helping him take some of his old stuff. She won't listen to me, but maybe she'll listen to you. Try to get her to drag her ass down to Concord and take care of her son. Ty needs her." He leans forward to watch my reaction.

Do I really have a choice? I don't think I do. And even if I had a choice, a part of me is dying to see Ty's mother. It might sound pathetic, but she is a piece of him. Who knows? Maybe I can actually get these two to get back in touch. Wouldn't that be something? The fact that I'm not even thinking this through is enough to tell me how much I love him, still.

"I'll need her number." I shift on my stool.

Jesse makes a face. "I think you're better off driving to her place. A face-to-face meeting will have more impact."

This sounds like a recipe for disaster, but I have to man up. I want this. I want to help Ty.

I want a chance to see him again.

৵৽

Mary Wilder lives in Redwood, NorCal in the kind of neighborhood that would make even an MMA champion fear for his life. I don't know what drove her here, but I sure know it couldn't have been a real-estate upgrade. The house is small and wooden, and desperately needs a coat of paint and a new roof. The yard hasn't been mowed in months—or years—and all the plants, trees and weeds are either yellow, orange or covered in mud. Random junk clutters the yard— children's bicycles, empty carton boxes, rusty pieces of metal, rotting wooden pallets. Man, this place looks rough.

How could Ty let his mom live this way?

I make sure my Mini Cooper is locked and push open the rusty gate, cursing as I stumble my way past stacks of moldy newspapers and crates of empty cans and climb the porch stairs to her front door. The door has a dirty, yellowing window with a torn curtain. I bang twice and sneeze when dust wisps into the air.

No one answers, but I think I hear a muffled cough inside the house. I rap on door again, this time harder.

"Go away," a miserable voice moans.

"Open the door, Mrs. Wilder," I yell. I hope I convey some kind of authority, because she may be my only chance to get Ty out of the head-deep shit he sank into.

The porch shakes as her footfalls approach. I hear her grunting, rustling the chain lock.

She thinks the better of it at the last minute and opts to peek through the curtain.

"Who the hell are you?" she demands.

I steal a glimpse of mother Wilder. She looks nothing like her son. He is tall, lean, athletic and has the facial features of a deity. She looks like a tired, overweight, unemployed mother of eight.

"It's about your son." I push my Wayfarers up my nose.

The curtain drops back in place.

"I ain't got the bail money to help him out. Go away."

Jesus Christ. I shake my head and squeeze my eyes shut. So much for maternal instincts. I kick an ugly frog ornament next to her door. Big, throbbing mistake. It's made of cast iron.

"He doesn't need money, Mary. He needs help. He's all busted up inside, and I don't know who to turn to." I bang her door with my fist. I wait impatiently and rub my wounded toes as she opens the door and stands in front of me, her eyes hollow with disinterest.

"He hasn't spoken to me in three years, how the hell can I help him?" She leans on the doorframe and folds her arms on her chest.

I allow myself a second to take in the sight of her. She looks a mess. Father Wilder must have been an Abercrombie model, otherwise I can't see how Ty and this woman are genetically linked.

She takes out a soft pack of Camel Lights from the back of her stained sweatpants and lights a cigarette, motioning with her hand to ask me if I want one. I shake my head, and she shrugs, covering the Zippo lighter with her hand.

"You his girl?" She sounds amused and billows a trail of smoke directly at my face.

"Why is this funny?" I dodge the question.

"There's always a girl trying to save Tyler. And all of you think you can. You girls are dumber than I was when I married his father."

"No point in asking how that one worked out, huh?" I push her away from the door, inviting myself in.

If her house looks like a mess from the outside, the inside could accurately be described as hell. She is a hoarder of some kind, and the place is crammed with shit I didn't even know still exists. And there is this rancid, awful smell of a stale fart and bad canned food.

"Nice place." I don't bat an eye, taking a tour around the house. I can't believe Ty used to live in this place. I know he moved around. Martinez to Redwood, Redwood to Concord. I can see why he ran away. Living in this place looks like a nightmare.

Mary plops down into a recliner and puffs on her cigarette. It was a bitch to find her place and it's going to be a bitch to get her to drag her sorry ass to Concord to be there for her son, and I know it.

When I started dating Ty, I imagined my first encounter with his mother would involve me asking her what the hell she was thinking when she decided to give him a name that rhythms. Tyler Wilder. Now I'm beginning to see that there's a lot of more pressing issues than Ty's name.

"How do you want me to help Tyler?" she repeats. "And what makes you think that I can?"

"I want you to come with me to Concord and take care of him until he comes around. He's been drinking and not eating and..." I trail off, fighting the urge to nibble on a fingernail. "He is not well."

"Tyler made it very clear that he doesn't consider me his mother."

"Ty says shit so you won't pick up on his pain. You're his freaking mom. Get your ass to Concord and live up to your role, because your son has a drinking problem that would put an Irish sailor to shame."

Mary offers me a shrewd smile. And that's when I see them. Those dimples. Ty's dimples. I take a good look at her, Photoshopping off years of poverty and misery. She was definitely a hottie before life hit her with a giant shovel and junk food did the rest of the damage.

"You're not one of the stupid bimbos. Guess Tyler has changed a little since I last saw him."

"Yeah." I take a few steps forward, making eye contact. "Now it's your turn. Get into the shower. I'll wait here. We're going to Concord."

Mary Wilder is her son's mother, alright. Just like him, she presents the demand list of an angry IRA terrorist before she'll agree to cooperate. She wants me to take her to the supermarket and buy her groceries, and also asks for a carton of smokes and a manicure before we leave Redwood.

I slam my Mini Cooper's passenger door, cussing under my breath, and slide behind the wheel. I know my mother can be a pain, but she also cares. She wants me to be happy, even if our definitions of "happy" are very, very different. Ty's mom definitely puts things in perspective.

"What the hell did you just say?" She lights up another cigarette, not bothering to ask if it's okay to smoke in my car. I roll down my windows.

"I said I'm surprised you didn't get any Mother of the Year awards yet." I start the engine and follow her directions to the nearest strip mall. It's a good thing my Wayfarers are dark enough to hide the disgust in my eyes.

I can't believe Ty had to suffer her as a mother. I just hope she'll step up to the plate now.

"I'm also getting some beer, just so you know," she tells me when I park outside the grocery store.

"Alcohol is off limits. You're not going near his house with beer." I put my foot down.

"Yes I am. He won't notice. I'll hide it from him." She flashes me a dimpled smile. Damn it.

"That's cheating," I point out.

"If it ain't worth cheating on, it ain't worth winning."

Yes. Ty has clearly inherited some traits from his mom. All she seems to care about is how to get her way while screwing people over.

I just wish her son wasn't so literal about following in her footsteps.

When it's all done and dealt with, and Mary walks out with two huge bags, and has new, glossy red nails, I finally drive to Ty's house. She's sitting next to me, completely consumed by the content of her new bags. She looks like a kid who just raided Toys R Us and asks zero questions about Ty. It's becoming more and more difficult for me not to dislike her. I'm convinced that she'll bail on me at the last minute.

"So what happens now?" She tears open a bag of corn chips and tosses one into her mouth, munching loudly.

"Ty's drinking too much. He needs someone to drag him to the shower, put some food in him and give him a hug. You think you can do that?" I flick my gaze to watch her briefly before turning back to the road.

She shrugs. "What set him off?"

"I dumped him."

Mary finds this so amusing she literally laughs until she cries. The smell of greasy chips on her hot, moist breath makes me want to throw the bag—and its owner—out of my car.

"Seriously, why's he depressed?" she finally asks, wiping her eyes. "Lost a fight again or somethin'?"

"He's depressed because we broke up," I repeat through gritted teeth.

"Look, Blake, you might be a cutie, but Ty doesn't get attached. Especially not to women. Look at me, I'm his mom and he won't even call me on my birthday. You think he's going to be heartbroken over some cute little thing?"

"Guess you'll just have to ask him for yourself." I feign a sugary smile and press the accelerator to the floor. That's enough bonding time for me with Mama Wilder.

I parallel park in front of Ty's house and immediately regret it. Why am I parking if I don't want to go inside? But I do want to go inside. I want to see him. I dragged his mom here so he'd have someone near him, so he wouldn't be alone. But frankly, I'm the one who should be helping him.

I glance at his fence. It's totally full of a new collection of souvenirs, courtesy of his female fans. Honest to God, if we ever get back together, the first thing I'm doing is tearing that fence down.

The Harley is off the porch and lying on its side in the yard. Judging by the high grass, the bike had been lying there for weeks. The curtains are drawn and everything is locked and dim, inside and out. If I didn't know better, I'd think he took off and abandoned the place.

Mary studies his house from the car window. She scowls at the fence. "Some girls just make it goddamned hard not to hate 'em."

I wrinkle my nose. "Men are worse."

I bully her out of the car after a five-minute pep talk. Yes, he'll want to see you, I assure her. No matter what happened between you two, blood is thicker than water. Honestly, I have no idea how Ty is going to react when he sees his mom. If I were him, I would be very suspicious of her. After all, she only agreed to see him after I bribed her with groceries and a manicure. But I so desperately don't want him to be alone right now, I'm taking a chance on her.

Mary finally sighs and opens her door. "Fine, time for us to go in."

"Us?" I raise an eyebrow. "This is where my journey ends. I'm not coming in with you."

"Like hell you aren't. I'm not going in there by myself. What if he throws me out? I'll need a ride home. Come inside with me and then leave."

"No."

"Yes."

"No."

"Yes."

I'm starting to see why women have such a hard time with their mothers-in-law.

"Fuck, you're so stubborn!" I rub my forehead, thumping one hand on the steering wheel.

"Ty never went for the wallflower type, but you really are a ballbuster, aren't you?" She smirks to herself. "I'm guessing by now you know that the Wilders are a stubborn bunch. Let's go."

"Yeah, okay," I finally say, killing the engine and reluctantly getting out of the car. The walk to his front door is agonizing. I'm happy and excited and sad and frustrated all at the same time. I'm the one who knocks on the door three times while Mary hides behind my back. No one answers, and there's no sound coming from inside. I knock again, harder.

Nothing.

I ring the bell multiple times, and finally walk around to one of the side windows, rapping against the glass with the side of my fist. I peek inside to his living room. The lights are turned off, and the place looks like it's been raided by the FBI, CIA and a pack of wolves.

"Ty!" I yell. "Open up. It's me."

I listen and hear a rustling noise and what sounds like an empty can rolling across the floor. I catch a glimpse of his tall figure floating toward the front door like a ghost, so I run back to the porch. Mary is standing wide-eyed, obviously expecting instructions.

"He's coming," I mouth. She turns to face the door, running her hand through her frizzy hair. I hear a chain clinking and jump in front of Mary so she won't be the first face that he sees. He swings the door open and stands in front of me, shirtless.

And... well, he is definitely not the sex on legs I've gotten used to.

At his prime, Ty Wilder has out-hotted Brad Pitt and Charlie Hunnam. Combined. Yeah, he was that gorgeous. Now? Not so much. He's gotten scary-thin, frail and looks about as lively as a corpse. His skin clings to his bones like an oversized shirt, his eyes vacant, glazed with apathy. I want to kill myself for doing this to him, and kill him for doing this to me.

"Seriously?" His eyes shoot to his mother. "What's this, your little revenge on me?"

"Heard you were struggling—"

"So you thought, why not push him over the edge? Shit just got suicidal."

I feel like he shoved a knife in my stomach and twisted it real slow. "I want someone to take care of you, and that's what your mother wants to do. Tell him, Mary." I turn to her.

She takes a step forward. "It's true, son." She coughs, trying to meet his eyes. He doesn't acknowledge her existence.

Instead, he shifts his gaze back to me. "You want someone to take care of me? That seems like a first. Usually, you're the last to give a flying fuck. Now go away and take this fatty with you." He angles backwards and is about to close the door.

Instinctively, I jam my foot in the gap. I'm floored to hear him talk like this. Even though he swears, he'd never stoop as low as fat-shaming or talked to me like this. This is not him speaking.

Ty slams the door on my foot and I wince in pain, falling sideways and stubbing my toes. This is the second time today my foot is injured on a Wilder's porch. This family is trying to kill me.

"Fuck. You okay? That was an accident. Fuck." He sighs, his dimples peeking through when he speaks.

"You kiss your mom with this mouth?" I feign a frown, but my lips are curving into a faint smile.

"No, I'm not. That's the point I was trying to make." He rests his temple on the doorframe, looking down at me. The high school sweetheart who escorted me to Dawson's office the first time I saw him is here again. Sweet-Ty. I missed him so.

I take a step forward and put my hands on his chest. It feels so natural to touch his warm, silky skin, and his body immediately tightens and flexes, reacting to my hands instinctively.

"Actually, Jesse suggested this little reunion. And I think it's a good idea, because frankly, I'm going to become a sports journalist in less than a week, and I'd really appreciate a good headline. Something along the lines of Local MMA Fighter Wins the XWL Welterweight Championship. Think you can manage that?" I whisper the words into his chest, watching it moving up and down slowly to the rhythm of our shallow heartbeats.

He clutches one of my hands, bringing it from his chest to his lips and kissing the back of it while looking deep into my eyes. I'm sure he can see all the shit I've been through the past few weeks. We read each other like open books. I feel his pain pouring down on the floor in waves.

"I'm not done being mad at you," he says.

My heart sinks. "I'm not done being mad at you either," I retort.

He shifts his gaze to his mother for the first time, looking at her, but talking to me. "She kicked me out of the house and stole my money three years ago."

"And she's your mother and wants to start fresh now." I swallow my anger at Mary.

My body melts into his, and I need to stop this before we kiss. I can't take him back. Not here, not now. Plus, his mother is standing next to us, so grinding each other like rabbits seems like a fairly bad idea. I drop my forehead to his chest and feel his heart thump beneath my cheek.

"Do you want to talk?" I ask.

"Not right now," he says, and I could crack and break into a million pieces on his threshold. "I have to focus on getting better, and hopefully, on winning this fight."

I lift my head, remembering the conversation with Cameron.

Athletes are wired differently. He needs this win. He needs his space.

It was like that before the Eoghan Doherty fight, and it's like that right now.

"Okay. Good luck." I try to smile at him. "You know where to find me."

He nods wordlessly, which makes my heart split in two.

When I reach my car, I peek over my shoulder to see Ty still holding the door ajar for his mother. She limps into his place, but before she enters the house completely, stops and looks him in the eyes. I can't read their expressions from this distance, but I hope they can work it out. I hope she can be there for him when he picks up the pieces and rebuilds himself.

And I hope Ty and I can get over ourselves and do the same one day.

# CHAPTER 20

November 10th.

It's almost time for Ty's fight. This is the date when he's scheduled to walk into the Vegas cage and face the biggest challenge of his career, the biggest fight of the year.

The past three months have gone by excruciatingly slowly without him. Days melded into each other, sticking together like glued chunks of paper in a new book. I offer myself the dumbest excuses for Ty not contacting me. He doesn't have my new phone number. He's busy preparing for his fight with Jesus Vasquez. He's waiting for our anger to blow over. Or maybe he still hasn't gotten out of his binge-drinking phase.

No. I know that's not true. I know for a fact that he's doing better.

Mary visits Ty every weekend. She takes two buses to get to his house. She cleans, cooks and yells at him that he's an unbearable slob. (A bit rich coming from her, I know.) She rants when she washes his dishes and cusses at him when she does his laundry. But she's taking care of him, and I know that because I talk to her whenever I can.

Mary never brings up the subject of my relationship with Ty, and I never volunteer anything about how I'm feeling.

Career-wise, I'm doing better. Or at least I'm doing better than Shane, who continuously reports to me about his days serving coffee and being bossed around by people who are only slightly older than us.

Me, I spend the first week at my new job sitting in front of a dead computer (the tech guy didn't have time to sort it out before my arrival) and trying not to cry out loud. I miss Ned's so much. But then at the start of week two, when I stare at the black screen like an idiot through blurry eyes, I feel a hand resting on my shoulder. I look up and see Cam's knowing smile.

"Don't worry about it. I know what it's like to leave a safe job. I was a butcher at my local big box store all through high school. Out of state tuition fee."

I duck my head in embarrassment, annoyed that he's seen me cry. "Where are you from?" I sniff.

"Promise you won't laugh."

I shake my head. "I can't do that. I suck at hiding my feelings." I point at a damp trail on my cheek left by one of my tears to prove the point.

"Fair enough." He offers me his hand and when I grab it, he yanks me up so he can go and have a smoke. "Arkansas. I'd barely left the state before I came here for school."

I laugh, of course I do, because it's so out of the blue.

"What made you stay in San Fran? I'm sure it wasn't the high rent and crazy people the city has to offer."

"Too lazy to move again, I guess." Cam runs a hand through his hair. "Then there's this ex back home I dread seeing. There's always an ex, isn't there?"

I guess there is. I'm just not sure I need to hear about one from my new boss.

"Let's get you started and give you something to do," he says.

And that is how my journalism career officially started.

The first month was brutal.

Trying to catch up on years of history attached to the local football, baseball and basketball teams is a real bitch. Each team has so much legacy and its own little quirky traditions and important statistics. It's funny how I thought I'd get rid of homework once and for all after I graduated, but for weeks, all I seem to do is memorize more and more info about the Golden State Warriors, San Francisco Giants, San

Jose Sharks and San Francisco 49ers.

By the fifth week, I already have all the coaches' phone numbers on speed dial, and quite a few of those basketball, baseball and hockey players even know my name. I also realize that I love basketball and hate hockey. Same problem as I had with MMA—hockey is way too aggressive for me. The injuries, broken noses and the way players crash into each other intentionally... Ouch.

By the time October swallows up summer, I'm a sports expert who knows which college football players are injured this year and which ones are draft prospects for the spring. I know the name of every coach in the NFL, the NBA and MLB. I even know who Floyd Mayweather is, which impresses Shane. Not to mention that I've already written two articles for *Diablo Hill* magazine and contributed to the website, which updates on a daily basis.

And the best part? I know I'm good. To begin with, I suspected that my success on my journalism assignment was purely a fluke. Now? Now I'm even starting to like writing about sports, which is something I never thought I'd enjoy.

November is just around the corner, and so is Ty's title fight. He's going to be fighting in Vegas again, and I'm sure Cam will cover the event, but I try not to think about it.

The fact that Ty still hasn't spoken to me drives me nuts. I'm not going to chase him around. I offered to clear the air months ago, but he didn't seem too eager, and my ego is still wounded from the huge secret he kept from me.

But that doesn't stop me from wandering to the XWL website to check now and then to see if there are any updates on him. It's part of my job to know what's going on with local athletes. Right?

One chilly day, I'm scanning the site for news, when Cam stops at my desk. I don't have an office. I share a big, open area with a dozen or so people. I'm actually grateful for the constant company and prefer the hustle and bustle to being alone.

"Hey." I flash Cam a smile that I'm certain doesn't reach my eyes. My smiles never do nowadays. "Winter is coming."

"Sure looks like it. So... November 10th," he announces, looking down at a paper in hand. "Tyler 'The Zombie'

Wilder Vs. Jesus Vasquez. Wilder is from Concord. We have to cover this."

"We? You mean the magazine." My stomach knots, my cheeks flush, and my pulse speeds up.

"No, I want you to help." He studies me from behind his glasses. "Bumped into your name on TMZ the other day. You have history with the guy."

"I haven't spoken to him in months."

"But you're obviously following the fight." He glances at my computer and the XWL site on the screen. *Busted.* Dammit. Why couldn't Brain do its job and keep Heart and Hormones in control.

"You don't have to write the story," Cam continues. "I doubt you'd be objective anyway. All I'm asking is that you come with me to Vegas and try and get Wilder to let me interview him. He doesn't do interviews, as you're probably well aware. If we manage to get him to talk to us, we're going to get a lot of buzz and new readers."

So many things are running through my head right now. The first one is that I may see Ty again, in the flesh, only a few weeks from now. The second is that Cam is pulling something completely unethical. The third? The last time I asked Ty for an interview, he demanded a date from me in exchange.

"Cam..." I readjust in my seat, because it feels so awkward to share this with my boss, no matter how nice and supportive he's been until now. "Ty and I aren't really on speaking terms. If I ask him for an interview, it could even decrease the magazine's chances. I don't want you to get your hopes up."

"It's a long shot, yeah, but it's better than nothing. And we need to cover the fight anyway, right?" Cam combs his fingers through his messy shag, but his hair stands up, looking even messier. "I mean, you can still say no, but why would you? Free hotel room, free plane ticket, free first row ticket, championship fight." He motions at my computer screen. There's a picture of a very angry, very bloody Jesus Vasquez. "And you get to see your ex-boyfriend getting punched. Which, according to Emilia and a few more girls who work here, is a serious bonus."

I nibble my lip. "People know you're asking me to do this?" Great. More pressure. And most definitely more humiliation when Ty turns me down.

"Well, no. I was asking Emilia this hypothetically, because I didn't want to come off as an insensitive prick."

I fold my arms. He *is* kind of an insensitive prick for asking me to do this, but I'm not going to say anything because... well, because I totally dig this job.

A few seconds pass in uncomfortable silence before Cam speaks again.

"Just think about it."

"I don't have to go to Vegas for this. I can stop by The Grind and ask him face to face."

Or better yet, go straight to his house. If there's less of a crowd around us, there's less of a chance of me trying to hurl myself under a bus when this whole thing blows up in my face. But Cameron shakes his head, eyes shut.

"Wilder's not in Concord anymore. He set his camp in Vegas four weeks ago. So unless you want to do this by phone..."

Nope. I really can't do it by phone. One, because I don't have his number, and two, because even if I get it through Jesse, Dawson or Mary, there's a good chance Ty won't answer my call.

"I'll do it," I hear myself saying, and even though the words coming out of my mouth are freaking me out, I know that it's the right thing to do.

I love this job.

And I freaking love Ty.

Vegas was bad to me the last time I was there, but maybe things will be different the second time around.

Maybe I'm already over his secret.

And maybe, he still isn't over me.

# CHAPTER 21

I'm sitting next to Cam in a cab that's taking us to our Vegas hotel. I think the panic attack started on the flight and kind of escalated to this point. I'm sweating like a pig, and my clammy hands strangle my canvas bag like I'm trying to choke it to death. What the hell am I doing? If Ty wanted me here, he would have said so. He is perfectly capable of getting what he wants—when he *wants it*—and now I'm just going to barge into the most important night of his life uninvited. The last time I surprised him, it ended up with tears and a breakup. I can't believe Cam has talked me into this.

"I may be out of line here... okay, I'm definitely way out of line here, but for whatever reason, I just can't seem to picture you and Wilder together? You don't seem to have a lot in common." Cam is filling the silence with his words.

"And why's that?" The assumption that we are too different to be together is pissing me off, and I'm not even sure why.

"Well, you don't have much in common. Like, you and I for instance, we share some cultural background I guess. We go to the same gigs, watch the same movies, go out to the same bars. You know, we're alike."

I send a sweet smile his way. "I don't want someone like me. I want someone who will drag me out of my comfort zone and introduce me to new things. Different things."

"I completely agree." Cameron is not stupid. He knows he crossed a line and is now backpedaling his way into my good graces. "I also like a challenge."

Ty is not a challenge, but I don't want to pick a fight with my boss in the middle of this trip, so I let it go and nod, looking out the window.

When the cab driver drops us off at the hotel, I'm literally shaking. Cam offers to do the check-in while I clutch my suitcase, looking around the lobby and trying to keep my emotions in check. The place is packed and buzzing with laughter and excitement. Judging by the amount of people who wear credentials around their necks, most sports journalists have already arrived and are now mingling with each other.

The lobby is spacious and dazzling, with ornate crystal and golden hand-carved marble chandeliers. Cam disappears somewhere between the masses of people waiting in line at the reception desk, and I mess with my phone, trying not to think about Ty.

*Don't think about him.*

*Don't think about him.*

*Don't...*

I hear screaming and clapping, peppered with low whistles and some gasps. I raise my head and watch as an entourage of about ten men slices through the crowd. I recognize Jesse instantly. He is tall and muscular and enjoying the attention. Dawson is walking next to him, and between them and a few more men I don't recognize is Ty.

Fuck, I've missed him.

There's a lot of commotion around the group, and I'm rooted to the ground, completely mesmerized by my gorgeous ex, who is looking healthy and happy as freaking ever, by the way.

My eyes follow the entourage. Ty is chewing gum and not making eye contact with his fans or the reporters, his face partly hidden under a baseball cap. I may be imagining this, but seconds before he disappears, he clutches the left side of his shirt, where he tatted my name, with his fist.

Just then, a gloriously stupid idea pops into my mind. It's

so stupid I can't afford to think about it, because I know I'll change my mind. I turn around and race outside to the street, and head in the direction of the spot where Shane and I drank our Coco Loco and talked about Ty.

This is going to be so gloriously stupid.

ॐ

"Dude, I'm sorry, but I'm not doing it."

Her name is Nash, and she is seriously hot. She's got thick bangs, a septum piercing and the sweetest, most innocent face a twenty-something-year-old could have. And she refuses to take my money and just do what I tell her, which is driving me mad. This is America, woman.

"Listen, I'm not going to regret it," I say with conviction, pressing both my palms together as I beg her to tattoo me. I know that if she won't, others will, but for some reason, I really like her. Plus, the place is packed and if it weren't for the early hour, she probably wouldn't even have time for a walk-in customer like me.

"Dude, check out my ten commandments. I pinned them to my wall." Nash points at the wall behind her, chuckling to herself. Sure enough, she wrote ten rules she sticks by when she gives tattoos:

1. No drunk-tatting. Come sober or don't come at all.

2. A tattoo is not a pet. It lasts forever. I do not ink clichés. If you're into the shape of infinity or an anchor on your wrist, go somewhere else.

3. I am not a translator. If you want something in Chinese, Arabic, Hebrew or any other foreign language, check your spelling.

4. You will suffer for your art. Try not to fidget and move too much. I do not tattoo movers. Sorry.

5. No tattoos of the names of boyfriends/girlfriends. You will thank me for it someday.

I don't bother reading number six. Instead, I swivel back to Nash, smiling as I spot a loophole. "He is not my boyfriend. I just want to ink his name, regardless. So there you have it."

"Nope," she says.

"Yes," I respond. "Because I swear, even if I never get back with him, I'll still love it."

"So let me get this straight." Nash folds her arms, leaning over the counter, squinting as she tries to read me. She is all sass, yet not a pretender. I'm pretty sure that if I were playing for the other team, I'd totally be crushing all over her. "You want me to tattoo the name of your ex-boyfriend. On your body."

"That's right," I nod.

"And you're not drunk?"

I shake my head, bouncing on my feet excitedly. "Please, Nash. I know what I'm doing."

Nash is laughing hard, trying to regulate her breathing. She looks at me like I'm the craziest person she's ever come across, which is pretty worrying, considering the fact she works in a freaking Vegas tattoo parlor. She looks around her, checking that no other tattoo artist or co-worker is watching as she bends her own rules for me.

Damn, I knew our chemistry was on fire. Shane is about to get dumped in favor of a new BFF.

"This is sick, girl. But I'm totally on board with that if you let me pick the size and the place."

I hesitate, because in my vision, Ty will be inked across my heart, just like he did for me. But when I actually lie beneath Nash, and she has her black elastic gloves on, she curls her finger in my direction, signaling for me to flip onto my stomach.

"Tie your hair up. Like, really up," she instructs.

I do as she tells me, my heart drumming wildly. Nash picks a place right underneath my left ear and applies the stencil transfer she's made for the tattoo.

"Chest tats are very in if you're a jailbird," she says, turning on the machine, "but I think this spot makes far more sense."

The buzzing is making my head spin but I keep it together.

"You chose a tiny tattoo," I argue.

"My castle, my rules, baby." She laughs. "It's going to hurt, so take a deep breath, and remember that love hurts."

It certainly does, Nash. It most certainly does.

৽৵

The massive Las Vegas arena is jammed and full of people. Nobody even bothers to sit down, Everyone's standing, and the air throbs with a deafening roar of chanting and cheers. The atmosphere is buzzing with excitement mingled with the oppressive smell of beer, hotdogs and BO.

There are a lot of types of crowds, and they're all different. A football crowd is not the same as basketball crowd; a hockey crowd is different from a soccer crowd. And the MMA crowd? It's freaking nuts. The fans here have such raw, unrestrained passion.

Cam pushes through the masses, leading the way to the press area, which is literally only fifteen feet from the ring. I can barely hear myself think, which is great, because thinking is not my strong point at the moment.

It's too hot in the arena, so I take my jacket off once we find our seats. I'm wearing a cool, blue vintage dress, one of the few I own, paired with my denim chucks. There are still echoes of pain from doing the tattoo this morning, and Nash promised it's going to itch like a bitch once it starts healing, but I don't mind that at all.

"I'll go get us something to drink," Cam shouts in my ear. Then he takes a step back and stares. My new tattoo hasn't escaped him. He frowns slightly, but doesn't say anything, just pivots to the other side and walks away.

I plop down on my seat and take in everything around me. I'm pretty sure I saw Dawson walking around outside the ring, and I definitely saw Jesse sitting across the ring, on the opposite side, with a few other XWL fighters who came to see the show. There's an announcer who entertains the crowd every once in awhile, but I don't bother listening to what he has to say.

The reporter on my right accidentally elbows my ribs. "Oops, sorry."

I nod.

"Hey, do I know you?" He turns around.

"Not likely." I shake my head. "*Diablo Hill* magazine?" I try.

He frowns. "I'm from *MMA Madness*. Chris," he introduces himself and we shake hands. He is still frowning, still looking at me, and as the pieces fall together, I blush and turn away from him, desperate to avoid his next question. But I can actually hear Chris smiling behind me when he says. "Hey, you're Wilder's old girlfriend. I saw you on TMZ when I was doing research."

*Well, ain't that just grand.* I turn back toward him. I'm hoping to convey annoyance, but I'm way too agitated to control my facial expressions. "I'm sorry, Chris. I can't seem to hear you with all the background noise. Enjoy the fight."

I'm relieved when Cam takes the seat to my right. He's brought bottles of water, and I sip from mine, pressing the cold bottle against my forehead.

Vasquez is the first to emerge from the tunnel. He's probably as tall as Ty and built like a gladiator. Ty has been doing this for four years professionally, but Vasquez is older, thirty-two, and more experienced. He's already won three championship belts, and he's considered a Brazilian Jiu Jitsu master. The Brazilian crowd cheers him on loudly, while some of the Americans boo him. Vasquez doesn't seem to mind, though. He's fought enough bouts to look past the booing.

And that's what I'm afraid of.

When the announcer introduces Ty and it's his turn to walk out of the tunnel, my heart thumps with anticipation. I have goose bumps all over my body as the crowd goes wild, chanting his name and throwing cups in the air. He walks out to his usual angry grunge tune and winks coolly to one of the video cameras following him, flashing his black mouth guard. When he gets to the edge of the ring, he lifts his arms sideways and allows one of the referees to pat him down all over.

"I never really got why they do that," I tell Cam.

But it's Chris who answers from my other side. "Being fondled by another man tends to put you in a bad mood and makes for a more exciting fight."

I turn my head, cocking it to the side and narrowing my eyes at him.

"I'm kidding," Chris says. "It's to check the fighters haven't greased themselves to death to avoid being grappled by their opponents."

The ref squeezes Ty's shoulder, as if to say *you're good to go*.

I think I'm going to be sick. The idea of Ty getting in there, of him getting hurt (and let's face it, there's a one hundred percent chance he'll get hurt) is driving me nuts.

Dawson arrives at Ty's side, along with two more of his trainers, and applies a layer of petroleum jelly to his face to prevent cuts. Dawson is constantly speaking, as Ty stares into the raised cage and nods, looking like his mind is far away from everything and everyone else here.

Then he climbs the steps, pauses at the gate to the cage and does this thing again, where he touches the tattoo with my name and looks up to the sky.

*I love you too, baby,* I want to scream.

The lock *clicks*, Ty and Vasquez bump fists with their gloved hands and the fight begins.

My heart is about to jump out of my chest even before they touch each other. In fact, they spend the first few seconds jumping around in circles. I decide to look away, not wanting to see how this one plays out. I still think the XWL is human cockfighting. I feel Cam fidgeting beside me and hear a loud *Awwww* from the crowd. It echoes in the arena and it makes me want to faint and wake up when it's all over.

"You want to see this," Cam tells me. "Open your eyes."

I slowly open my eyes and watch Ty sitting on top of Vasquez, pounding on him for what seems to be at least two minutes straight. There's blood everywhere. I'm fighting the scream that's stuck in my throat, because blood makes me want to vomit. I get dizzy before blood tests, so this is definitely not my scene. To top that off, in a matter of seconds, Vasquez manages to flip Ty over, and now he's on top of him.

Through the wire, Dawson yells up to Ty, "Lock your foot down! Push your hip! Ty! Ty! I'm talking to you!" He is frantic, screaming loud enough to be heard even with all the chaos and noise around us. That's when the first round is over and I take a deep breath.

Four more rounds to go.

I don't bother opening my eyes even once during the next twenty minutes of fighting. I don't respond to any of the *ahhhs* and the *ohhhs*. I don't open my eyes during the rest periods between rounds. I wait patiently even when the place explodes with cheers and people scream their assess off at the end of the fifth round. That's when I hear the announcer officially crown Ty Wilder the XWL welterweight champion. He's won by a decision.

I open my eyes and watch the president of the XWL walk straight into the cage and hand Ty his new belt. The belt he's worked so hard for. The belt that broke us apart in a way.

"This is your cue to go try and ask him if he'll talk to us before they whisk him off for the official TV interviews."

At first, I can't seem to move, but when Cam literally shoves me out of my chair, I run toward the cage and hook my fingers into the net.

I wouldn't be able to get so close to the ring if it weren't for my super-great seat, but since I have a journalist tag, I can get away with a lot of things.

Ty looks exhausted, sweaty as hell, and there are fresh bruises and blood on him. Also, he's panting like crazy, the adrenaline pumping. He notices me after a few seconds and turns around to face me.

Heart stops beating. Brain shuts down. Hormones are raging.

He is coming over. Squatting down, he doesn't smile, just kind of wrinkles his forehead as if he's trying to figure out whether he is imagining this or not. He makes me feel home again. I missed this. I missed *him*.

"You deserve this," I mouth, tilting my head in the direction of the gigantic gold and silver belt. "Champ."

He leans into the net, and I lose sight of everything around us, but I'm pretty sure people are wondering who the hell I am and why is he paying attention to me, instead of celebrating his victory.

"Yrrr wamaminvivoo?" he asks.

"What?"

He spits his mouthpiece into his hand, this time asking clearly. "You want an interview, huh?"

I shake my head. "I'd love one, but I want *you* more."

His eyes soften immediately.

"You can start by giving me your number. You haven't done that in... well, never." He is slurring his words slightly, but I'm sure he'll be okay. He turns his back to me and before

I know it Jesse appears by my side with Ty's phone, handing it to me. He's opened a new contact. I enter the number with a grin.

Jesse bites his upper lip, obviously worried by Ty's behavior. "He grew his virginity back while you were gone, just so you know."

I can't help but grin even wider. My eyes cling to Ty as he talks to an attractive female TV reporter inside the cage. I don't care about her. I'm just so freaking proud. At the end, he won. And he did it all by himself.

Ty twists his head and points at me with this crooked smirk of his. There's a shitload of noise in the arena, but I'm close enough to hear when he shouts, "When you get that interview, don't forget, I've got ammo on you."

"What ammo?" My brows shoot up in surprise.

"First date? Your cell phone playlist. Ring any bells?" He sticks his tongue out at me.

Damn! He said he was going to use Phil Collins against me when I become a journalist.

And I did, partly because of him.

# CHAPTER 22

It's the middle of the night and I hear a knock on my hotel room's door. I know who it is. I've been waiting for Ty, and I haven't slept a second. It took time for him to get here, since he was caught up with all those interviews, the last one with Cam for *Diablo Hill* magazine. Yes, he met Cam in the lobby at 2 a.m., and then he even skipped all the after-parties just so he could come back to me.

My own personal, very unusual Prince Charming.

I open the door and lean on the frame. He has a black eye, swollen lip and a deep cut above his left eyebrow, but he is beautiful, absolutely perfect.

"Tired?" I ask, smiling.

"As shit. Thanks for waiting."

He walks straight into my bedroom and lifts his hand, showing me something... a ticket? I pluck it from his hand.

"I planned all along to beg you to take me back," he says quietly. "This is proof that I was getting my ass on a plane to come home the minute I was done with the fight."

And sure enough, I'm holding a one-way ticket from Vegas to San Francisco, scheduled to leave here in the morning.

"And this is the second piece of proof." He takes off his shirt, staring down at his tattoo. "You don't ink a reminder of a person if you're not willing to fight really hard to keep them in your life."

"I know." I grin, looking away and giving him my left side, flashing my new tat. The letter T is inked behind my ear, curling into a shape of a heart.

"Holy shit." He laughs, but quickly stops because smiling is painful when you have a busted lip. "I love it." He runs his finger tenderly along my jaw.

"I love you," I answer without blinking.

"And I love you too. Actually, not to be competitive— hell, I am a competitive sonofabitch—but I fell in love with you a lot quicker than you did me. You pretty much ripped my heart from my chest when you came to see me in July."

I throw my arms around his neck, diving my face into his chest. I can feel him wincing from the pain from the fight, but he wraps his arms around me presses me into him like all he wants is for us to become one.

"I shouldn't have judged you," I cry into his chest. "Not on what you'd done before we met. I know you never meant to hurt me."

"And I shouldn't have been so pissed at you for walking out on me." He strokes my head, whispering into my left ear, no doubt admiring the new tattoo. "I just got so attached so quickly it felt like a betrayal when you turned your back on me. I realized you needed the time, and I was more than prepared to give it to you. I always knew I'd come back. Always." He laughs. "This is the first time you're ahead of my game. I didn't expect you to surprise me in Vegas again."

"It's about time." I pull away so I can look at his perfect face. The face I've missed so much. Heart is pounding to the rhythm of Ty's heartbeat, Brain is enjoying the adrenaline rush, and Hormones are ready to make use of the big bed behind us.

All three parts of me are in sync, finally in perfect harmony.

"I haven't been with anyone else since we broke up," he says, his expression turning serious.

Every hair in my body stands up. I know that. I believe him. "Neither have I," I say.

He pulls me close for a kiss. His lips are warm and salty

and he's sweaty, but just inhaling his familiar scent makes me drunk. Completely smashed, more like. We kiss like it's the last time we'll ever touch each other again. Even though he's here and we're together—definitely together—I'm still heartbroken for all the lost time. Living life without him was hell on earth. Nothing felt good without him by my side.

He pulls me closer, and by the bulge pressing my stomach, I know exactly where we're heading.

"Are you sure you're not too hurt for us to...?" I drop my gaze to his erection. He looked like he could use a few days at the hospital when he walked out of that cage earlier this evening.

He nods. "It's been too long. Jesse said I grew my virginity back."

"I heard. I'm not sure men can do that, though. Like, physically. Not that women can, but..."

"My point is, I'm getting you out of this blue dress now."

"Okay," I agree, laughing.

"I love you," he says.

"I love you too," I promise.

And that's the last thing we say to each other before we collapse back onto the bed together. Forever tied.

-THE END-

# ABOUT THE AUTHOR

Author L. J. Shen lives in NorCal with her small family, consisting of her husband and chubby cat. She's a self-proclaimed TV and movie buff, and she reads about three books a week. Her hobbies consist of gymming, watching UFC fight nights and sushi (yeah, okay, sushi is not a hobby per se, but it's a great part of her life).

Her debut novel, *Tyed*, is available on Amazon and paperback. She loves to talk to her readers (fine, she likes to talk, and doing so with her readers is just a bonus), so feel free to contact her on Facebook or Twitter.

She is now working on book number two, due early 2015.

Twitter: https://twitter.com/lj_shen
Facebook: https://www.facebook.com/authorljshen

92996953R00133

Made in the USA
Columbia, SC
03 April 2018